RINGS OF DEATH

Ricki Thomas

A Wild Wolf Publication

Published by Wild Wolf Publishing in 2014
This second edition, 2016
Copyright © 2014 Ricki Thomas

ISBN: 978-1-907954-38-2

www.wildwolfpublishing.com

Also by Ricki Thomas

Hope's Vengeance
Unlikely Killer
Bloody Mary
Holiday of the Dead (contributor)
Bonfire Night
Black Park
Wild Wolf's Twisted Tails (contributor)
Deadly Angels

To Mum: an adventure for you.
And, as always, for my children.

Chapter 1
Friday 20th September, 2014

Sammy's head pounded and her mouth was parched. She opened her eyes, slowly adjusting to the darkness, and realised she was lying in filth on a freezing, concrete floor. She raised herself onto her arms, wondering where she was and how she had got there, and soon became aware that she wasn't alone; three other girls lay to her right, dazed, their breathing shallow.

She reached to the wall - damp to the touch and ice cold - to steady herself as she struggled to sit, and surveyed the door, heavy and wooden, the only exit to the windowless room. Using the meagre strength she could muster, she groggily pulled herself up, rattling the handle, and the clanging echoed from the walls.

Weary, Lydia groaned. "There's no point making all that racket. Nobody can hear you and he won't be back until later."

Sammy turned to see who had noticed her, taking in the dark skin and unkempt afro curls. "Who is he?"

Lydia closed her eyes, tired from the ordeal that had stolen the past three months of her life. "We don't know. We call him Dick because he *is* one, but who he really is, I don't know."

Sammy had a million questions and they tumbled out, one after the other, but her fellow captives, drugged and woozy, weren't forthcoming with replies. Soon the incessant questions and jarring banging were enough and Lydia snapped. "Look, I know you're new to this, and we all know first-hand how scared you are - we've been where you are now - but the only advice I can give is to do what he asks, keep quiet, and eat as much of the food as you can manage."

"But we're caged up like animals in here, don't you care?"

Lydia rolled her eyes at Sammy's naivety. "Get used to it, because it's your life from now on." She collapsed back on the ground, too exhausted to prop herself up any longer.

The terseness shamed Sammy and her eyes dropped to the floor, wet with urine and faeces. She shivered, holding back the tears that threatened. Noticing her distress, Sying reached out a hand, a friendly gesture in the midst of terror. "Lydia doesn't mean to be harsh," her words were slurred, "but she's been here the longest and she's already seen me and Neeraja hauled in after her. My name's Sying, by the way, what's your name?"

"Sammy. Do you know why we're here?"

A door slammed outside the room and Sying put her finger to her lips, quieting to a whisper. "No. Shush, he doesn't like us talking."

Indignant despite her fear, Sammy shook the handle again. "Dick? Why have you brought me here?"

Sying winced and closed her eyes, awaiting an angry tirade, but the gentleness in the reply shocked her; they had always been too scared to talk to him. "Sammy, is that you?"

"Let me out, let us out."

"Calm down, Sammy, it's going to be okay. It'll all be over in a couple of weeks." He unbolted a small flap at the bottom of the door and pushed it open, sliding a chipped bowl of unappetising food through.

"What will all be over in a couple of weeks? What are you doing with us?"

"Just eat the food I've given you and go to sleep."

"No, I reckon you'll have put drugs in it. I'm not touching it." Footsteps receded on the other side of the door and, terrified, Sammy shouted, "Don't go, Dick, please, just let us out." But it was futile, he had gone, and the door that served as a warning to his approach slammed behind him. Thumping the wall with a weak hand, confused tears began to flow. "Please, Dick, my parents will be worried…"

Gerda slammed the receiver into its holder, angry and unheard. "Why won't they take this seriously? Our baby's been missing for over fifteen hours and they still aren't doing anything."

Rob Cooper pulled his wife to his chest, his heavy heart filled with the same angst and helplessness. "What did they say?"

Frustrated tears broke through and coursed over her cheeks, choking her words. "Forty-eight hours, that's what they keep saying. Forty-eight hours until they take her disappearance seriously. She'd never run away from home, you know that. Our Sammy's just not that girl."

"I know, love, but there's no point in worrying."

"No point in worrying!" Gerda pulled away, flummoxed by his calmness. "I've tried every friend of hers we know of, I've put endless messages on Facebook, I've contacted uni, the running club and the gym. Nobody's seen her since eight yesterday evening. Sammy's out there somewhere and she needs help, and the bloody police won't give me the time of day. And why? Because she's probably 'run away from home', which you know as well as I do is ridiculous. Plus, as if they're not insensitive enough with all that crap, they've insinuated there must be problems at home."

Rob sighed, he hated to see his wife so distraught and couldn't disagree with her. Sammy's night away from home was uncharacteristic. "Look, why don't we go down to the station, they might listen if we kick up a bit of a fuss."

Jill unfolded the cumbersome table and clicked it easily into place, draping a clean towel over it. "Up you get then." She waited patiently as he clambered on, flinching with the twinges that only a massage seemed to help. "You look like you need this today, what have you been up this time?"

He settled onto his tummy, his brow on the cushion, face down. "It's that project I've been working on, I got the last but one piece yesterday. It was heavy. Well, not heavy, but awkward to carry."

Jill pumped fragrant oil onto her hands and began to pummel his bare shoulders, gently easing the muscles and searching for knots to dispel. "I've told you before, you need to be careful." Her fingers ran along his spine, gentle on the down stroke, firmer as she pushed upwards. "So, this mysterious project, are you still not going to tell me anything about it?"

He exhaled lazily, unwinding with her touch. "You'll know soon enough. It'll be a masterpiece, I've been planning it for years."

"You know how dreadful my memory is, but I'm sure you said you'll be displaying it publicly."

"Yes, I'll be unveiling it on the sixth of October, just two weeks and two days to go. I'm pretty excited about it; you'll be seeing photographs of it everywhere."

She chuckled, her fingers working their way over his skin, feeling the tension melt as his body relaxed. "You're such a tease. Go on, tell me, I promise I'll keep it to myself."

Tired from the events the previous night, his voice was low and slurred, the blissful massage seeping his consciousness. "I can't, it's a secret, you know that."

She found a knot and deftly worked it upwards, away from the backbone until it snapped away. "I was at the library this morning."

"Mmmm."

"I've always had a keen interest in architecture, especially Victorian."

"You're interested in *everything*, Jill." Her capacity for soaking up facts had never ceased to amaze him.

Her palms pressed against his back, soothing and softening, the scent of lavender reaching his nose as her fingers curled into his neck. "I was seeing what I could find out about the buildings you mentioned last time, the old Fubarre factories. I found it quite romantic."

"Lazy, more like. From what I know of my ancestors they'll have done it to save the pennies."

"Maybe so, and why not? All the same, I think it's lovely that there's a building in Manchester which is exactly the same as the one here. Have you ever been there?"

"No."

"Does your family still own them?"

"Mmmm." Jill realised sleep was drifting over him. He often succumbed when the pain had been worse than usual.

"It's all ruins now, isn't it, the old industrial estate here. I might take a drive out there one day."

He pushed himself up, sudden and forceful. "No. You must *not* go there, Jill. Promise me." Concerned by his outburst, he added, "It's just it's dangerous, the brickwork's falling to bits and I don't want you getting hurt."

Shocked. "Okay." She waited for him to settle again, reasoning that the stress of the curious project and the unrelenting pain he suffered must be wearing for him, and continued working on her favourite client without another word.

"These are the non-urgent cases that have come in overnight. You know what to do." DC Boswell dropped the reports on Jo's desk and she glanced over the summary, before moving it aside to reveal the first file. "Oh, I recognise this girl, she was in Teejays yesterday lunchtime."

"You mean to say you're idiotic enough to eat in that vermin-ridden hole?"

Jo glanced at her colleague, irritated that was he always so spiky with her. "I have to eat downmarket, the pathetic wages I get won't allow any different."

She returned to the photo before her, the wholesome smile that crinkled the edges of green eyes underneath a pale, yellow fringe. Sammy Cooper's parents had filed a missing person's statement the night before, but no investigation had started yet; teenagers often disappeared for a few days, eventually returning to the folds of their families.

Boswell gave an exaggerated sigh for her benefit. "Look, we're busy enough without you wasting time on a self-solver, it's not important so deal with it and move on. We've got a full caseload at the moment. What is she?" He leaned over and scanned the report. "Just a missing kid. Log it, sign it, and get some work done."

Jo saluted him sarcastically, tapped Sammy Cooper's name and details into the computer, and tossed the report aside.

Lydia, Sying and Neeraja, fragile and listless, reached for the bowl with their hands, filthy from the squalor, and scooped the grey gruel to their mouths. Sammy gasped. "You're kidding me, right?" Her question was ignored and she grimaced with disbelief. "You're all drugged up to the eyeballs and he must be putting it in the food. What the hell are you eating it for?" She touched her forehead, her brain still fuzzy and aching from whatever he had given her to knock her out when he had abducted her.

Neeraja swallowed, the bland casserole, tasteless and cold, sticking in her throat. "We've got no choice, we're starving. And, anyway, it's easier that way. More bearable."

Sammy noticed for the first time how skinny the girls were, but was still incredulous that they were allowing themselves to be poisoned. "But if you stop eating whatever's drugging you, we might be able to find a way out of here."

Lydia had seen it all before with the other two prisoners and was intolerant to it happening again with a third. "You don't get it, do you, coming in here as if you know exactly what to do. I'll tell you why we eat that shit: we've been locked up for weeks on end, starved and scared, and left to sleep in our own crap. It's disgusting, it's soul destroying, and the only time we get relief from this hellhole is when whatever it is he's feeding us works."

"So you enjoy being doped up on…"

The black coldness in Lydia's glare silenced her. "We eat it so we can sleep, full stop. When we're asleep we get a break from this nightmare, it's the only relief there is. Now shut up. Eat if you want, don't if you don't, but don't flounce in here criticising what we do when you have no idea what we've been through."

Sammy leant against the damp wall, determined not to give in to temptation despite her growing hunger; she wanted to stay sober and alert. "Well, I'm not giving up just like that. I'm going to find a way and get the hell out of here, and if you lot are too out of it to come with me, then that's tough."

The desk sergeant was getting annoyed. He could understand the desperation the couple felt for their missing daughter, but they were being unreasonable and he was running out of ways to pacify them. As a last resort he picked up the phone and waited. "Jo, could you help me out with something? I've got the parents of a missing girl downstairs and they want to speak to someone... Yes, Samantha Cooper, went missing last night."

His emphasis on the latter words needled Gerda and she crossed her arms defiantly. "It's not like her; how many times do I have to repeat myself?"

Bob's shoulders sagged with relief now the problem was no longer his and he replaced the receiver. "Constable Ellis will be down to see you in a minute to discuss your concerns. If you'd like to take a seat while you wait." He gestured to the row of hard, red chairs - plastic and ugly - and dismissed the couple to acknowledge the reporter who had just come through the door to collect her weekly round-up of crime and misery for the local paper.

"Good afternoon, Bob, what have you got for me this week?"

Scanning the list of reported crimes for the previous seven days, he tucked his pen over his ear. "Four burglaries, one assault, a house fire, suspected arson, one hate-crime and," he hushed to a whisper, mindful of the pained couple who sat nearby, "two missing girls, but one has turned up safe and sound after a fun night out with her boyfriend."

"Is that all? Hardly worth keeping the station open for at the taxpayers' expense." As always, Nancy grated on him, her manner brash and abrasive. "Are there any details you can give me?"

Bob checked his watch; his shift ended in five minutes and he was keen to delegate the mundane chore with the unpleasant journalist, so hearing Jo's footsteps on the stairs was a welcome diversion. He smiled at her when she came into view and pointed to the distraught couple. "Mr and Mrs Cooper, the parents of the missing girl."

The reporter's reaction was exactly what he had hoped for: she excitedly raced across the reception area before Jo could reach them. "Hello, my name's Nancy Blaine, I work for the Southside Express. I understand you've reported your daughter as a missing person and I…"

"Not now, Nancy." Jo hated the woman as much as everybody, with her nosiness and lack of consideration, and she sat beside Gerda and Rob. "I'm Constable Ellis. Would you prefer if we went to a private room to have a chat?"

Rob eyed the reporter suspiciously. "I think so."

"I think not," Gerda had other ideas, "if she's a reporter we can give her pictures and details about our Sammy to publish, at least that way *someone* will be taking her disappearance seriously." A marked glare at Jo showed her feelings about the police loud and clear.

Jo knew the likelihood of their daughter returning home without a care in the world was strong, and press involvement would be a meaningless waste of time, but she was powerless to exclude Nancy from the conversation. Her displeasure obvious, she scanned the scribbled notes before her. "So Samantha…"

"Nobody calls her that, call her Sammy." Gerda was irked that they hadn't even listened to such a basic detail.

Shocked and a little amused, she continued, "Right, no problem. So Sammy was last seen at eight yesterday evening. Was that by you?"

"No, she'd been to the gym for training, she's competing in the Raymouth Marathon next month so she's always there nowadays. She's a brilliant runner. Anyway, as far as we know, her coach was the last to see her, we called him at eight-thirty when she hadn't come home."

"What's his name?" Nancy scrawled in shorthand on her notepad.

"Peter Camber, he's a good friend. She's been running since she was five, competitively since she was nine, and Peter's like a member of our family now. He said he waved her off at eight after training ended."

"Thanks. Did he say anything about her mood? Was she tired? Happy?"

Jo put her own smaller notepad on the empty seat beside her, wondering what the point of her presence was; the Coopers and meddlesome Nancy seemed to be doing fine without her. "He said she was as bouncy as normal. She's a very cheerful girl, sees the good in everyone and everything. She would never make us worry unnecessarily, this is all so unlike her. Our Sammy always called when she wasn't going to be back on time and she wouldn't dream of staying out a night without checking with us first."

Jo sighed, having seen it all before. "Mr and Mrs Cooper, Sammy is eighteen, she's an adult. Childhood rules don't apply when…"

"They do in our house." The curtness in Gerda's voice was harsh and her controlling personality clear. "I know my daughter better than anyone and she's a good girl. She may not *have* to adhere to our rules, as you cuttingly pointed out, but she does anyway because she knows why we've set them."

Jo knew she shouldn't, but not only did she have too much work to do and not enough time, she knew Sammy was bound to come home soon. She stood and walked away, leaving Gerda speechless.

Whatever drug their tormentor had laced the food with had taken effect swiftly, and Lydia, Sying and Neeraja slept peacefully on the hard, fouled floor. Sammy, hungry and thirsty, hadn't let anything pass her lips since she had arrived and had no intention of doing so; she wasn't a quitter like the other three.

She had no idea how - or why - she had been brought to the stark, dank room. All she could remember was leaving the gym and saying goodbye to her trainer. She had not been aware of anyone's presence as she had made her way towards her home and had no memory of being attacked. Her mind was blank. She had checked herself over and could find no injuries or signs of indecent behaviour, so could only assume she had been drugged and bundled into a vehicle. But why?

Her head had been woollen when she had first awoken, but gradually her coherence had returned, and having no recollection of the man who had imprisoned her meant she couldn't give a reason to the horrifying predicament she was in.

After the other girls had slumped into drug-fuelled comas, Sammy had tried to find something she could use to pick the lock, but she had been stripped of her watch and jewellery, and a quick inspection of her fellow inmates showed they had too. Now she sat on the cleanest piece of floor she could find, amongst the faeces, urine and sick, wondering what else she could do to free herself, but short of their jailor actually opening the door himself, she was out of ideas.

Sammy felt for the mobile phone that she already knew wasn't there and desperately wished she could call her mum.

After the policewoman had so rudely left the interview, Nancy had suggested they take their meeting to a nearby café, that the coffee would be her treat, and the Coopers had had no objection. Neither was hungry, but Nancy hadn't had lunch and ordered a chicken salad sandwich, which she ate hungrily in between taking notes for the story she hoped to prepare in time for the next day's issue.

"So, this Peter Camber, the coach, you know he'll be the first port of call for the police if Sammy hasn't returned by tomorrow night? The prime suspect is often the last person to have seen the victim."

Gerda sipped her coffee. "Peter wouldn't hurt our Sammy."

Rob shook his head. "Never."

"He ran for the country in the nineteen ninety-six Olympics, and he can spot talent when he sees it. He saw

Sammy's star quality at an early age and has helped her since. Peter would never do anything to hurt her."

"Never," Rob agreed.

"Okay, if you say so. Did Sammy have a boyfriend?"

"There have been a few lads here and there, but nothing serious. She's too committed to her running to have time for a relationship."

"So you don't think she'd have done something spontaneous like many kids do - meet a boy, fall madly in love, want to spend the weekend in bed?"

The Coopers were stunned by the blatant suggestion and cried 'no' in unison, before Gerda added, "I don't think she's ever slept with anyone. I think she's still a virgin."

Rob shook his head. "She's never mentioned a boy to me and we've always been close."

"It would be totally out of character for her to do something so rash anyway, she's a planner, not a whimsical floozy."

"That's fine, you two know her better than anyone. You say she's a keen runner, what about the rest of her life? What else does she like to do? So I can build a picture of her for the article."

The Coopers eyed each other, shrugging. "Well, nothing really. Running is her life. Even at uni she's taking a physical fitness degree, she wants to be a PE teacher in the long run, once she's achieved her running goals."

"And what are they?"

"She's determined to run in the two thousand and sixteen Olympics."

Nancy grinned widely. "Commendable. This is going to make a great story, I can see the headlines now."

Jo was aware of Boswell's eyes boring into her as she crept to her desk and hoped he would leave her alone for once, but, "Sneaking off for a fag while the boss is out?"

She glared at him, already annoyed from Nancy Blaine's intrusion. "I don't smoke."

17

"So what were you doing?" Boswell approached her desk, nosily eyeing the paperwork next to the photo of Sammy, and her skin crawled. "Is it something to do with this?"

"Her parents were downstairs and they wanted to talk about it. Fat lot of good that was."

"What the hell were you thinking? The kid's just gone off the rails a little and needed a break, end of. It happens all the time, you know it does."

"I know, but Bob called up and..."

"Blah, blah and bloody blah. I don't give a shit about your reason for getting involved, because you know you shouldn't have."

And now she'd had enough from the man who was barely her superior. "You know what? It's none of your sodding business, you're not..."

"What's going on?" Returning late from his brief lunch break, DI French hurried through the door, concerned by the angry interchange he had heard from the stairwell. "Oh, not you two children again. What is it now? In fact, don't tell me, I'm not interested in six of one and half a dozen of the other. Shut up and get some work done, the pair of you. It's like being in kindergarten here."

Reddened from the scolding, Jo considered that if her boss were annoyed now, he would be fuming when he found out about the reporter sticking her nose in, and she resolved to be the messenger. "Guv, I think there's something you should know." French's eyebrow raised and he steeled himself for the latest cock-up. She swallowed, composing herself. "Nancy Blaine was downstairs and she picked up on the story about the missing girl."

"What missing girl?" He didn't care, he was too busy.

Jo held the photo up. "Her name is..."

"Sammy Cooper. Shit." French looked left to right, furtive. "Give me the file, I'll take it from here. We're going to have to start the investigation early, even if it's just for show, otherwise heads are going to roll."

18

Boswell chuckled as he sat behind his own desk, listening, but not obviously, and Jo was confused. "Why? Who is she?"

"That's not important. Look, give the Southside Express a call and tell them not to run the story just yet, tell them you'll give them everything in a couple of days, statements, photos, whatever they want. I'm sure she'll be back home safe and sound by them. Go on then, get on with it, I need to make a call."

Nancy had been with the Coopers for ages and had gleaned all the information she needed to make local headline news. After waving them goodbye, she hurried to her car to make her way back to the office. It was mid-afternoon when she arrived and she headed straight to her desk to type up the story. She had compiled half of it when Lewis shook her shoulder and she jumped; she hadn't noticed him approach. "I hear you've been talking to a Mr and Mrs Cooper about their daughter."

"Yes, they reported her as a missing person last night." Nancy tugged her long fringe behind her ear, the errant chocolate curls springing back immediately.

"We can't run the story, so you might as well find something else instead."

"What? Why?"

"We just can't."

"But I've spent over an hour with Sammy's parents and I feel like I know her already. They're convinced, and so am I, that something's happened to her. Surely the more coverage this gets, the sooner we'll find out where she is."

"Nancy, I'm being firm on this one, the order's come from very high above."

"How high? This is smacking of conspiracy, Lewis," he sighed but it didn't deter her, "she's an eighteen-year-old, well-respected girl with a bright future ahead of her and an impeccable past, I don't believe for a second she'd abandon her devoted parents to run off for a spot of shenanigans. I'm an investigative journalist; I'm trained to do this."

"I acknowledge that, but not in this case. I can't say it any clearer: if a word about this appears in my newspaper then you're not only sacked, but I'll make damned sure your career in journalism is finished."

She knew the words were empty, he didn't have the esteem or power to do such a thing, but she was still rankled. "Who's behind this cover-up?"

"I mean it, Nancy. This has come from Chief Superintendent Brown's office and I can't afford to lose my job just because you don't know when to keep your nose out."

His piece said, he stormed away and Nancy saved the file before slumping back on the chair. His emphatic refusal to interfere even slightly in this particular case could only mean that somebody, somewhere, knew more about Sammy's disappearance than they were admitting to, and her curiosity reached fever pitch. If the Southside Express wasn't going to run the story, she knew someone who would.

Nancy picked up the phone and dialled her home number. "Phil, darling, it's me. I've got something that may interest The Daily Review, but I need you to find some stuff out for me. This research you've been doing on Benedict Brown," she explained about Lewis's odd refusal to run the story, "see what link, if any, you can find between him and a teenager called Sammy Cooper."

Chapter 2
Saturday 21st September

Dan French slammed on the brakes when he spotted the headlines scrawled in black marker pen on a board outside the newsagent and, after waving an apology to the disgruntled driver behind, he ran inside in the hope he was wrong. He wasn't. A picture of a smiling Sammy Cooper shone from the front cover of The Daily Review. Collecting a copy to study once he arrived at the station, he wondered if he would even have a job by sunset; the previous evening he had received strict orders from Sussex Headquarters in Lewes that the investigation into Sammy Cooper's disappearance was confidential and the press was not to be involved under any circumstances.

He jumped in his car and raced as fast as the rush hour traffic would allow to Southside Police Station, and by the time he had parked and hurried to the incident room, his fury was simmering. He tagged Jo on the shoulder and indicated the spare room, unable to speak for fear of exploding.

She closed the door behind her, confused. "What's up?" French threw the newspaper on the table and she gasped. "Guv, I know nothing about that, really I don't. I called the Southside Express myself and told them not to run a story."

"And they didn't, but a fucking national did instead. Either someone leaked the story from here, or that fucking Nancy Blaine's had something to do with this."

Jo was amazed to find his tirade had stopped and she kept quiet to avoid causing him to lose his temper again, but when he sagged onto a chair, clearly troubled, she felt an uncommon sympathy and wondered if his job was on the line. She had to ask. "I don't get the interest in her disappearance, though. There's nothing to show that she's been hurt and she's only been gone for what," she calculated quickly, "thirty-six hours, if I've worked that out correctly."

French tapped the revealing article with his finger. "She was dating Chief Superintendent Brown's son."

"Oh, I see. Now it makes sense. What are you going to do?"

"Obviously I'll have to check with those in the know, but we'll probably have to start a proper investigation into her disappearance immediately, and aside from that, just see if I've got a job left when the Chief Super calms down. I want you to go and see Nancy, find out what she knows about this. In the meantime, I'll get a team together to start the investigation. Can you get me a copy of the missing person report?"

Gerda was relieved when she saw the headlines about her daughter's sorry tale in the national newspaper she had bought instead of the Southside Express that morning. Nancy had promised they would take the plight of her missing daughter seriously - unlike the police - and they had. However, she was shocked that the article stated Sammy was having an affair with a man, whose name, Joshua Brown, was unfamiliar. She was sure the smear on Sammy's perfect reputation had been fabricated for titillation, as her daughter told her everything.

She reread the detailed story, which covered three pages, but the words blurred before her, having been unable to sleep the past two nights from intense worry. She picked up the phone and dialled. "Peter, have you seen The Daily Review this morning?"

He sounded shifty and spoke hurriedly. "This isn't a good time, Gerda, the police have just walked in."

"They'll just have to wait. Is there any truth in the ridiculous claims that Sammy was in a relationship with some guy called Joshua Brown?"

He sighed, annoyed, a betrayer of confidence. "Yes, it's true."

For nearly fourteen years she had considered him a friend, but the trust melted easily. "Why didn't you tell me? Did you think I don't have the right to know what my daughter's getting up to?"

"And this is why she didn't want you to know. I'm sorry, Gerda, but you do have a tendency to run her life. She's eighteen now, nineteen in four days - an adult - and she just wanted a smidgen of privacy, something of her own that she didn't share with you."

"She shares everything with me. I never even have to ask; she offers it of her own accord."

"She tells you what she wants you to know."

"No, she tells me everything, we're best friends. I can't believe you've been this irresponsible, and you have the audacity to claim you're our friend. Now I look like an idiot thanks to you and your bloody meddling. You should have told me or Rob." Cutting the call, Gerda immediately dialled the police; she needed to know exactly what was going on.

Nancy lounged back against the cushions and stroked Phil's arm gently. She had not bothered to go to the office, aware that Lewis would probably fire her now the forbidden story had made national news. She didn't need the poky job on the worthless rag now anyway, the pay out her husband had received for the details he had provided to his contact at The Daily Review, on top of his healthy income from freelance journalism, was more than enough to keep them going for a while.

"How did you know about Sammy dating Joshua Brown then? I hadn't a clue when I called you, I was just being pig-headed because Lewis told me not to run the story."

"We've been fishing for something on him for ages, you know, a bit of negative press to bring the spoilt idiot down a peg or two."

Confused, Nancy laughed. "Yeah, I get it: Daddy's high up in the police force, he probably went to private school and had plenty of holidays and all that caboodle, but really, what can you possibly find on a teenage guy?"

"Babe, Joshua isn't a teenager, he's thirty-five."

She chuckled. "Dirty bastard. What could Sammy possibly have seen in him, she's a pretty girl?"

"Money, of course. She wanted to be in the next Olympics and he has the money to make sure she gets what she wants. As long as she was sleeping with him."

"You're talking about her in the past tense, do you think she's been hurt?"

"The more involved she'd got with him, the more needy she'd become and he wanted her out of the way. That's what Raoul told me, anyway, but surely he'd just dump her, not, well, you know."

"Goodness. So why didn't their little fling make the news anyway?"

Phil shrugged. "Grown man dates teenager, it's not news. Chief Superintendent's arse of a son dates promising athlete: minor news. Chief Superintendent's arse of a son dates promising athlete, who disappears in mysterious circumstances - big news. Raoul nearly bit my hand off for the information."

Raoul laid the handset on the desk and leant back on the swivel chair; the call had flummoxed him. The unexpected news could be extremely beneficial for his burgeoning career in the media, but any profits from it would be blood money. The idea that a serial killer may be on the prowl was sickening, yet exciting too, and he wanted to be the one whose name was behind the revelation.

He formed a pyramid with his fingers as he relived the call, adding to the notes he had sporadically taken when necessary. Mr Sharma had been polite, but his voice had been filled with sadness as he had related the details of his daughter's disappearance on the fifth of August - six weeks and five days ago; he had been mournfully counting as he and his wife had gradually tried to come to terms with the possibility they may never see Neeraja again.

Mr Sharma had explained that he had read the article about Sammy Cooper in that morning's Daily Review, that the circumstances of the girls' disappearances were frighteningly similar.

Neeraja Sharma was seventeen and had excelled at school, entering college to study mathematics, computing and chemistry, and was also an avid runner, having completed three full marathons in as many years. She had recently applied to run in the Raymouth Marathon, which was being held on the sixth of October, and had been training heavily.

On the last day her parents had seen her, she had been training with her personal coach and he had gone inside a shop to purchase some drinks at about eight in the evening. When he came out, Neeraja wasn't there. Mr Sharma, her father, had reported her disappearance to the police immediately.

Like Sammy's parents, he had insisted she would never have gone anywhere without telling either him or his wife, that she was a good girl who obeyed her father. He believed his daughter had been abducted and was either being held somewhere against her will or, worse, had been killed.

Raoul knew he should contact the police, but he wanted the scoop, and they would find out soon anyway when The Daily Review ran the story the next day. In the meantime, he had some digging to do.

Gerda and Rob were seated together on their plush, chintz sofa, anxiously awaiting the policeman who was on his way. They knew the early investigation into their daughter's disappearance was happening because her disappearance had hit the national headlines that morning, but as long as Sammy was in possible danger, they would do whatever it took to bring her safely home. The doorbell rang and they stared at each other before Gerda trotted to greet their visitor.

"Mrs Cooper?" She nodded, nervous. "I'm Detective Inspector French, I believe my colleague informed you I was on my way." She nodded again, moving aside to let him enter the homely house. "I take it you've still not heard from Samantha?"

"For God's sake, Sammy. Everyone calls her Sammy." Gerda indicated the matching armchair as she returned to the

25

warm spot beside her husband on the sofa. "Nobody has heard anything, it's like she's fallen off the edge of the planet."

"Okay, please try not to worry, I'm sure she'll turn up safe and sound."

"Are you? Because I don't feel so sure, I know my daughter…" Her voice tailed off as she remembered the vastly older boyfriend she hadn't had a clue about. "Sammy would never willingly hurt us like this."

"When was the last time you saw her?"

"Rob, make a pot of tea, will you?" He jumped to her command and left the room.

"Is there something you don't want him to know?" French leant forward, intrigued, but she shook her head, dismissing his concerns.

"No, we share everything, I'm just thirsty. The last time I saw our Sammy was at about nine in the morning. I gave her a lift to uni; it's on my way to work."

"Which university is she at?"

"Southside, she said she wasn't ready to leave home and was lucky enough to get a place there studying Sport and Physical Education. She wanted to minimise the debt she would graduate with and we were more than happy to help as much as we could. We still are."

"And her mood when you last saw her, happy? Normal?"

"Absolutely normal. She's always a bit grumpy in the mornings, but aren't we all? She didn't say much, but she didn't *not* say much either, you know what I mean?"

"Yes. I assume you've seen the coverage in The Daily Review this morning?" Gerda nodded. "Yet you told my colleague yesterday she didn't have a boyfriend."

Gerda's face clouded, shamed. "I admit she hadn't told us about him, it came as a big shock. I thought she was pure. Is he going to be interviewed?"

"At this stage I'm afraid both he and her coach are suspicious to us, we'll be interviewing them as soon as possible, but obviously we wanted to hear from you in the first instance."

"Suspicious, what does that mean? You think something bad has happened to her, don't you?" Behind her, Rob appeared at the doorway, wiping his hands on a tea towel, concerned.

"Please, you need to stay positive. The most probable outcome is that Sammy will return home soon after some wild adventure, it's highly unlikely someone has taken her, but obviously we have to take precautions and keep that line of enquiry open."

"So what happens now?"

"We talk to everyone who could possibly have information about her whereabouts - friends, teachers, members of the gym - and try to piece together her day before her disappearance. We'll build a profile of her personality and lifestyle and, if necessary, encourage the public to come forward if they've seen anything that may help us. Obviously her details will be forwarded to the Missing Person's Bureau."

Rob stepped forward and laid a hand on his wife's shoulder reassuringly, knowing her heart was breaking, regardless of her confident composure.

"I've been asked to come and see," he glanced at the scrap of paper in his hand, "Detective Inspector French. My name's Peter Camber, it's about Sammy Cooper. I'm her coach."

Bob rang the incident room to inform his colleague, before indicating the row of seats to the tall man before him. He busied himself at the desk but found himself glancing at the visitor - a prime suspect in a possible murder enquiry - every now and then, wondering if he was ten feet away from a cold-blooded killer.

Peter Camber was well over six-foot-tall - probably six-four, six-five - and was lanky, gangly like a child, but his excellently defined muscles showed his extreme fitness. Was he strong enough to abduct and kill a girl? He was balding and had shaved the scant hair he hadn't lost, leaving a dull shadow at the base of his skull. His skin was deeply tanned and leathery with age, which Bob guessed must be mid-forties, and his eyes were a cold blue. He seemed agitated, frequently shifting position and fidgeting.

Bob wished he could be part of the interview rather than sitting at the front desk meeting mindless members of the public and taking mundane phone calls. On cue, the phone beeped and he sighed before taking the call.

French, harassed and overworked, stepped through the door to the reception area and greeted his guest, leading him to an empty interview room on the first floor. Several members of his team waited outside, behind the two-way mirror, eager to hear what Suspect Number One had to say, just as they would when Suspect Number Two - Joshua Brown - arrived later.

French showed Peter to a seat behind the central table and sat on the other side, and was about to begin his inquiry when the lofty man burst into tears, sobbing like a baby. Nonplussed, the inspector's jaw dropped. "Mr Camber, are you okay?" It was a redundant question.

"I know you think it was me who did it, but I loved her like a daughter, I'd never hurt a hair on her head." Tears coursed through his wrinkles and he wiped them away with the back of his hand, ashamed by the unwanted outburst. "I'll do anything I can to help, but please believe me when I say it wasn't me who took her."

"You seem to think something's happened to her?"

Now the fitter man's mouth gaped, eyes wide and scared. "No, at least I hope not. It's just not like Sammy not to be in contact, I don't think she's just had a tantrum and run away, it's something she just wouldn't do. I'm praying to God that she has, though, because the other possibilities are horrendous."

"Possibilities such as?"

Peter's shoulders sagged, despondent and trapped. "I don't know, that she's hurt somewhere, that she's scared, that someone's taken her. That she's..." it wasn't worth him continuing, French knew what he meant.

"Can you think back to Thursday evening after your training session with Sammy? We understand you were the last person to see her. Can you tell me what happened?"

"Yes, I'll try. I work at Southside Gym, I'm a personal coach, and because of her talent, Sammy was allowed to use the facilities for free, so she was there most nights. Thursday was no different. She'd finished uni early - she often did on Thursdays and Tuesdays - and had gone straight there. As you'll know from the photos, Sammy is a skinny little thing, she's sleek like a greyhound, and I checked that she'd eaten that day. It was an in-joke, I was always saying she'd break if she didn't put on weight, but she knew I was kidding, she just takes after her mother in build."

"And had she eaten?"

"She said she'd been to Teejays with some friends and had had a tuna jacket potato. She was watching her food intake keenly with the Raymouth Marathon coming up. We did some warm-ups and then went for a run, just a short one as she'd had a stressful day."

"In what way?"

"Oh, I don't know. Teenage things, boyfriend trouble, I think. She didn't say much, just that she was looking forward to going to sleep so tomorrow would come sooner."

"Do you know her boyfriend?"

Peter sighed deeply, aware that the secret he had been keeping for Sammy from her overbearing mother was exposed. "Yes, unfortunately. Joshua Brown is a repugnant waste of space and I have no idea what she could possibly have seen in him."

"You don't like him then?" State the obvious.

"I detest him. He comes to the gym two or three times a week, more to be seen than to exercise. He'll half-heartedly use the facilities, eye up the women, generally sour the air with his presence, and no doubt goes back to being a pompous couch potato as soon as he leaves, because he certainly isn't fit."

29

"Was he there on Thursday?"

Peter shook his head. "No, I think Sammy would have gone home earlier if he had been, he wasn't in her good books."

"Why?"

"I don't know any details, she just said his name with scorn a couple of times, you know how teenage girls do."

"So, you went for a run, then what?"

"She said she was going home, simple as that. My working day was over, I had no evening clients, so I was packing up and she waved me goodbye."

"And that was the last you saw of her?"

"Yes."

Jo had located Nancy Blaine easily, her former employers - as of that day, due to the headlines only she could have supplied - at the Southside Express had been delighted to hand her contact details to the police. Jo rarely managed to get out of the station, deskwork occupying most of her hours, and was relishing the freedom, but not the abrupt woman she was about to speak to again. She knocked on the door and waited.

"Who is it?" Jo instantly recognised the shrill tone of the woman she had been unable to avoid the previous day.

"My name is Constable Ellis, I'm sure you'll remember me from yesterday. I wonder if I could have a chat with you?"

The door opened wide and Nancy grinned. "I knew you lot would be round sometime, I bet your tails are well between your legs back at the station." She moved aside to let Jo in.

"What do you mean?"

"A beautiful girl goes missing and you guys do nothing. Come on, what do you think I mean?"

"Was it you who leaked the details to the national press?" Jo had followed her host into a small and chaotic kitchen.

"Might have been. Does it matter?" She took the kettle and half-filled it.

"It does to my boss. Apparently Chief Superintendent Brown is furious that his son is now implicated in Sammy's disappearance and it's possible heads are going to roll. My boss may be old-school, but he's a brilliant cop."

"Oh dear, such a shame. Look, sweetie, if your little boss has a few problems at work, why is that suddenly my concern?"

Irritation growing, her face reddened. Nancy Blaine was a revolting woman, a selfish bully, and Jo wasn't about to be browbeaten. "Because an eighteen-year-old girl is missing and my boss needs to put all his energy into finding her, not worrying about whether his neck's on the line."

Nancy turned back to the kettle, now boiling, and smiled smugly. "Hmm, I see where you're coming from, the Chief Super's got quite a temper on him, hasn't he. Coffee?"

"No, thank you. Please, Nancy, do the right thing."

She poured water into a mug and stirred. "Oh, if you insist! Damn you for shaming me into confessing my sins." Nancy stared into Jo's eyes, unsettling and deep. "It wasn't me who submitted the details to The Daily Review, but I know who it was and I can assure you he or she does not work for the police in any capacity."

"But you won't name names?"

"Of course not, I'm a journalist, but next time I see good old Benedict Brown, jocular cherub that he is, I'll be happy to let him know that the boys on the East Sussex force are watertight."

Jo couldn't help herself. "You know him?"

With a mischievous chuckle, Nancy winked as she replied. "I've rattled his cage on many an occasion."

As the reporter led her guest back along the hall to let her out, Jo glanced through the open doorway to the living room and noticed a man in a wheelchair, and she stopped, issuing Nancy a questioning look. It wasn't answered, but another side of Nancy's vulgar personality became clearer: she was tough, but life had obviously been tough back to her. Maybe she wasn't so bad underneath the hard exterior.

Chapter 3
Saturday Afternoon

Until he'd had the displeasure of meeting Joshua Brown, French had been certain Sammy would be found safe and well, but his conviction had been challenged by the odious man who had swaggered into the station, with a prominent lawyer by his side, as if he owned the place. The two men had been shown to the interview room recently vacated by the distraught personal trainer, and the preliminary details asked, but now they appeared to have reached stalemate. The majority of questions posed to the arrogant, fleshy man had been fended off with a 'no comment' from the solicitor.

French was agitated. "Why aren't you co-operating with us; it's your girlfriend who's missing."

"My client is co-operating with you, but your line of inquiry is mostly irrelevant. He's agreed he was dating Miss Cooper and had been for three months, and he's assured you that he didn't see her on the day she went missing. He's voluntarily come to see you and it's obvious he had no involvement in her disappearance. How can he make that any clearer?"

"By telling us his movements on Thursday the nineteenth of September, with credible witnesses who will collaborate to his whereabouts."

Joshua's voice was as slimy as his persona. "In my work as a councillor I meet a lot of people who would be furious to be involved with such a distressing case. You don't need to know my movements, nor do I need to tell you whom I was with. The last time I saw Sammy was on Wednesday evening when we had a silly tiff over something ridiculous."

"Oh?" French finally felt he was getting some answers.

"I've made no secret of the fact I was tired of her and I repeatedly told her our relationship was over, but she just wouldn't listen. She'd become a pain in the backside, and being eighteen, she had the looks but not the mind to hold my interest. Quite simply, she bored me."

"So you wanted her off your back?"

Joshua leaned forward, his chubby arms on the table. "Not enough to kill her, if that's what you're getting at. Girls like her are ten-a-penny to me, they throw themselves at me all the time and I'm not stupid enough to think it's me they want. I know they're after the celebrity lifestyle and my money, but hell, I get enough shags from it so everybody's happy."

French's stomach churned and again he wondered how a pretty little thing like Sammy Cooper could possibly degrade herself to be with such an oaf; the money he put her way must have been substantial. "Where were you on Thursday night?"

"I was at a black tie event for a charity. Can't remember which one, that's never been important to me, but there were plenty of people there who would vouch for my presence."

"I want to know which charity it was and I want the names of anyone who can confirm you were there."

Joshua reached into his jacket pocket and produced a business card, as tacky and loud as the man whose name it bore. "My card has the phone number of my office. If you dial it on Monday as she doesn't work weekends, you'll get through to my secretary and she'll be able to give you the event details and guest list."

"Monday's not good enough, Mr Brown…"

"Councillor."

"Sammy is missing and possibly hurt. I'm not sitting here all weekend twiddling my thumbs while her safety is compromised, just because it may be inconvenient for you. Get your fucking arse to the office and get me the details. Now." He checked his watch. "It's just gone three now, I'll give you two hours. Get me the information by five this afternoon. Interview over, Detective Inspector French is leaving the room."

Sammy had gradually weakened since being locked in the unsanitary room; the lack of food and water had drained her energy and was now affecting her comprehension. She had tried everything possible to escape, but had reached the stage

34

of not knowing if it was day or night; the windowless prison, dark and disgusting, gave no clues.

The sound of the warning door made her jump and her heart beat faster. She listened to the approaching steps, hoping he would unlock the door this time, but when another bowl of unappetising, cold stew was fed through the flap, she cried out, "Who are you? Why have you got me here? Let me out."

His breathing was audible, yet he said nothing. "Please, I don't know why you've picked on me, I haven't done anything wrong."

He breathed louder, quicker, and she hoped his resolve was weakening. Sammy tried another avenue, "These girls in here, they're ill. Have you seen how skinny they are?"

Silence. She wondered if he had tiptoed away and with consuming frustration let the tears flow, heavy sobs of pure misery. A cough hushed her. "I'm sorry, I don't want you to be sad, but I have to do this, it's for my sister. It won't be long now, there's just one more to go, then it'll all be over."

His talking could only be a good thing, especially as he seemed repentant. She could work on that, couldn't she? "Who are you?"

No reply came, but she felt his presence and continued, "Do you know me? Us? What's your sister got to do with it?" It was important she tried to engage him somehow; if he saw her as a person rather than a captive, maybe he would have some compassion and forget whatever vengeance he was seeking. "It must be hard for you, having to feed four girls, and the smell must be revolting, it's pretty damned bad in here I can assure you." She chuckled, friendly yet forced. "Why don't you tell me about what happened to make you take us?"

"It won't be long now." The footsteps dissipated behind the locked door and the warning door slammed. Sammy broke down again, wrenching, heartbroken tears dripping from her clammy skin.

"At least you tried." Sammy felt a hand on her shoulder and she spun around to see Sying, eyelids drooping from the drug-fuelled coma she had awoken from. "He's not talked to any of us, well, not that I know of, but we have all been sparko most of the time."

Sammy reached across and the two girls fell into a reassuring cuddle, both needing the human contact desperately. "You'll be awake for a while, won't you, Sying? Please stay awake a while, I need to know what's going on."

Sying looked at the dish of grey food, her stomach hurting from hunger, but resisted, sensing that the new girl was about to lose the plot. "What do you want to know?"

"Tell me your story. Tell me about Neeraja and Lydia. What's led to us being here in this disgusting prison?"

"I don't know much about them, we're asleep most of the time. And glad to be, I hasten to add. Lydia was the first, she's been here for ages. She'd just finished training at the gym and…"

Sammy's eyes widened. "I'd just been training when I was taken."

"We all had. That seems to be the one thing we have in common, that we're all keen runners, because as you can see there's nothing similar in our looks. Lydia was abducted on the twenty-first of June, and I've been here since the thirtieth of July. We've got no idea how long ago that was. What was the date when you were taken?"

"Nineteenth of September."

"Shit. The days just blend into one another, what with the drugs and no way of seeing outside. That means I've been here nearly two months." She quietened, the impact of the realisation - the waste of her life - overwhelming.

"What about Neeraja?"

Pulling herself together, Sying continued, "Fifth of August, nearly a week after me."

"God, you poor things, I've barely been here a minute compared to you guys, no wonder you're all so keen to sleep through it. Have you any idea why he's got us, what his plans are?"

She shook her head, the mane of black, greasy rat-tails skimming her bony shoulders. "Like I said, Dick hasn't spoken to any of us but, then again, none of us tried to engage him in conversation like you did, we all just shrieked and shouted at him until we realised he never intended to respond. Then we just gave up and ate the drugged food just to get out of it."

"So it's definitely the food, not the water?" Sying nodded and instantly Sammy got up and began to drink from the bucket of what she hoped was tap water. The wetness against her dry lips, her parched tongue, was an utter relief and pure pleasure; wine of the Gods had never tasted so good. Satiated, she fell back into the comforting hug, both girls benefiting from each other's support. "I'm going to find a way out of here. How, I don't know, but I promise you I will."

Beside them, Lydia's hand, the dusky skin covered in grime and sewage, reached towards the bowl and scooped some drug-laden mush to her mouth.

"That fucking wank-stain is clean." French stormed into the room, throwing his jacket over the back of Jo's chair. She glanced at him timidly, unsure whether to speak or let him continue his rant, but reasoned that the latter was probably safer. "Joshua fucking Brown, slime-ball that he is, has a solid alibi. There are photos and witnesses to prove he was at a charity event all evening, and he was actually giving a speech at eight pm."

"What about Peter Camber?" Although she could feel his fury, she also sensed his despair.

"Well, Boswell was checking out his movements and I haven't heard from him yet, but my gut says he wasn't involved in this. You know, this could all just be a mountain out of a molehill, Sammy's probably in bed with some young whippersnapper right now enjoying the trouble she's causing. If it hadn't been for that fucking reporter meddling, we wouldn't all be wasting our bloody time."

"I might be out of place, Guv, but whatever I say is wrong with everybody anyway, so I won't..."

"For goodness' sake, Jo, get to the fucking point, I'm a busy man."

"I don't think you really believe this is a waste of time. I know I don't. I went to lunch at Teejays on Thursday and she was there. She was talkative and happy; in fact, it was her laughing so loudly that made me notice her in the first place."

"You never told me that."

"You never asked, and anyway, I told Boswell."

He heard his name and butted in. "Don't hang this one on me, Jo Ellis, you come out with so much crap there's no point listening to you most of the time."

"Pack it in, children. Are you sure it was Sammy? I mean, Peter Camber said she'd had a stressful day and that tends to stop people from having a good time."

"Maybe her mates were cheering her up. They seemed like a nice bunch, and that's what friends do for each other." She flicked a loose strand of chestnut hair from her face, eyes fixed on her boss to avoid Boswell and his nastiness.

"Oh, is it? I wouldn't know." Jo almost felt sorry for him, unsure whether it was sarcasm or not. "There's your next job, then, I want you to find those friends and ask about the lunch, you know, the conversation, what she ate…"

"It was a tuna jacket."

"I know what Peter's said, but people lie, you know?"

"No, Guv, it was a tuna jacket potato. I know, I was there and I coveted it, it looked gorgeous compared to my bowl of cheap, soggy chips."

Irritated still, and uncommunicative with it, French waved his hand dismissively, grabbed his jacket and stomped towards his office. "I've given you orders, go and do what you're told." The door slammed behind him.

"Yeah, do as you're told, *Constable*."

"Piss off, Boswell."

Raoul had worked long hours collecting as much detail as he could from Mr Sharma and his wife, collating it with what he knew about Sammy, and writing and editing the article. He sent the file to the crime editor, Jonas Mildenhall, knowing that when the newspaper hit the stands the next morning his reputation as a journalist would take a big leap in the right direction.

He clicked the computer off, the blackening screen reminding him how dry and tired his eyes were, and snatched his anorak from the hook. He was about to leave the office, darkened and empty of staff due to the late hour, when his desk phone rang. For a moment he debated answering, but his curiosity was strong. Grasping the receiver, he answered bluntly, "What? Oh, Phil, you're calling late. What's up?"

"Nancy's been doing some digging, in fact, we both have. I've got plenty more stuff on Sammy Cooper and that knob, Joshua Brown."

"Too late, mate, tomorrow's edition has just been sent to press. I'll give you a call in the morning; it'll have to wait until either Monday or Tuesday, depending on how good the scoop is."

The disappointment in Phil's voice was clear, but as a freelancer he was used to knock-backs. "Yeah, sure thing, I understand. Can I not just tell you now."

"No, I'm tired. Send it in an email if you like, then it'll be there when I get in. Did you get the cheque, by the way?"

"Yeah, nice one, thanks. Nancy took it to the bank this morning."

"No probs. Look, I've got to go, I'm so exhausted I think I may already be asleep. Send the email, I'll look at it first thing and if there's anything Jonas or I want to run with, I'll call you. Oh, and make sure you get the paper tomorrow, you're going to be swept off your feet by what's headlining."

"Unlikely in a wheelchair, Raoul."

"Shit, yeah, sorry mate."

Chapter 4
Sunday 22nd September

Boswell tentatively opened the door to French's office, aware that - as was everybody in the incident room - he was in a foul mood due to the newspaper headlines that morning. "You wanted me, Guv?"

"Why did we not know this? Hasn't anyone been in touch with the Missing Person's Bureau? Surely they should have flagged it up to us? Now we look like complete imbeciles to the bloody public, plus I'm getting hammered from above. Get on the phone to that bloody organisation and find out if there are any more we should know about. And get in touch with whatever police force is dealing with this," he pulled the paper closer to find the girl's name, "Neeraja Sharma's disappearance."

"Yes, Guv, I'm on it."

"Too bloody late," French said under his breath, but not quietly enough to stop the cocky man hearing, and he sloped away, closing the door behind him. "And Boswell," he was shouting now, "send Jo in, if you can manage that without bickering."

Everyone in the busy room heard the demand and Jo received plenty of sympathetic stares as she reluctantly left her desk and mooched to the door, signing the cross on her chest with a despondent shrug before entering the 'room of doom', as it was affectionately dubbed when French was in one of his frequent bad moods.

"Guv, you wanted me?"

"Sit down." She followed his instructions, tense and apprehensive. "Have you seen it?" He tapped the newspaper on his desk with a finger and she nodded. "I want you to get hold of Nancy Blaine again. " Jo sagged; her dislike for the arrogant journalist was intense, despite the unseen caring side that must exist deep down. "She knows who's feeding these details to The Daily Review and I want you to find out who it is. They need to be stopped before this becomes a national panic."

"Why not just tell the newspaper not to print anything on it? They must have a code of conduct."

"Whoever it is will just move on to the next paper. No, we need Nancy to tell us who the source is and there's every possibility it's her, anyway. I think it'd be a good idea if you and Nancy become best buddies for a short while."

"Guv, she hates me and the feeling's mutual."

His hazel eyes settled on her, stern and intolerant. "That was an order." As she walked out, chided, he called after her again. "And tell Barbara to come in."

Barbara had been given the task of arranging a press conference for the following day, a command sent through the ranks by Chief Superintendent Brown in order for him to explain the police force's actions in the embarrassing situation, an attempt to regain some respect from the judgemental public. She had prepared press statements and sorted the venue, time and refreshments to suit Brown's full diary. Her phone had been humming, and impromptu colleagues bothering her with random, often unimportant questions had taken minutes she didn't have. The twenty-seven hours she had been given to arrange the event were proving to be taxing and she was already exhausted.

Beside her, Boswell was having an obviously tough conversation on the phone. "Yes, yes, I know we didn't classify her as high risk, but we should have, and now the news about the other girl who's missing... I know she also wasn't classified as high risk; I've spoken to the team dealing with her case. Look," suddenly his voice was commanding and the room hushed around him, "I've admitted all our faults here, no, don't talk over me," pens dropped as eyes everywhere watched his performance, "we need to know if there are any other girls who have disappeared under similar circumstances; running and age seem to be the key here. If you would send your findings to us as soon as they're done, and please do so quickly, because this is a possible multi-abduction enquiry and there's a very real possibility that these two girls may have been harmed. I appreciate your help, thank you."

He slammed the phone down and the room erupted with laughter at his uncommon outburst; Kenneth Boswell may be the size of a rugby player, with an orange peel face littered with scars, but to everybody except Jo Ellis - the apparent nemesis he fancied the pants off - he was gentle, kind and considerate. It was rare for him to raise his voice.

Jo had spoken to Nancy, much to the older woman's amusement, and they had arranged to meet for lunch an hour later at a place Jo couldn't possibly afford; Nancy's refusal to eat somewhere so lowly as Teejays meant that, unless the reporter offered to pay, Jo would have to manage on just a beverage, if she could even scrape enough pennies together for that.

French's office door opened and he came through, his face paler than normal and a slight tremor to his hands. He didn't have to speak to gain attention, his pained expression was enough to make the team take notice. The room fell quiet, apart from a couple of officers locked into phone calls. "I've got some news and it's not good. The Met have just spoken to Gates, there's another girl, Lydia Wilson, who's been missing since the twenty-first of June." His tone saddened. "Lydia is also a keen runner."

A troubled sigh came from the doorway and all heads turned towards the source: Detective Superintendent Gates. "So was Sying Cheng."

"There's another?" French was horrified, he had never headed such a grave investigation.

"Sying was abducted - I think we can lose the 'disappeared' and 'missing' tags now - from a nearby park where she was training alone for the Raymouth Marathon."

Jo, young and excitable, sprung up. "So was Sammy Cooper, I read it in her mother's statement."

"Coincidence." French was bitter and couldn't control his temper.

42

"I'm not so sure. That sounds like a good lead to follow up. Make sure someone takes care of that, Dan. Now, back to Sying: she is eighteen, Asian - well, Chinese - and had been about to start at the University of Sussex, studying for a Sports Science Degree. Her friends and family all insisted that her disappearance was highly out of character, but due to the fact she hadn't taken well to leaving home, on top of desperately missing her family in Leeds, her case remained low-risk. Obviously the classification has been changed now."

"Are we now thinking serial killer, opposed to stropping teenage girls?"

"No. *We're* not, the Met are, though. They're officially taking the investigation off our hands."

Groans and expletives erupted through the room and Gates waited a minute for the commotion to die down. "Yes, I know, I know, but, to be honest, it's probably for the best. Lydia Wilson went missing from central London and she was the first - well, that we know of, anyway. The good news for some of you is that they want a team from here, and one from each of the three forces involved with the other girls, to join their investigation."

Again the room was buzzing, this time with a positive vibe. Gates raised his voice to regain control. "Obviously Dan French will be the team leader, but it's now his job to pick another five people to go with him on this all-expenses-paid manhunt." He strutted towards French and spoke quietly. "They're rank specific, so don't make up your mind until you've seen the conditions they've set. I'll get my secretary to send a copy down to you." He turned to leave but stopped in afterthought. "Oh, by the way, Dan, they want you to start tomorrow at ten a.m."

Barbara glanced at her desk, piles of details and arrangements strewn haphazardly in an order that made sense to her. "What about the press conference?"

French shook his head in reply and she sank into her seat sulkily, having wasted hours of her time for nothing.

43

Jo intended to be late for the lunch date with Nancy Blaine to avoid having to buy a drink, but she was dismayed on arrival to find the reporter absent. Reluctantly she ordered the cheapest drink on the pricey menu: a pot of English breakfast tea.

Sipping it slowly, she waited at the pre-booked table, but after a further fifteen minutes had passed she became concerned that Nancy wasn't going to show. She decided to wait five more minutes before heading back to the station and was pleased when, moments later, a flurry of movement caught her eye. The woman entered, flamboyantly dressed and colourful.

The maître-d led her to the table and the two women shook hands. "I got delayed in traffic, there are road works all along Truman Street, not that I saw anybody working. Anyway, I'm sure you're enjoying the relaxing break from your duties back at the station."

Jo seethed inwardly; not even an apology. Nancy Blaine clearly thought her time was more important than everyone else's, and she wanted to point out that she had also travelled along Truman Street, yet had managed to arrive on time - well, as suitably late as she had planned to arrive to avoid spending the money she'd had to spend after all. Instead she smiled, concealing her irritation.

Nancy bustled about, taking her cardigan off and arranging the many layers of clothing, before sitting across the small table from the policewoman. "I must say, you look very young for a copper; they always say you're getting old when the police look too young to be in the job. How old are you?"

The arrogance was palpable and Jo bristled. Somehow Nancy always seemed to press her buttons, but she had been ordered to be friendly, so friendly she would be. "I'll be twenty-four next month, but everyone tells me I look young for my age."

Nancy shrugged, dismissive. "People always say that but it's usually a lie. What did you want to meet up for this time?" She opened her handbag and took out a brown bottle of prescription tablets, dropping one into her hand. "Pesky allergies. I have to take these damned pills or I end up having to use my EpiPen. Lactose, if you're wondering." Jo couldn't have cared less.

The waiter approached, pen and pad in hand ready to take the order, and Nancy hastily grasped the wine list from the table, scanning it masterfully as she swallowed the tablet without water. "We'll just have a bottle of Clos des Fous for now. Come back in ten minutes to take our food order."

"Of course, madam."

Jo was uneasy, embarrassed by her poverty, and she spoke in a low whisper. "I don't think I'll be eating..."

"My treat, my dear, I remember what it's like to be starting out with no money." Even when offering a gift, the woman managed to be patronising and Jo was further shamed. "So, what did you want to see me for? It must be about the whole missing girl thing. I hate to admit it, but I didn't know about that. Let me see, you've been told to be my friend so you can find out where the damning revelation about the police force's shortcomings came from. Am I right?"

Startled and in the spotlight, Jo reddened, belying her guilt. "No, no."

"Yes, I'm right. Well, befriend me if you like, I can always use an extra police contact, but I still won't be breaking any confidences. How's the case going, by the way?"

Jo scratched her head, belittled and confused by how easily Nancy had turned the questioning back onto her. "I can't say, I'm afraid."

"Are you dear? Don't be, I don't bite." Nancy sniffed and took a sip of the taster the waiter had dribbled into a polished crystal glass, rolling it around her mouth, savouring the expensive chardonnay. She held a hand up to indicate her satisfaction and the waiter furnished both women with a full measure. "Anyway, before we start becoming 'friends', we'll get the elephant out of the way: I don't know where the details came from about Neeraja Sharma, it was a shock to me too.

All good fun, though, I've never investigated a serial killer before."

Jo choked on her wine, the indifference unbelievable. "We have nothing to say the girls are dead."

"You will, don't worry." She raised her glass and chinked Jo's affably. "Exciting, eh?"

Sammy felt as if she were going crazy. The growling hunger that made her retch as it tore through her, combined with extreme fatigue, was awful, and being trapped, away from friends and family, was worse. She had tried to convince Sying not to eat any more of the debilitating food, to stay coherent and help her find a way to escape the treacherous prison, but she had succumbed. Be it to appetite or boredom, Sammy wasn't sure.

The warning door clanged and Sammy dragged herself, weary, across the sticky floor, too tired now to stand unless necessary. She had managed to talk to the man - the other girls called him Dick, but she hadn't yet joined their sad joke - another time. It seemed to be hours ago, but was possibly only minutes; she had lost all track of time. As she waited for him to reach the door, she glanced at the other girls, drugged and asleep as they always were.

"Are you awake?"

It was the first time the man had instigated conversation and Sammy was nervous. "Yes."

He coughed, a deep rattle that sounded painful. "You'll sleep if you eat."

"I know, that's why I'm not eating. Please tell me, why are you holding us here?"

"I'm sorry, but I have to. It won't be long now, and I'll have a treat for you soon."

"The biggest treat you could give me is freedom, don't you see that?"

"No." He was angry and he coughed again, before, "The biggest treat I could give you is for you to live."

Sammy gasped. She had tried to avoid the possibility, tried to keep upbeat, but now he had suggested murder and she was terrified. Broken and timid, "You intend to kill us? But why, we haven't done anything wrong?"

"I know and I'm sorry." Forlorn again.

Sammy realised that common sense mattered more than ever before and instinct told her that building a relationship with their captor was essential if they were to stay alive. "You don't sound like you want to keep us here."

"No, I feel sorry for you all, I really do, but I feel sorry for my sister too."

"The other girls call you Dick, what's your real name?"

"I can't say."

"Why? It's not like we can tell anyone."

"Because I like you and I don't know if I can kill you. The others, yes, but not you. If I tell you my name and then set you free, you'll tell the police."

Sammy felt dizzy with relief and the safest she had been since her abduction, but then her eyes settled on the three painfully skinny girls - teenagers like her whose greatest love was running - and knew that if she were saved the fate he seemed to have planned for them the guilt would be eternally unbearable. "I can see your point. What are your plans for us?"

Abrupt. "You ask too many questions." Sammy heard Dick stride away and tears brimmed as the warning door banged. Selfish in her own grief, she failed to notice that Lydia had awoken and, unmoving on the floor, her energy level so low, was also crying. "Oh my God, Lydia, I take it you heard that?"

Sammy shuffled to the anguished girl and wrapped her arms around her, hugging her close, letting her spill nearly three months of sorrow. "We'll be fine. I know we will. Shush. Shush." She gently stroked Lydia's wiry curls, ignoring the embedded dirt and grease, comforting her; a mother and her child.

Eventually Lydia had no tears left. "You don't get it," she sniffed, swallowed, "he likes you because you're white." A detail Sammy had never considered. "I'm Jamaican, Sying's Chinese and Neeraja's Indian. He likes you because you're white and we're going to die because of the colour of our skin."

Raoul hadn't had a day off work for over two weeks. He adored his position as Deputy Political Editor at The Daily Review and had toiled relentlessly to achieve success, but it had its pitfalls. He sat behind his desk, rereading what he hoped was now a finalised article that Phil Blaine had prepared about Joshua Brown, dishing as much dirt as he could about the revolting man. The only downfall, as far as he was concerned, was that the piece absolved the councillor of any involvement in the missing girl's disappearance. Raoul would have loved to be able to pin that one on him.

Jonas Mildenhall entered and Raoul rested back on his seat, welcoming the chance to stop focusing on the screen he had stared at all day. "What's up?"

"I thought I'd let you know that I've had an email from the Met, they're holding a press conference tomorrow evening about the investigation into Sammy Cooper and Neeraja Sharma's disappearances. I know it's not in your job remit, but because you gave me the article blowing their cock-up, I thought you'd be interested."

"Is it invitation only?"

"I'm sure I can squeeze you in as my plus-one if you fancy going. We could go for a drink after, make a night of it." The Crime Editor dragged a chair forward, clearly enjoying the break from work.

"Nice thought, but I've got an early start tomorrow and…"

"Raoul, I know you're excited about your promotion and all that, but I'm worried about you. You've been working so hard recently we barely see each other." He leant over the desk and patted his partner's hand lovingly.

"I know, but I spent so many years wanting this job that I feel I've got to give it my all."

Jonas, practical and optimistic as always, smiled as he concocted a compromise. "I'll tell you what, come along with me anyway. This case is unusual in that our jobs are linked, you with the Joshua Brown part and me, obviously, with the abduction side of things. Maybe we can work together for a bit, which would make more time for us to give our relationship the care it deserves."

"That sounds like a plan." Raoul clasped Jonas's hand, fingers entwined.

The phone trilled and Jonas nodded for his lover to answer. "Raoul, it's me, Phil. You're not going to believe what Nancy's just told me."

Raoul held his hand up for quiet and listened intently. "Send it to me now, everything you've got." He dropped the receiver into its holder and stared at Jonas, who was curious. "You haven't sent tomorrow's edition off yet, have you?" Jonas shook his head. "Apparently two more girls have been linked to the case, Phil's sending the details through now."

"Phil Blaine? He's not an investigative journalist."

"No, but his wife is and she's good. Very good."

Chapter 5
Monday 23rd September

French was fuming as he puffed up the stairs, The Daily Review in his hand, and as he passed Jo's desk he demanded, "You. My office. Now."

Worried, she followed him through, closing the door. "Have I done something wrong?"

French threw the paper on the desk and it unfolded, revealing the bold, black headlines: *Two More Victims*. He gave her a moment to digest the words. "I think we can safely say you have."

"I didn't tell anybody, I swear. If there's a leak it wasn't anything to do with me."

"I asked you to get details *from* Nancy, not feed her them. And before you pipe up some lame excuse, I've spoken to the dreaded woman myself and she was happy to drop you in it."

"But I didn't say anything." Jo recalled the conversation with Nancy the day before, desperate to clear her name. She was sure she had not said anything out of place. But there it was: '*and the other two*'. She had mentioned it without meaning to and was now in big trouble. "Oh shit. Guv, I'm so sorry. Oh my God, are you going to drop me from the London team?"

French glanced at his watch, hassled already. "We've only got one fucking hour before we're supposed to be at Scotland Yard and there's no one else to take your place, so no, I can't drop you from the fucking team. But I forbid you to talk to Nancy Blaine again and from now on I'll be keeping a close eye on you. Are the others ready?"

"I think so, we were just waiting for you." The timid sigh of a chastened child.

"Well, I would have been here five minutes ago if I hadn't had to stop and pick up the damned newspaper. Because of your big gob. What about transport to the train station?"

"Barbara's arranged it."

"At least I can rely on one of my members of staff. Get the fuck out of here. Get everyone downstairs and I'll be down in a minute."

The journey to London was uneventful and the team of six arrived just on time. They were led to an incident room - massive compared to the one in Southside Station - and offered refreshments, which they accepted gratefully. Three other teams were grouped in the room, one from Slough, another from Brighton, and the largest were the Metropolitan Police, who had already set up several whiteboards, each littered with documents and photos. Each group spoke amongst themselves for a while, sipping tea and coffee, munching on biscuits, until a hush settled over the room and all eyes settled on the doorway.

Superintendent Brannigan had entered and his authority and presence were striking. He strode in purposefully and retained the attention despite saying nothing. The members of the Met Police who worked under his command shuffled forward, sitting on chairs or desks, and the alien groups followed their lead. Eventually, when the fidgeting and fussing died down, he spoke. "Good morning everybody, and thank you for coming."

In normal circumstances Nancy kept her composure no matter what, but today was different; she was attending an interview with Jonas Mildenhall, the esteemed Crime Editor at The Daily Review. He had emailed her late the previous evening, having heard that it was she, through her husband, who had provided most of the details for the paper's latest headline, mentioning he had been impressed by her investigative abilities.

Nancy had worked for a national newspaper - albeit a less popular one than The Daily Review - in the early days of her career as a reporter, but she had disgraced herself and been fired, and the damning reference her former employer had issued nailed the coffin lid on her fledgling Fleet Street career.

She had moved many miles from her home town, away from the wagging tongues of bitchiness, and found the part-time position with the Southside Express, at the same time tentatively - quietly - setting herself up as a freelancer, and she submitted the majority of her stories through her husband of fifteen years; Phil had a far better reputation in the media world than she probably ever would.

But somehow, despite the mud attached to her name, she was now in line for an amazing position at the country's biggest-selling national newspaper. Nervous was an understatement; she was petrified.

With seven alternative outfits scattered over the bed, Nancy gave herself a once over in the mirror and decided that the taupe Harvey Nichols two-piece would have to do; she was running late for her train already. She dabbed her face with a tissue to collect the most recent smattering of sweat and patted on a final coat of powder. Steeling herself, she grabbed her briefcase, took a deep breath and left the bedroom.

"You look lovely, just the job. Are you excited?"

"Terrified."

Phil pushed his wheelchair away from the article he was working on and patted his knee. "Come and have a cuddle before you go."

She debated for a moment and reached in for a quick kiss before heading for the door. "I'll be fine. You get yourself back to work and I'll be back before you know it, hopefully with good news."

He smiled after her, enjoying the breeze her departure created on his cheeks, the sweetness of her expensive perfume tickling his nose. How he would cope if she was in London every day, he didn't know, but she had been such a blessing to him since the accident and it was time for her career to fly. She had helped enough with his, after all.

French was impressed with the efficiency and organisation within the Met Police, it put Southside Station to shame, but he had noticed there was less camaraderie between the officers and hoped some would develop with time as they got to know each other. Superintendent Brannigan had detailed the investigation concisely to the vast team - more than thirty in total of varying ranks - and left each man and woman with a clear outline of their expected tasks.

DCI Barry Harner had taken over the meeting on Brannigan's departure and allowed them to briefly introduce themselves, before heading back to his office to let the next stage of the investigation begin. As soon as he had left the room the gossips began to whisper, and soon all the newcomers knew that Harner had headed the Black Museum Bunch in the search for the notorious Kopycat Killer five years previously and had cocked up big style: his mistake had led to the distressing death and mutilation of a woman named Adelaide Smith.

French remembered the case well – he had been a Detective Sergeant based in Eastbourne at the time and had been part of the investigation into Maud Blessing's death - and felt sorry for Harner. It had been a dreadful case to be involved with. The country had been in uproar and the police had taken the flack. Apparently, poor Harner was still taking it, and from his own people, which seemed harsh.

French's first job was to contact the organisers of the Raymouth Marathon for a detailed list of all the women currently registered to run in the next race. Officers had contacted the parents of Sying Cheng and Lydia Wilson on the matter and they had confirmed that both girls had intended to run. Thus, it was probable that the abductor had access to the list and was picking his victims from it, one by one.

The nation was already gripped with the case, having read the unofficial details in the Sunday Review, and the television and radio news programmes frequently mentioned the press conference due to be held by the police that evening.

The newspaper had contained no specifics regarding the two latest missing person cases to have been linked to those of Neeraja's and Sammy's, no names or dates - Jo hadn't supplied details when she had inadvertently leaked the news to Nancy -

but that was irrelevant to most people; they were counting numbers, not identities.

French made the call from his makeshift desk area and was grateful that Roberta Robinson, the Chairwoman, was helpful and proficient. Within minutes of the conversation ending an email popped into his mailbox and he clicked on the attachment to reveal a file containing nearly three thousand names, along with their contact details. He swiftly forwarded the email to Harner and Barbara, the only civilian on his team, before printing a copy for himself.

Collecting the numerous pages from the printer, he neatened them, taking them to Harner. "I've just emailed you the list of people registered for the race, there are two thousand nine hundred and forty-three due to run. Do you want me to get my team to contact each one?" He hoped not and was relieved when Harner shook his head.

"No, there are way too many, it'll take forever and we haven't got the time. I'll make sure the Super's aware and get him to mention this tonight. If it's all over the news tomorrow, then the women will know to be on their guard when they're training. In fact, perhaps we should suggest they don't train. I'm surprised that the organisers haven't already decided to cancel the race this year, all things considered."

"Maybe they will, after all, they've only just been told that their register links the victims. The woman I spoke to seemed pretty shocked."

"Did you ask her about the other committee members, whether she had anybody in mind who would be capable of something as disturbing as this?"

French nodded. "She said that they were a friendly bunch and she didn't suspect any of them, but she promised to send their details to me anyway. The email should have come through by now."

"Print it out and give me a copy as soon as possible. I'll want backgrounds on everybody with access to the register." Harner's discussion with French ended swiftly, another officer needed his attention.

Sammy sat to attention when she heard the warning door, wondering if Dick would talk to her again. Unusually, Lydia, Sying and Neeraja were awake, albeit groggy, but they tended not to speak; they had nothing new to say. The footsteps approached and presently a bowl of grey-speckled mush was fed under the door. Sammy, starving, still refused to eat, but the other three delved in, welcoming the gruel that would send them to sleep again. "Are you going to eat this time?"

He had instigated contact with her for the second time and Sammy was pleased, it made her feel safer. "You know I'm not, I don't want to be drugged."

"I'm worried about you. You've had two days without food."

His concern was refreshing, but now she knew how long she had been captive for, and how much longer it seemed to her, she understood why the girls welcomed the intoxicating food. However, she was adamant she wasn't going to end up like they had; she still had hope. "Why won't you let us out, Dick? I know you're a good person."

Brusque and angry. "You know nothing about me." He started coughing and grumbled.

"I know that you care about me, because you talk to me, and I know that you care for the others because you make sure they don't go hungry." She dragged words from nowhere, determined to keep him in conversation. "And I know you love your sister, because whatever you're doing, you're doing it for her."

Sammy was aghast when she realised that the scraping noise she had heard was Dick - their tormentor - slipping down the wall and sitting on the floor near the door. It dawned on her that this chat could be instrumental in saving her life. He didn't speak and she realised she had hit a nerve.

"Dick, it's not too late to stop this. I don't know what you're planning, but I'm scared - we all are - and if you were just to let us go…" she quietened, straining to hear his mood. "It's not too late. We don't need to know what you look like,

55

your name, we don't need anything. Just set us free and the police will never know who took us."

An anguished wail, followed by a harsh rattle in his throat. "I'm in too deep now, I've got to follow this through."

"No, you don't. Dick," she had another avenue to try, knowing she was getting through to him, "you know the others think you're doing this because they're coloured? They think you won't kill me because I'm white."

And now his mood was unmistakeable, voice raised and indignant. "Racist? I am not a racist. Race, colour, religion, they mean nothing to me."

She had him and could work this to her advantage. "So prove it, Dick, let us go. Let the black girl, and the Indian, the Chinese girl, let them go, prove that their colour isn't a problem. You'll never be caught, we won't let you be, because we'll not say a word."

The hacking cough took over again and Sammy waited, holding her breath, hoping for a response. But she heard him clamber to his feet and her heart fell. "I've fed you all early today because I have to go somewhere."

"Are you seeing a doctor about that cold you've got? It sounds pretty harsh."

"Sort of. It's not a cold, it's from an old injury and I have a lady massage me when it gets bad. She's coming over tomorrow. Don't worry about it, it's nothing. Afterwards is where the fun starts, because I'm collecting the treat I promised you."

His footsteps hastened away, followed by the slamming door and Sammy realised she was screaming, loud and frustrated, scared and lonely.

Rhiannon Hughes couldn't avoid the news that two more girls were missing but, flippant and fifteen, she didn't care. What went on around the world was no concern of hers and current affairs were boring. Her friends at school were fanciful and romantic about the disappearances, but Rhiannon only cared about two main things: the way she had been mistreated all her life, and running.

The product of a broken home, her father in prison for grievous bodily harm and his ex-wife, her mother, an alcoholic and frequent drug abuser, she had learned the hard way that feelings were dreadful things that got in the way of life, and she had effectively placed mental barriers between herself and everybody she knew to protect herself from being hurt. Again. The only time she felt peace was when she pounded the pavements, the elements whipping around her, freeing her mind from the turmoil and violence she had witnessed over the years.

At her own insistence, family life having been so troubled, Rhiannon had been placed in a foster home the year before, but when she had caused the family trouble she had been taken to a care home for teenagers. It was run by do-gooders who she had no respect for, and her constant bad behaviour had vexed them to the point where they no longer cared about her toing and froing from one spot of bother to the next. She hadn't told anyone she was training tonight, let alone where or for how long.

The wind was blustery and the hot evening sun that edged closer to the horizon failed to stop the cooling gusts biting as she trotted through the outskirts of Knole Park. Although originally from Wales, her mother had taken Rhiannon and her siblings to start a new life away from their father, fearing for the family's safety. She'd had friends in Sevenoaks who had helped the Hughes to settle in, but slowly and surely Vivian's nightly forays into drunkenness had alienated her from every person who had supported her. Eventually her children had joined the crowd.

Having been in the town for over five years now, and a keen runner for most of those, Rhiannon knew the National Trust beauty spot well and it was her preferred place to train. The backdrop of trees, colourful at this time of year with a variety of oranges and yellows as the leaves dried and fell, had always somehow made her feel secure, comforting her in a life where no fellow human did.

She glanced at her watch. It was late, but no one would notice if she kept running all night, even into next week, because not a single soul on the planet gave a shit for her. Despondent and in need of a break, she saw a bench ahead and trotted, sweating and pink, intending to sit for a minute. Only then did she notice another jogger behind her.

Unthreatened by the innocuous man, she was stunned when he lunged at her, thrusting something grey towards her mouth. She struggled, her streetwise ways showing their use for once, and almost overpowered him, but the fumes from the rag he held seeped up her nostrils and, seconds later, her body gave up the fight. Dick cradled the girl in his arms, her shiny and wild auburn hair billowing in the squally wind, and with every gasping breath he took, Sammy Cooper's pleading returned: *it's not too late*.

Phil sighed with relief as he clicked the button to send the email to Raoul. Although he was a freelancer, most of the work he did was for his old friend's benefit, their shared passion for politics - specifically left-wing politics - gave them common ground with their work.

Phil had worked for The Daily Review before the accident, had been a 'valued member of staff' according to his team leader, but apparently not valued enough, because they had paid him off like a shot when he had lost his legs in a terrorist bombing in the final year of the millennium, despite his mind remaining intact and functional. They had labelled him with post-traumatic stress disorder, but he had never considered himself troubled. The truth, he felt, was that his wheelchair didn't match the office's contemporary decor.

He heard keys in the door and his heart beat faster. His beloved Nancy, the only person to have supported him regardless since that fateful day, was back. "Babe, how did it go?"

"Oh. My. God." Nancy dashed into the room, simultaneously kicking her stilettos from her feet and discarding the smart jacket. "They want me to start Wednesday, can you believe it?"

He grinned, genuinely delighted, despite concern about how he would cope with her away every day, and she hopped onto the lap she had rebuked earlier. He basked in her intense, loving, excited cuddle. "I am so, so proud of you, Mrs Blaine."

"And I'm proud of you, Mr Blaine."

"Really? Why?"

"Because you carried on fighting when everyone else gave up on you. Retained your dignity." She kissed him three times on the face and he pulled her closer.

A minute became two, and finally they stopped clinging to the person they loved most, basking in the knowledge that they were lucky to have each other in a world filled with cruelty, suspicion and intolerance.

Sammy knew something was wrong. Lydia had become paler than she had thought possible and her breaths were erratic and laboured. She weakly dragged herself across the floor and cuddled her, protective and warm. "Lydia, are you okay?" But Lydia didn't reply, struggling to breathe.

Sammy reached out to Sying, jostling in an attempt to wake her and when she didn't respond, Sammy tried Neeraja. "Please wake up." Without warning, Lydia threw up; a vile-smelling bile that cloyed Sammy's throat, but even sickness didn't revive the girl. Sammy shook her patient, but there was no response, and suddenly Lydia began to fit, convulsing in impossible and frightening positions. It didn't last long.

Sammy checked Lydia's pulse, but had already guessed that her fellow prisoner had taken her final breath. Gently, she lay the empty body of her friend on the floor and cried, unrelenting and wrenching, ridding herself of the hopelessness and grief that had escalated intolerably since her abduction.

As the tears eventually subsided, her face blotchy and damp, Sammy felt that nothing had any meaning any more.

She would have to face facts, come to terms with reality, and accept that Dick, whoever he really was, was her captor and had no intention of setting her or the two remaining girls free. She reached out and scooped up some stew, desperate for the drug to take the beastliness - the truth - away.

Chapter 6
Late Monday Evening

It had been a hard and busy day and French was exhausted. Everyone was. Staff at New Scotland Yard had arranged accommodation for the three visiting teams and implemented staggered shifts so the incident room would always be buzzing as long as the girls remained unfound. French was notorious for working long hours, but the pressure put on his and everyone's shoulders was tougher than normal. Operation Bandicoot was the biggest investigation he had ever been part of.

Only the elite few had attended the press conference and the rest had half-watched it on the news while working, following leads, making phone calls, building pictures of the victims that would hopefully lead to the man who had taken them. Superintendent Brannigan, his presence still palpable from the television screen, had done a sterling job of defending the police's initial inaction in all four abductions and, a master of public relations, he came across as sensitive and thorough, leaving the nation with no doubt that the girls would be found safe and unharmed.

Of course, everyone watching at New Scotland Yard knew the reality was very different. It was probable they were looking for bodies rather than young women with their lives ahead of them, but a smidgeon of hope and a lot of excitement kept their spirits up.

French glanced at the clock on the wall; it appeared to have four hands and he realised how tired he really was. He checked the address of the shared house his team had been allocated - Barbara and Jo were already there due to their early starts the next day - and left. He wasn't due to start until midday the next day, but guessed he would be in earlier.

He was about to step into a black cab he had flagged down when his mobile chirped and he held his hand up to the driver in apology. "French, it's Spencer, how far have you got?"

"I'm outside. What's happened?"

"Can you come back? Another girl's been taken. We've got an eyewitness this time, they're bringing her in now. I've been told to do the interview with you."

"Me? Why me?" He was already retracing his steps, the disgruntled taxi driver waving a fist behind him.

"I don't know. I'm just following orders."

Shortly, the two men introduced themselves. Although they had seen each other in passing over the course of the day, this was the first time they had spoken. Spencer, if a little arrogant, seemed friendly enough. He led French to his workspace and furnished him with the details of the latest girl.

"We haven't had any girls reported missing yet, so we don't know much about her. It seems this woman saw a girl being bundled away in a place called Knole Park, which is in Sevenoaks. She thought at the time it was just kids playing about, which it still may be, but when she saw the press conference on the news she decided to call in. Obviously we're treating this as a possible abduction."

"Has anyone alerted the press?"

"Why?"

"If she's not been reported missing then people need to know her description, then they might notice that their daughter, or sister, or friend hasn't come home." French's words were laced with venom and Spencer nodded, irritated himself.

He waved a young policeman over and instructed him to contact the major daily newspapers with the scant details they already knew: the girl was between sixteen and eighteen, very tall, and had long ginger hair, tied in a ponytail. She had been wearing a navy track-suit and trainers and had been running when a man dressed entirely in black, face and hair shadowed by a hood, had approached her from behind and put his hand over her mouth. She had appeared to collapse in his arms and he had dragged her into the bushes.

Having now heard the details, French was appalled. He waited for the rookie to leave before speaking. "You're telling me that some old biddy saw all that and thought they were just messing about?"

Spencer strolled to the refreshments table and poured from the coffee jug, needing caffeine to stay awake. "You know what people are like, scared to get involved unless they can get something for themselves out of it."

"So now the old biddy gets her fifteen minutes of fame?"

An officer waved from the doorway and Spencer took his drink, walking towards her. "Well, I think the old biddy must have arrived. Come on."

Rhiannon was far taller and heavier than the other girls and, a dead weight under the influence of chloroform first, then intravenous ketamine, Dick was struggling to get her limp body from the car to the door of the empty, ruined building he had all but taken up home in for the duration of his plan.

Eventually, after many attempts to carry her, and coughing harshly, he gave up and dragged her by the arms, wincing at the thought of the grazing to her legs and lower back from the gravelly ground. He hadn't realised when he had researched her that she was such a solid, muscular girl; there had been barely any personal detail on her application.

Although he felt as sorry for his latest captive as he did for the others, he was also relieved. This was the final one and in less than two weeks he would give the girls their freedom back with the ultimate gesture that would avenge his sister's mistreatment. Nobody had listened to his beloved Bubby when she had pleaded for help, not until it was too late, and now their paltry attempts to make amends weren't enough for Dick. He wanted justice.

Dropping Rhiannon's shoulders, he took a key from his pocket and unlocked the heavy padlock, and he dragged her through the doorway. The building was in complete silence and he wondered if rebellious Sammy had succumbed to taking the drugged food. Although he was fond of their short chats, she would have to be asleep when he brought the latest girl into the room.

In torchlight, he dragged Rhiannon along corridor after corridor, the maze to the cell where he kept his prey, less heavy now she was on a smooth floor. Soon he opened the warning door, ensuring he was quieter than normal to avoid waking the girls. In a whisper he said, "Sammy?"

No response came, but he wasn't confident she had taken the drugs, after all she hadn't before, and decided it would be safer blitzing the room with gas first, unwilling to risk any of the girls being awake when he delivered their new roommate. He settled Rhiannon on the floor and retraced his steps to collect the equipment.

Once he had donned the breathing apparatus and filled the room with Fluothane gas, Dick quietly unlocked and unbolted the door, the stench of excrement mixed with vomit and body odour not filtering through the mask. He dropped Rhiannon and pushed her in with his feet, just far enough to close the door behind her. He pulled the bolt across, relocked the door and made his way back to the car. Hopefully the fish and chips he had bought on the way back from Sevenoaks would still be warm.

"Fuck me! That's no old biddy." Spencer turned and saw French had had a similar reaction, only not so vocally. He stared through the two-way mirror at the elegant woman who sat at the central table, wide-eyed and nervously clutching her handbag.

"I think we'd better take a few deep breaths before we go in." They stood, gazing at the gorgeous woman, her huge eyes glistening like melted chocolate, her perfect pout enhanced by seductive red, two children coveting a sweet shop.

Aware of their presence, the policewoman who had brought the beauty in came through the door. "Tongues away, lads, she's married."

"I wasn't planning to marry her, just..."

"Shall we go in?" French cut in.

The policewoman laughed as she strutted away and French followed Spencer into the room. They introduced themselves, shaking Ms De Boucher's dainty, excellently manicured hand, and she told them what she had seen, but the elaboration didn't give them much more than they already knew.

She had been walking her dog in the park and was resting on a bench when the girl had run past. She had been drawn to watch her into the distance because the girl was so striking, Amazonian. Penelope mentioned she ran an agency for models - catwalk, not anything tacky - and kept a lookout for unusual features. Shortly after, a man had come from the bushes a fair distance from where Penelope sat and had fallen into a trot behind the girl. She had stopped for a breather, and he had suddenly pounced on her from behind and dragged her away from the track into the trees.

"What I don't understand is why you didn't report this to the police as soon as it happened. I mean, it seems obvious to me that the girl was in trouble."

Penelope sighed. "Look, I've been in that park many a time and the amount of girls who scream things like 'rape' and 'help' when they're not in any form of trouble is shocking.

"The first time I saw it happen, some youngster - twelve, thirteen-ish - was walking along when a boy jumped on her from behind. She screamed 'help me, help me' and I immediately called the police. However, I was hugely embarrassed to be told later that the girl hadn't been in trouble at all; the lad was her boyfriend. After that, I stopped taking notice. But when I saw the news tonight, I thought it would be appropriate to inform you and here we are."

"Have you seen her before?"

"Sevenoaks is a big place and I spend most of my time in my office in London, so no. But I hope I see her again, she could be the next Cara Delevingne. I just wish I'd stopped her there and then instead of being my usual, unspontaneous self, because the thought that such a beautiful girl could be in trouble..."

Opposite her, Spencer mouthed, 'the next what?' to French, who shrugged, before returning his focus to Penelope. "The man who approached her, what can you tell me about him?"

She sighed again, checking the time on her mobile, which lay on the table. "I've already given a detailed description to the officers back home. Well, as much detail as I could, I was quite far away. And that policewoman, the one who was in here before you, told me they're preparing an e-fit as we speak."

French shoved Spencer's arm and whispered, "Can we nip outside for a minute?" He led, and Spencer followed him from the room, closing the door. "If they've got all the details, why did they need two detective inspectors to do the interview? If she isn't a suspect - and I'm sure she's not - don't you think that's a bit excessive?"

"I agree totally. I don't get it either."

"So, what do we do?"

Spencer gawped through the window. "Well, she's great eye-candy, but I must admit I'm shattered, could do with some shuteye."

"I'll offer her a drink or something, you go and have a word with Harner. That's if he's still here."

Minutes later Penelope nursed a black, sugarless coffee and Spencer called French from the room with a smile. "Lucky bastard. He didn't say as much, but I think he's getting it on with her."

"Never!" French glanced through the window, admiring the beautiful woman who was way out of his league. "What did he say?"

"He was adamant they'd brought her in because she's the only person to have seen the attacker, but he also mentioned he wanted her out of Sevenoaks while there's a possible serial killer on the loose. He slipped up and called her Penny."

French chuckled. "And from that you deduced they're sleeping together?"

"He lives in Sevenoaks too, he's a handsome man, and I'm a bloody good detective. Trust me, he's keeping her warm at night."

Sammy lay on the cold floor, unable to move without her head pounding as if it would explode, and wished she hadn't eaten the food that had made her sleep for however long it had been. Once more, resolve set in. No matter how hungry she got, she wasn't going to touch the poisoned offerings again. Then she remembered Lydia. Poor, dead Lydia, an empty shell with no dignity amidst the foul mess on the floor. Clutching a hand to her head, shuddering from the dull, throbbing ache, she pulled herself up and rested against the wall.

Lydia was lying just as she had been when Sammy had blacked out, crunched in a foetal ball with a thin trail of blood, now drying, on her cheek, and her body was rigid with rigor mortis. Beside her, Sying was in a drugged coma, fitful, and Neeraja simply lay, eyes open but unseeing. A noise by the door startled Sammy and she gasped when she saw another girl had been brought in. "Oh my God."

Sammy scrabbled to her feet and staggered, dizzy and uncoordinated, to the new girl - a giant compared to her tiny frame - and fell back to the floor, the brief spell of strength gone. She shook the girl's shoulder, lightly at first, but becoming more frantic. "Wake up."

Rhiannon's eyelids flickered and she let out a low groan. "Where am I?"

"You've been kidnapped. We all have." Rhiannon's eyes closed and Sammy shook her harder. "Please don't go to sleep. You've been drugged, you need to stay conscious and not eat the food. He puts something in it that makes you sleep."

Rhiannon's eyes opened, fearful now as Sammy's words registered. She grimaced, moaning. "What is that disgusting smell?"

"We don't have a toilet. We try to keep it all in one corner, but he doesn't seem to clear it out. Lydia said he cleans the floor every couple of weeks or so, but we've all lost track of time."

Rhiannon tried to get up, but her head was fuzzy and painful and she struggled. Sammy helped her to sit. The new prisoner slowly panned the room, taking in the sewage and squalor, the cold and damp. For minutes she said nothing, digesting the horror she had awoken to. Eventually, her voice small and confused, she managed, "No. No!"

Sammy hugged the girl, but Rhiannon pushed her away, not used to being comforted or cared for. "My name's Sammy, I've been here... Actually, I don't know how long, what was the date when you were taken?"

Rhiannon shook her head, willing her memory to return. "It's all a blur. Everything's a blur. I was out running, yes, I was running. I was in Knole Park, but I don't remember what happened."

"It's the drug he gives you. I can't remember anything about being taken either, but I do know that it was on the nineteenth. What's your name?

"Rhiannon. Who is 'he'?"

"We don't know. I've never seen him. He comes to the door a couple of times a day with food, and every time the other three eat it and sleep until the next lot. I refused to eat anything, but I was so hungry, and then Lydia died and I knew I couldn't cope with that, so I had some. I've only just woken up."

Rhiannon held her hands up to stop the confusing words, struggling to understand the situation. "Whoa, whoa. Too much, too quick." She breathed deeply, calming herself, regaining control. "Did you say someone died?"

Sammy pointed to the coloured girl and Rhiannon gasped. "He killed her?"

"No, no, she just died. She started convulsing and died. She's been here three months, so maybe it was the build-up of drugs in her system or something. I was with her, I cuddled her..." The memory was harsh and she wiped away a tear with the back of her grubby hand.

"So you're telling me that we're locked in a room with no windows and toilet, with a dead fucking body?" Sammy focused on the floor; she understood the range of horrified emotions that were pulsing through the new girl, had been there herself not so long ago. "Oh, fucking hell, you said your name was Sammy. Now I get it. It's that fucking bloke that's all over the news isn't it? I didn't pay no attention to the papers, but I'm sure the last girl that went missing was called Sammy."

"You're right, that was me, Sammy Cooper, then there's Lydia, Neeraja and Sying." She indicated the other prisoners one by one. "What was the last date you remember? You've only just come in and I want to know how long he's had me here."

"It was the twenty-third of September. Monday."

"Four days, is that all? It feels like a lifetime." She was forlorn until she considered what Rhiannon had said. "You mean it's in the papers? Like The Review and The Mirror type papers?"

"And the radio, and the telly, they even had a press conference, I think."

Sammy was happier than she had ever been, knowing that everyone was searching for her - for them - and she couldn't withhold a grin. "I'd never heard about the other three, so I thought nobody was looking for us. Thank God, that means they'll find us soon and we can get out of this disgusting dungeon."

Rhiannon was the more realistic of the two. "Only if they know where to look. Right," having grown up essentially on her own, with no care or love, she had learned to be streetwise, "what exactly have you done to get out of this place?"

"There's nothing we can do. He keeps the door locked and it's bolted on the outside, and there are no windows. The floor's solid concrete and, well, I tried everything I could think of. In fact, if I hadn't eaten the food and got myself spaced out, I would have been awake when he brought you in. Shit, I could have tried to escape then." Damn her bloody lack of resolve.

"There's never *nothing* we can do. What about the ceiling? It might be plasterboard."

They glanced at the greying paint through the darkness they had become accustomed to, a single bulb that shed no light on a wire hanging from the centre, cracks running this way and that. Rhiannon rose unsteadily to her feet, gripping the wall for stability. With her height and long arms, it was easy for her to touch the plaster, and she sank back, dropping to the floor next to Sammy. "No chance, it's solid. What about kicking up a fuss, screaming and shouting?"

"Sying said they'd done all that at first, but it didn't bother him. From what they say we must be somewhere remote, otherwise somebody would have heard them."

"Fuck my life, I didn't think things could get any worse than they already were. Fuck this."

"Don't lose hope, it's all we've got."

Rhiannon sneered, tossing her mane of auburn waves. "You're one of those whiny little things that always sees the good in everything, aren't you?"

Sammy was embarrassed and close to tears. "I'm just trying to survive this, that's all."

Chapter 7
Tuesday 24th September

Roberta was furious as she sent an early email to the members of the committee. Her baby, the Raymouth Marathon, had been linked to the disappearance of four girls, plus a possible fifth. The local police had called, suggesting the event she had worked so hard towards for the best part of a year should be either postponed or cancelled and she couldn't see the reasoning behind it. However, despite being the figurehead of the charitable race, the popularity of the annual marathon had grown so much over the past eleven years since she had singularly organised the first one, and it was no longer a decision she could make alone.

The email was terse, belying her aggravation, but necessary. No matter what plans the other six members had, their presence at the meeting, to be held in a small restaurant in the town centre at lunchtime, was essential.

With only five hours to go, she busied herself with the stack of newspapers she had purchased early that morning, reading each article about the missing girls thoroughly; information was the key to getting her own way.

Jo Ellis had been given the tedious task of logging the names and contact details of the female entrants to the Raymouth Marathon onto the computer. Suddenly she jumped up, excitable. "I've got one in Sevenoaks, a girl named Rhiannon Hughes." Harner approached her desk, alongside several other officers, listening intently as she related the details. "She's fifteen, according to this."

"Younger than the others. What else have you got on her?"

"There's a mobile number, an address. Well, that's it. There's no next-of-kin or home number, not even an email address."

Harner instructed a colleague to try the mobile number, and to get the local police to visit the address as a matter of urgency if he didn't get through to anyone. "I've already tried the number." Barbara, seated beside Jo, was known for her efficiency and had dialled as soon as Jo had flagged the details. "It went straight to voicemail."

"Get on it, Dave." The officer trotted to his desk to find the number for the nearest police department and Harner nodded a thank you to Jo. He strode to the refreshments table and threw a teabag into a mug, topping it with hot water from the urn, and Jo followed him, thirsty herself.

Spencer was preparing strong coffee. "How's Penelope?"

Harner's eyes widened and he coughed. "She stayed in a hotel last night. I didn't think it was safe to have her taken back to Sevenoaks, not with what's going on."

"That's quite unusual."

"It's not what you're thinking, you and your filthy mind." Harner glanced at Jo, embarrassed, hoping she hadn't heard the insinuating conversation.

"I understand, you know. I mean, I would if I got the chance."

"There's nothing going on and starting rumours like that can be dangerous. Leave it, Gordon, I mean it."

"But you admit you know her?"

Reddening and shifty, Harner squeezed the flavour from the teabag, ignoring the impertinence. Spencer walked away with a smile, convinced his deduction was right: married Harner was involved with Penelope somehow, and secrets were always good ammunition.

Nancy was a master of laziness when she wanted to be, but despite the cosy, warm covers, she couldn't relax. Resigned, she laid her book on the bedside cabinet and dragged herself up, feeding feet into slippers. So much for a leisurely day before starting her new, high-powered job in the morning. "Phil?"

"Babe, you're awake at last." His voice came from the living room and Nancy went through, kissing him gently on

72

the forehead. "Why aren't you staying in bed? I thought you loved having duvet days."

"It's those missing girls, I can't get them off my mind." She sat on the arm of the sofa beside his desk.

"Did you know another girl was abducted last night?" He threw The Daily Review towards her. "There was an eye-witness, but they don't know who the girl is yet."

Nancy read the article and sighed deeply. "So if that girl was abducted by the man, then someone's seen him now. Does it give the identity of the witness anywhere?"

"No, they haven't released the name, probably for his or her own safety."

"I've got to find out who it was, I can feel an article coming on."

Phil smiled lovingly and pulled his wife close for a hug. "It's good to see your fire burning again. I think losing your job at the Southside Express hurt you more than you let on."

She chuckled. "What? That two-bit job with a poky local rag. I don't think so. No, I've enjoyed a couple of days' rest, but I'm going to relish being back at work. If I get started on something now, I can have it nearly ready for my new job tomorrow, impress them on my first day. Have you got any more details, or is it just this?" She tapped the discarded newspaper.

"If you google 'missing girls UK', there are pages and pages about it. It's the trending news, it seems."

She stood, stretching to easing her aching joints, and plodded to the kitchen, turning her computer on as she passed. "I'll get some coffee brewing and then get started. Do you want a cup?"

"That's my girl, yes please."

Sammy had slept in bursts, the wooziness from the drug she had consumed ebbing and flowing, and she noticed that Rhiannon had done the same. Feeling better than she had for a while, she sat up and realised that Dick hadn't visited for what seemed to be ages. Had something happened to him?

Would they be locked in this abominable trap forever? No longer noticing the defecation that soaked into her clothes, putrid and vile, she crawled to the door and concentrated carefully.

"What are you doing?" Rhiannon wearily pulled herself upright.

"Just listening to see if he's out there. He hasn't brought any new food for a long time and I'm scared he's just left us here to die."

"Well, he'd better not have. That, that…" she pointed to Lydia's body, mottled and spent. "I think she's started to smell."

"I'm surprised you can tell, what with all the shit we're sitting in. Excuse the pun." Neither girl laughed, unable to see the funny side of anything any more. Across the room, Sying stirred and they turned to watch. "Sying, wake up. Lydia's died. And he's brought another girl."

Groggy, Sying opened her eyes, soulful, rich coffee underneath impossibly long eyelashes. "What?" She slowly raised her head towards Lydia's body. "Dead? How?"

"She just died. It wasn't him. Now you've *got* to stop eating the food, I think it was the drugs in it that ended up making her body give up and I don't want that to happen to you."

Four unlikely friends from completely different backgrounds, united in their desperation to survive. Sammy knew the bond she had with the girls could never be broken.

Sying leant across and shoved Neeraja heavily, and she groaned. "Get off me."

"Neeraja, you've got to wake up. We've all got to be awake. The drugs have killed Lydia."

Neeraja gasped and propped herself against the wall, weak and emaciated. "What?" She tried to focus but everything was blurred.

The warning door sounded and they silenced, waiting as the steps approached. Soon the flap opened and Dick pushed another bowl of unappetising food through. Sammy put her

74

finger to her lips to hush the others, before, "Dick, I need to talk to you."

He didn't speak and Sammy held a forbidding hand up at Rhiannon, noticing her urge to say something. "Dick, one of the girls has died." He gasped, and she continued, "She's in here and she's starting to smell."

"Which one?"

"Lydia, the black girl."

Dick let out a pained wail, deafening and outraged, and the girls waited, on tenterhooks, to see what he would do next. The silence seemed to last forever, but finally, "She was the hardest to get, now I'm going to have to look for another."

His footsteps resounded and Rhiannon couldn't contain herself any longer. "You can't just leave us with a dead body in the room." The footsteps stopped. "She's decomposing. It's disgusting."

"I'm sorry, I never thought of that. You must be Rhiannon; I don't recognise your voice.

"You know our names? How?"

"I picked you out individually. I trailed each of you for weeks, learning your habits so I could pick the optimum time to bring you home."

A sickened silence fell, the girls stunned by the sinister revelation. "Please, Dick, please let us go." Neeraja could only mumble.

"Are you all awake?"

They chorused: "Yes."

"Then there's nothing I can do about Lydia until you're asleep. I'm not opening this door. Eat your dinner, it'll help you forget." The footsteps dissipated and he was gone, the warning door slamming behind him.

The four girls glanced at each other, not knowing what to say, but eventually Rhiannon broke the spell. "So, it's simple: we don't take the drug, pretend we're asleep, then when he opens the door... Bam."

Sying and Sammy nodded in agreement, but Neeraja choked back tears. "I can't stay awake. I can't handle this any more, it's too hard."

Despite her tender age, Rhiannon was a strong and feisty woman. "Oh, pull yourself together, will you, and stop being pathetic. If you don't fight back that man is probably going to kill us, and if you keep taking that shit," she pointed to the food, wrinkling her freckled nose, "then you're going to end up like the nigger."

Three sharp intakes of breath, a multi-cultural assembly disgusted with her blatant racism. "What?" she asked innocently, holding her hands palm up.

Constables Pickering and Kauser strode to the door of the children's home, familiar due to the unruly residents who mostly came from broken homes; the police were frequently called out for one disturbance or another. Kauser knocked and presently a young girl - lips and eyebrows pierced, hair multi-coloured - answered. "What is it this time?"

"We need to speak to Mary, is she here?"

"No."

Churlish and unhelpful, she tried to close the door but Pickering leant forward to stop her. "Is there anyone else with you?"

"Fred's out the back." Swiftly trotting up the stairs, she disappeared from view and a door slammed.

Shrugging, they entered the hallway they had seen many times before and made their way to the back garden. The aging carer was hammering some nails into a wooden structure and he stopped when he saw them. "Oh no, which one's in trouble now?" He smiled, but inside felt dread.

"We're here about Rhiannon Hughes."

Fred stood and stretched his back, tired from building the rabbit hutch that nobody was interested in; he had thought the youngsters would benefit from caring for a pet, but they had other things on their minds. "For heaven's sake, can she not just behave for once? What's she done this time?"

Kauser and Pickering glanced at each other, feeling sympathy for the man and his impossible job. "Have you seen her?"

"Not since yesterday afternoon, no. Has she gone AWOL again?"

"We have reason to believe she may have been abducted."

Fred chuckled, this time with genuine mirth. "She'll just have stayed over at a lad's or something. She'll keep doing that until she gets knocked up, then they'll house her and give her an income. That's what all the girls do."

Kauser was shocked by his utter disillusion with the children he cared for. "Fred, you're not listening. You must have seen in the papers that five girls have gone missing?"

"Five now, is it?" Fred shook his head, intrigued, and then paled as the meaning behind the statement dawned on him.

"Well, we think Rhiannon is the fifth girl. There was an eye witness and she matches the description. Do you have a recent photo of her so we can show it to the woman who reported the struggle?"

"Probably, somewhere. If I don't have one then Mary probably does, she's always taking pictures of the kids on her mobile." He took a mobile from his trouser pocket and searched for a while. "No, I don't have one. Mary's in the kitchen, I'll ask her." Kauser was about to inform him that they had been told she wasn't in, but realised he had been lied to by the surly, pierced girl and his cheeks reddened.

They followed the carer into the large house and greeted Mary, who wiped flour and dough from her hands while beaming a friendly grin, but the smile waned when Fred repeated what the constables had told him. "I took a picture of her a couple of days ago." Her voice wavered as she sifted through her phone, leaving smudges of raw pastry on the screen, and finally found an image, which she showed to the officers. Rhiannon Hughes, tall and slender, pale and freckled, with wild, dark-ginger curls framing a strong-boned, strangely attractive face. There was no disputing she was the girl.

"We're going to need a copy of this at the station. If I give you my mobile number, will you send it to me?"

"Of course. Here, have my phone and do it yourself, I can't get to grips with how to do all these things." She handed it over.

"Also, we'll need to speak to everybody to find out about Rhiannon's movements yesterday."

"Yesterday? But I saw her in bed this morning... Oh, those damned girls! I'll bet they stuffed pillows under her quilt to make it look like she was there." She huffed over to the kettle, filling it, turning it on, blasphemous under her breath. "We can't leave the kids so you'll have to question us here."

"No problem. We'll need to talk to the kids too, especially the one she shares a room with. That's if she shares a room."

"She does, there's four to a room until they're sixteen."

People considered Roberta a fussy person, but she didn't understand the label. Fastidious, organised and hardworking, more like, and what was wrong with that? Organising the Raymouth Marathon was a dream come true now her teaching career had been laid to rest through age and disability - nothing serious, just wear and tear on joints that were now painfully arthritic.

Nodding to the waiter she knew well, she sat at the table she had reserved first thing in the morning and he brought her a bottle of sparkling mineral water. She was ten minutes early but this gave her time to prepare.

Presently the co-members of the committee arrived - no one would dare to be late for a meeting with Roberta - and once the food orders were settled, the talking began. Roberta started by reiterating what she had already emailed to them. "So I've been totally cooperative with everything the police have asked for, yet they still want us to cancel the event. I think it's disgraceful. All those charities who should be benefiting, all those people who've been training for months."

Elliot choked on his tea. "So you're going to do as they ask, then?" Stubborn and direct, Roberta wasn't one to back down.

"That depends on the outcome of this meeting. The police say that every girl who's gone missing - five now - was registered to run, and obviously that's dreadful, but I can't see how it affects the race. They'll still be missing, but there'll be nearly six thousand unhappy runners and a lot of disappointed charities. I think we should go ahead with it."

"In my opinion I think we absolutely should not."

Roberta's mouth gaped. People rarely disagreed with her and Elliot was on her side with most matters. He had been her right hand man for a decade and they had always worked well together, chalk and cheese. Her insides tensed, steeling herself for a fight - bring it on. "Oh, and why's that then?"

He adjusted his glasses and cleared his throat. "If the abductor is getting the details of the girls from the register, then it's got to be one of us, because we're the only people to have seen it."

A couple of members chuckled uncomfortably, the idea ludicrous but the point valid. It was an aspect Roberta hadn't considered and she glowered. "Of course it's not one of us, that's just silly." The members' eyes darted suspiciously, each wondering if they really knew the others as well as they thought they did. "I suppose we'd better ask the questions just to rule ourselves out. Who has seen the register?"

Elliot sighed; Roberta already knew the answer. "We all have, you know that."

"Has anybody shown the register to anyone else?"

He was becoming weary with the waste of time; he was due to start coaching in less than an hour and needed to prepare. "We all know that would break the confidentially agreement we have with the runners, and nobody here is dumb enough to do that."

79

Meek in the corner, Lily raised her hand apologetically. "Um, I know I shouldn't have, but my daughter wanted to know if her friend's registration had been received, so I," she swallowed, embarrassed, "let her read through rather than find it for her. I was so busy that day."

Roberta's eyes bulged, a steaming, angry bull. "Are you stupid or something?"

Lily shrunk, chastised, but Elliot came to her defence. "Look, Karen's only what? Thirteen, fourteen?"

Her voice was a whisper. "Thirteen."

"Exactly, it's not like she's going to go and start stealing girls just because she's had access to our records. Be realistic."

"Has anybody *else* seen the register?" Roberta glared at Lily, who became even tinier. Around the table each head shook in answer, knowing the police would ask them the same question later.

Chapter 8
Midday, Tuesday

DCI Jeremy Barker had taken Monday off to attend his father's funeral, making it a long and sad weekend, and had not arrived at work until late morning the next day, after sorting through the numerous wreaths and cards, sent in honour of the popular man, at his bereaved mother's house. For the first time since Friday he checked his emails and was shocked to see one from his old friend, Gordon Spencer, who had remained in London when Barker had moved to the coast.

A priority, he opened it and scanned through, before rereading in detail. "Damn." He immediately dialled the number at the bottom of the screen and waited. "Can I speak to DI Spencer, please?"

Operation Bandicoot was all over the newspapers and Barker guessed his friend would be busy, but he was still impatient, eager to get on with the task Gordon had asked him to do on Sunday. He explained the situation to Spencer, who was sorry to hear about the deceased man whom he had known since childhood, and assured his friend he would arrange the interviews immediately.

He replaced the receiver and beckoned his colleague over. "I had an important email sent to me about those girls who've gone missing, why didn't you check my inbox while I was out of the office?"

"Because you told me last week you didn't want me checking your emails." Laced with sarcasm.

"For God's sake, Carl, you know that was said in anger, I didn't mean you to take me literally."

"You made it loud and clear last week that you'd rather I wasn't a self-starter, you said I cock too many things up - your words - and should leave the police work to the competent guys."

Barker ran a hand through his hair, frustrated. How long did his blasted colleague hold a grudge for? "You're bloody infuriating, do you know that? Okay, if it means we can let go and return to being grown-ups, then I'm sorry I shouted at you last week. In my defence, I was grieving for my dad, remember?"

Carl hadn't and was sheepish. "Oh, yeah, how did it go?"

"Very gloomy, very sad and I'm worried about my mum. We all are."

"I guess you don't want to talk about it, then."

"You're like a bloody woman, you are, you read everything the wrong way. God, I'd hate to be married to you."

"Ditto. Sir."

Barker grabbed his jacket, shrugging it on, and reached into the pocket for his car keys. "Come on, I've got to take a couple of statements, they're urgent." Carl crossed his arms and remained standing, while Barker darted for the door. He stopped and turned back. "What now?" Incredulous.

"Oh, I was just wondering if you might prefer to take someone else, I mean, you don't have any respect for my work."

And exasperated. "Get in my fucking car. Now."

Minutes later they arrived at Roberta Robinson's house, a nondescript semi on a featureless estate, the only individuality being the resplendent hanging basket by the front door. They parked and strode up the path. "Her car's not here so it doesn't look promising. That's if my opinion's of any relevance, of course "

Barker rolled his eyes, fed up with the attitude but reluctant to address it for fear of making things worse. Like he had last week, clearly. "Yes, I do value your opinion, Carl." He hammered on the door. "Maybe she's gone for a walk."

"Mrs Robinson's got severe arthritis in her knees so she doesn't - can't - walk much."

"Oh, I never realised that, she's never shown any signs when I've met her."

"Then she won't have been on the move. Once she's seated, she's fine."

"Do you know her?"

"Yes, she was my PE teacher at school and we kept in touch when I left. She's a friend of my mum, too. I think she's even older than you, if that's possible."

Barker raised a fist, growling at the impudence; Carl loved getting a reaction to his banter. As they reached the gate, Roberta's car turned the corner and Carl said, "That's her."

She was concerned as she parked but, guessing what they were there for, smiled affably. "Carl, how lovely to see you." She reached in for a friendly hug and kiss on the cheek, and turned to Barker. "I've met you, but I can't remember your name, sorry." He introduced himself and she grinned. "I've just had lunch with the committee members to discuss your suggestion."

"What suggestion?" Barker and Carl followed the woman into her musty-smelling home.

"I had an email from you lot this morning asking us to consider cancelling the run due to the missing girls and their link to our register."

"I haven't been told about that but I kind of agree with it." Barker sat by the kitchen table awaiting the tea she was preparing busily.

Roberta couldn't understand why everybody was so determined to stop the race. "How can cancelling the marathon possibly benefit the missing girls?"

"Out of respect for their families, of course."

Another aspect that Roberta hadn't considered during her successful meeting to keep the race on, as planned. "Oh. Well, I'm sorry, but we put it to the vote and have decided it will go ahead."

"Okay, you have the right, I suppose, unless the council object." And another point. Roberta seethed inwardly at the next battle she would be facing. What was wrong with everybody? "Anyway, I don't know if you've been reading about the case in the papers, but we need to interview the committee members to see if the details have been leaked to someone. We need to find out how the abductor got hold of the girls' names and contact details."

"We already discussed that at lunch. Apart from the seven of us, only one other person had access and she's a thirteen-year-old girl, so highly unlikely to be responsible. It wasn't one of us, I can assure you."

"Five girls are too many to be a coincidence, though. Some psychopath is out there with the list in his hand, picking out young girls and abducting them, and we have to find him before he takes another."

Roberta brought a tray over and served the drinks. "We're all law-abiding citizens who work our proverbials off to raise money for charity, year in, year out. We don't know any psychopaths."

Carl fixed his eyes on his boss. "Don't be so sure."

Barker was about to chastise Carl, but stopped when a chilling thought descended on him. "Dear God. The police."

"Yep, in my experience most of them have that tendency." Grinning, Carl hadn't grasped Barker's meaning and was keen to keep the jokiness going.

"After the Boston Marathon bombings in April, didn't we ask you to copy your register to us as a security measure?"

"Well, I'll be damned. Yes, you did, I remember now. Elliot is in charge of registration, so he'll be able to tell you more about that side of things. I'm surprised he didn't mention that at the meeting, it seems so obvious now."

Carl had paled significantly as the suggestion had sunk in; could he be working alongside someone deranged enough to take young girls off the street and keep them captive - if not worse? Unwanted thoughts of his colleagues - of their tempers - resounded in his mind during their brief spell at the elderly woman's house, and as they returned to the car, out of Roberta's earshot, he voiced his concerns. "You don't really think it could be someone from our nick, do you?"

Sighing, Barker opened the door and climbed in. "I've known of Roberta and the gang for many years, they're all such good and honest people and they raise a fortune for charities every year. I can say, hand on heart, that not a single one is involved, they just don't have it in them."

84

"Not even that Elliot she mentioned?"

"Especially not him, he's a lovely man. Look, when we get back, I want you - discreetly - to find out who the keeps the copy of the register, it's probably someone in admin."

Carl began the journey back to the station, and Barker found Gordon Spencer's number on his mobile. The revelation was disturbing and he knew there would have to be an external investigation. At the moment, there was nothing he could do, because everybody, including himself, was under suspicion.

The warning door sounded and the four girls, wide awake and alert, kept their breathing under control as planned; they had to make Dick believe they were sleeping. They had concocted the idea after his promise to remove Lydia's body if they took the poison and each girl had been praying it would work. The steps neared and stopped.

A few moments passed before they noticed that the end of a hosepipe had been pushed under the door and, horrified, the girls realised they were being gassed. Seconds later, they had succumbed to the noxious fumes.

When he was certain the girls were unconscious, Dick turned the key and unbolted the door. He wore a PVC boiler suit, and a mask fed him pure air from a tank strapped to his back to ensure the Fluothane wouldn't affect him. He stepped around the prisoners to reach Lydia's body.

She had only been a small woman at five foot four and the running she had loved had left her body toned and fat-free. More so now after months of barely eating. Dick lifted her with ease, regardless that her body, in a foetal position, was in full rigor mortis, and faeces and urine smeared the protective clothing. He carried her from the room, laying her on the floor of the corridor, and placed a bowl of drugged food inside for when the girls woke up, before securing the door again. Hoisting the coloured girl into his arms, he marched away.

85

As soon as Spencer ended the call from Barker, he informed his boss of the developments and Harner arranged for two new officers to join Operation Bandicoot to replace Spencer and French, whom he was sending to the south coast for an internal investigation into Raymouth Police department. French was familiar with the area, Southside being ten miles from Raymouth, and they arrived just over two hours after the alert.

A storm approached from the English Channel, the sky grey and cloudy and a strong wind blustering, unobstructed, over choppy waves until it battered the town's colourful seaside buildings. Carl, shivering in the cold and annoyed that his immaculately gelled hairstyle was mussed, trotted across the car park when the unmarked car arrived. French opened the passenger door. "Are you Carl Tramontana?"

"Yes, come with me. We haven't told anyone about you coming, as requested."

The two visitors glanced at each other as the young man led the way; Carl was effeminate, with the campest walk they had ever seen and they struggled to restrain their laughter.

Officers stopped and stared as they entered the station, curious, but no explanation was offered, and after the group had closed the door behind them for a brief with Barker, rumours about their presence started.

Once they were settled and Carl had brought refreshments, Spencer took the lead. "Where do you keep your copy of the register?"

"I spoke to Elliot Jacobs, who keeps it up to date, and he says he sent a copy, via email, to Alice, our admin clerk. He said he emails her weekly with the most recent list."

"Are we setting up the inquiry in this room?"

"If it's big enough for you."

Spencer nodded and turned to Carl. "Can you go and get this Alice, please, we'll need to speak to her in the first instance." And now to French. "Dan, you can take the interview with her, you know what you're doing."

"I can take him to the admin department if you want?" Trying to be helpful, Carl was intimidated by the confident and suave London detective.

"No, any interviews must be in private, you never know who could be listening."

Barker was aware people judged his colleague because of his appearance and manner and was protective when the cruel jokes started, and he noticed the amused smiles shared by the two visiting inspectors. It rattled him more than usual; he had always thought Spencer to be unbiased, but had been wrong. "Carl, when you come back with Alice, can you take her and Inspector French to an interview room, I need to speak with Gordon alone."

Carl smiled his thanks for the support he knew his boss was giving him and left the room.

Dick was having a bad day. Until now, everything had been going to plan, although he had to admit that if he could do it all over again he would have snared his trophies closer to the planned date of the finale. There were still nearly two weeks to go and he desperately hoped there would be no more deaths, because replacing Lydia with no prior planning was going to be hard. Risky. He needed to see the register again, but how, he wasn't sure. It was imperative nobody suspected him if that bitch, Roberta Robinson, was to get her macabre humiliation.

Sighing with both tiredness and reflection, he set to work on Lydia's body. He had hoisted her through the corridors to the Victorian washroom outdoors, modern and fashionable when the building had been built, state-of-the-art, but now lime scaled and mouldy. Luckily the water pump still worked.

He stripped the fouled clothes, having to rip some seams because of her cramped position, and scrubbed her skin, hair and nails until she was respectably fresh and clean. He undressed, throwing the boiler suit on top of Lydia's discarded clothing, intending to burn them later, and pumped more water into a ceramic sink to wash with.

Feeling refreshed and wearing clean clothes, Dick now had the arduous task of deciding what to do with Lydia's body. He hadn't a clue where to leave it. If he dumped it there was a risk of being seen, but if he didn't she would rapidly decompose in the autumn warmth and the familiar, permeating odour would trigger horrendous memories of Iraq. He couldn't handle that; it had taken too many years to find stability after he had been retired from the Army on health grounds.

Eventually Dick decided to leave Lydia where she lay for now, it wasn't as if she was going anywhere. Her skin would have a chance to dry after the wash and maybe the stiffening would ease, leaving her easier to manoeuvre when he dressed her in the cheap tracksuit he intended to purchase. It was important to him that she didn't have the indignity of being discovered in the nude.

Despite thoroughly scrubbing, his skin still crawled, a morbid, unclean sensation. He drew his foot back and booted the body, once, twice, again... "You selfish fucking bitch, why did you go and die? Now everything's got too hard."

Issuing a final kick, he spat on her and left. He still needed to cook another pot of stew for the girls and, if he had time, google 'rigor mortis' to see how long it would take to wear off.

He would go home and soak in the bath, ready for his massage appointment at six. Jill was a good listener.

"I'd never have thought of you as a homophobe, Gordon, especially as you work in London."

"What?" The statement from his friend came out of the blue.

"Carl's a damned good officer and I don't give a shit that he's overtly gay. What he does in his own bed is none of my business, or yours."

Spencer hung his head, chastened; he had been rude and was ashamed. "You're right, Jez, I was out of order."

"What were you thinking? Is this how the Met behave? Zero tolerance to anybody who doesn't fit the norm." Spencer tried to speak but Barker was on a roll. "Because I'll tell you what, if that's what they teach you in London, then I'm bloody glad I moved away. As far as I'm concerned, and as far as you should be too, a person is a person, no matter what race, sex, religion or sexual orientation."

He broke off, but this time Spencer made no move to defend himself. "If I see or hear one more slight towards Carl from you, or Dan French - or any other officer you may bring into this investigation - then I swear I'll report you all the way to the top." As an afterthought he added, "And I'll personally give you a bloody good hiding."

"I'm sorry, Jez, I don't know what I was thinking."

Calmer now, having said his piece. "Don't do it again." Barker took a pen from the desk, fidgeting, allowing time for the severity of his reprimand to sink in. Finally, he sighed. "Anyway, back to the case in hand. You'll no doubt need to investigate me alongside everyone else, but it would be unethical if you did it personally, considering we're friends. Is Dan going to do the job?"

Spencer was a hundred percent certain the inquiry would find nothing untoward in Barker's history and hadn't planned to investigate him, but after the lecture realised he would have to be squeaky clean. He nodded lamely. "Yes, he'll interview you after he's finished with Alice."

Barker stood, stretching. "I can assure you I've never seen the register, but that's for you guys to verify."

French entered, closing the door behind him. "I've had a word with Alice. She showed me her system and where she keeps her records, and she's very conscious of security. The file has a password, an unusual one, at that, and I'm confident she hasn't allowed anyone access."

"Has she left it open at any stage, like when she's left her desk to go to the loo, or get a drink, you know?" Spencer was relieved French had returned, the atmosphere had lightened.

"She says she's only opened the file once, when it was first sent to her. She says that whenever Elliot Jacobs sent her an up-to-date file, she simply replaced the old file with the new without looking at the details."

"Well, it looks like this might be the quickest internal investigation on record. Your computer techies must be able to access the files, though?"

Barker shook his head. "They can only access confidential files with permission, and I imagine that, because of the confidentiality laws, this one was restricted."

"Yes," French agreed, "Alice said she labelled it amber, which means it can only be opened with her say so."

"And she hasn't given anyone authorization, or the password."

"No." French sat, propping his foot over his leg, relaxed. "However, I would suggest that before we rush back to London with another closed avenue, we check the system history. That will tell us if the file's been accessed and by whom."

Spencer laughed. "Looks like you've found yourself your next job, then."

"What about me?" Barker wasn't guilty but preferred to be completely exonerated of any wrongdoing before the officers headed back to the City.

Relieved, Spencer smiled. "We don't need to check you out if the records show you haven't accessed the file."

Although the parents and relatives of the five missing women were suffering deeply, their wonderful girls lost to them with a real prospect they may never be seen alive again, they were pleased Operation Bandicoot had been set up, that their fears were being addressed and the girls searched for.

Like the other parents, Cantrice Wilson was informed of any developments with the case, but had so far heard little. There wasn't much to tell. Every night since her daughter hadn't returned home from her daily run, she had lit a candle and prayed for Lydia's safe return, but her god seemed to be

90

ignoring her and her spirit had worn low. At first she had cried like a baby, wishing her beloved husband, deceased for three years after a battle with lung cancer, was there to comfort her, hold her in his arms and make the hurt go away.

More than three months had passed since that dreadful, confusing and scary night, and she was a shadow of the woman she had once been. Years before - the happy years, when she had been a mother of two young daughters and cherished by her husband - she and Emmet had set up a small business, which had been instantly successful, giving the family enough money to live a comfortable lifestyle. But illness had stolen him and her grief after his death had stopped her giving the company the arduous work it needed. With regret, she had sold it and now lived on the dwindling money she had been paid in return.

But money no longer mattered, though. With her husband gone and her relatives in Port Antonio, unable to support her as they wished they could, and now her eldest daughter possibly dead, all she had was her sixteen-year-old, Sophia. Cantrice was numb, locked in a world of uncertainty, loss and fear. Only Sophia, bright and friendly, loving and generous, kept her going.

She dimmed the lights and lit a candle - cheap, yet symbolic - and prayed once more that her precious daughter would return to the family home, safe and unharmed.

Chapter 9
Tuesday Evening

"Thanks for letting me get things off my chest, Jill." Dick waved to the elderly woman who was carrying her portable massage table to her brand new Smart car.

Grinning kindly, she waved back, loading the boot. "You know you're always welcome, I love our chats. I'll see you next week, if not before, and keep an eye on that cough."

"I will." He closed the door, rolling his tension free shoulders, and went to the kitchen to stir the stew. He had methodically deliberated the unexpected problem during the massage, eventually formulating a plan, which comforted him. He liked routine, and preparation was a necessity, whatever the task at hand.

Outside, the sun descended over the horizon, the sky a dramatic red. He still had to buy a tracksuit to dress Lydia in and load her in the car, and he planned to leave her at a remote spot beside the River Ray, where she would inevitably be found, hopefully with her dignity intact. He had read that the rigor mortis would start to recede roughly twelve hours after death, which should make handling her easier.

He poured the latest batch of stew into a lidded container and propped it securely in the boot of his car, before driving the short distance to a supermarket on the northern outskirts of Raymouth.

He had barely seen the girls since locking them in the room, and even when he had, they had been unconscious, crumpled heaps. He had trailed each one before snatching them and knew their individual styles, and could picture Lydia in a smart, albeit cheap, blue tracksuit he had seen in passing when buying groceries. Although Lydia was slight, he chose a medium size for ease of dressing her, in case her body was still rigid.

The next stop of the busy night was the dilapidated factory that had once been a hive of activity, with noisy machines pumping and grinding and creaking in their productivity, buzzing workers controlling them and the output. The company, Fubarre and Sons Ltd, established in the industrious Victorian era, had closed in the nineteen twenties due to financial difficulties. The official story was that they hadn't been able to produce fabrics cheaply enough to compete with imports, and the premises had long since been abandoned and left to ruin.

But the derelict building was perfect to house his prisoners, too far from town to interest curious children, and far enough from parks and nature trails to avoid dogs sniffing around. He locked the door behind him and navigated the corridors to the room he used for himself in the hours he spent there. He set the container of food on the side and stirred in a few of vials of ketamine, stolen from his workplace, and dished a quarter into a bowl, taking it to the girls.

While Dick had been away, the effects of the Fluothane had worn off relatively quickly and the girls had awakened, pleased that they no longer shared a cell with a dead and decomposing body, but deeply disappointed they had not escaped. Sying and Neeraja, who had long since stopped caring, had immediately reached for the bowl of food to knock themselves out again, but Sammy - starving now, her stomach endlessly painful and griping - and Rhiannon still had hope and had resisted.

They heard the warning door and glanced at each other, ready to instigate Plan B. During the coherent hours, Sammy had told Rhiannon about the relationship she had started with their captor, that he had mentioned he didn't want to kill her, which she assumed must be because he valued the bond between them. Despite Rhiannon's desire to create havoc, she eventually conceded that moving gently may provide the best outcome for them all.

Sammy waited until the flap opened and the latest batch of food posted through, checking that Neeraja and Sying were still asleep, before, "Dick?"

"Hello, Sammy, I hoped you were still talking to me. Just for the record, I always use gas before I unlock the door, so you have no chance of escaping that way."

"Why do you think we were trying to escape?"

"It's obvious you would try." He paused for a moment. "Why do you want to escape anyway, I thought you liked me?"

Sammy chose her words carefully; what she said now could influence the outcome of the dreadful situation. She was only eighteen - nineteen tomorrow, but with no daylight entering the windowless room, she didn't realise that - and had no experience of psychology, but her mother was a counsellor and this gave her guidance: keep him talking. "I do, but it's dirty and smelly in here and the floor is so uncomfortable to sit or sleep on."

"I know," guilt grated his voice, "but it won't be for much longer. What if I brought you a bucket or something to do your business in, would that make things better?"

Both Sammy and Rhiannon's shoulders dropped with relief. "Yes, that's a start. Dick, why did you take us?"

He didn't reply for a while and Sammy became nervous. Eventually, quietly, he said, "Is the new girl still awake?"

Sammy shook her head and held her hand up to silence her cellmate. "No, she's taking whatever you put in the food, just like the others. They told her it was the best way."

"Good, because I like our time alone together." She guessed from the scraping sound that he had sat down and relief flooded her; the plan was working so far. "Just me and you."

"So why did you take us? Were you lonely?"

"I'm doing it for my sister. She was horribly mistreated and this is my way of rectifying that."

"In what way? Badly treated, that is." Sammy's heart beat so hard she considered it might explode, but concentrated on keeping her voice steady, friendly.

"She used to run, like you, she was really good. A promising athlete, the papers called her, but the other girls were jealous and that bitch of a sports teacher hated her, made that quite clear. They made her life a living hell."

Rhiannon and Sammy had so many questions but didn't speak; the more detail he gave them, the more ammunition they had. "Then there was the accident. At least that's what they called it, but it wasn't, it really wasn't."

He was careful to keep names and dates from his speech, aware the girls could be found, and if that happened he wouldn't have said anything to incriminate himself or his beloved Bubby, the pet name he had given his sister as a baby. "She was on an athletic team, she was a great all-rounder, and they were in training for the London Triathlon. It was a huge thing for her as places were limited, and the four of them had been lucky enough to be accepted before they closed the register. She said it felt as if she'd lived her whole life to lead up to that moment." He tailed off, the memory still raw.

"So, what happened?" *Keep him talking.*

Some scuffling. "I've told you too much already."

"No, Dick, I'm really interested. Honestly."

"Are you? You know, whenever I mention this to anyone their eyes go blank. No one wants to hear."

Emphatic. "Well, I do. Please tell me, don't make me have to beg."

The only sounds were four girls and one man breathing and Sammy was patient, wary of scaring him off, but his guard was back up. "I haven't got time. I've got to get rid of Lydia's body."

Desperate now. "Dick, please, you're the only company I have. I thought Rhiannon would be different but she just sleeps like the others. Please talk to me."

"I've got a busy night. Eat some food, it'll make the hours go quicker. I won't be back until tomorrow morning."

Sammy and Rhiannon had no choice but to accept the brief conversation was over and they sadly listened to his retreating footsteps, the warning door banging, sealing them away from the world once more.

Nancy had tried every avenue she could think of to find the name of the mystery witness to Rhiannon Hughes's abduction, but the hassled Metropolitan Police were nowhere near as cooperative as the local forces tended to be. She was due to start her prestigious job with The Daily Review the next day and had wanted to start with a bang, but it was proving difficult. Eventually she bit the bullet and called Southside Station; Jo Ellis was a weak newbie, easy to manipulate and the only chance of saving Nancy's day. She was told, however, that Jo was away on business, and further probing found the constable was part of the massive Operation Bandicoot in London.

Impressed, and now hopeful due to the new door into the investigation, Nancy found Jo's mobile number and dialled. "Jo, it's Nancy - don't put the phone down."

A long, tired sigh came down the line and Nancy grinned. "I promise I won't get you into trouble again. The thing is, I need to know the name of the witness who saw the latest girl being snatched."

"We're not giving names out and I owe you no favours."

"Jo, you and I have a common goal: we both want that madman caught and locked away. I can help you and you can help me."

"I don't need help. I'm part of a team of experienced detectives who have all the details I need. And I don't want to help you." Jo was careful not to inadvertently give anything away as she had the last time she had spoken to the interfering woman.

"Congratulations, by the way, for getting onto a major investigation. You must be good at your work to be given an opportunity like that."

"Flattery won't get you anywhere in my case. There's a reason her identity is being kept confidential."

It was so easy to probe the youngster; now Nancy knew the witness was female. "Is she in danger?"

"I don't know the reason, but the orders came from DCI Harner."

"Barry Harner?"

Jo swiftly recapped every word she had uttered, but couldn't see that giving his name would cause problems. "Yes. I take it you know him, just like you seem to know everybody?"

"No, I've never met him, but a friend prepared an exposé on him a couple of years back that held my interest."

"Oh, right. That'll be about his cock-up on the Kopycat Killer investigation. Old news."

"Actually, no, he was having an affair with some posh totty, but when my friend submitted the article they wouldn't publish. Things like that always involve big money so somebody was looking out for him. Anyway, his marriage is intact, although I doubt it's happy, and as far as I know his wife never found out. Poor woman."

Spencer's insinuating remark about Harner and Penelope having a fling suddenly fronted Jo's mind and she gasped. "His mistress. That explains it, no wonder he booked her a hotel."

"Who?"

"Pene… Oh no, I see what you did there. Well, you're not getting anything else off me." Jo slammed the phone down, angry and exposed, and on the other end of the line Nancy was grinning. Yes, the mistress had been Penelope De Boucher, and now Nancy knew the name of the witness. Bless little Jo, so innocent.

The best part of the revelation was that Nancy hardly needed to do any research. Phil had a box-file brimming with Penelope's life and habits, her tacky affair with Harner, her husband's multi-million business. Was it ongoing? Did it matter? The dirt was there, all she had to do was hone it into an article to supply to her new boss the next day. As she had wanted, her first day was going to start with a bang.

Dick took care dressing Lydia's body, ensuring the seams were straight and the zip securing her decency, but it was difficult as she was still stiff. Not as much as when he had removed her

97

from the room she had taken her last breath in, but enough to hamper him severely.

While stalking the girls, he felt he had come to know them, their habits, personalities, but he wouldn't have time to learn such information about Lydia's replacement, and this disturbed him. Why did she have to die? It had all been going so well. He was angry, finding it hard to accept that his first captive would no longer be part of the elaborate display he was working towards. He took a final look at her before taking her to her temporary resting place.

In death she didn't look the same. Her dark skin was tinged greenish-blue under the harsh torchlight that showed her in such detail, and her closed eyes were hollowed, haunting. The unmistakable odour of death had escalated during the hours she had laid on the stark floor of the toilet block and he had to force the dreadful, consuming memories of his time in Iraq from his mind.

He roused himself from his thoughts; he had a job to do. With force, he curled her body into a moveable position and lifted her. She seemed lighter than ever and although her head fell back, her mouth and eyes remained shut. He carried her from the washroom and through the maze of corridors that were well known to him - he had been visiting the disused building since childhood - and finally to the yard outside. Her body wasn't heavy, but cumbersome, and he struggled to click the car boot open. He folded her inside and slammed the lid, glad to be away from the permeating stench that would get stronger in time.

The drive to the River Ray was short, the once booming industrial estate that Fubarre and Sons stood on had relied on the waterway for both power - many of the buildings had waterwheels - and transport in the booming Victorian era. He climbed from the driving seat and scanned the open area through binoculars, watching for signs of movement to suggest a witness.

Convinced he was alone, Dick opened the boot and recoiled from the trapped odour that had been enhanced by the autumn heat. When the air had cleared, he reached in and manoeuvred her into his arms. A final glance at her face raised no emotion this time, he had already said his goodbyes, and he dropped her body over the bank, ensuring no part showed through the surface of the water.

Rubbing his hands together harshly in a subconscious attempt to remove the cloying smell, Dick climbed into the car and started the engine. He drove back along the dirt-path to the main road and made his way to the sports hall, where he knew Elliot Jacobs would be training his team. It would be impossible to access to the register without suspicion now the police were involved, so he would have to find a girl and hope for the best. As long as she was black and a runner, nothing else really mattered at this late stage.

Parked in the corner of the car park, shielded from suspicion by a low-hanging oak tree, he watched the athletes arrive one by one, mostly dropped off by overprotective parents, and finally a black girl stepped from a car. Now he had a target.

"Okay, guys, settle down." Elliot Jacobs waited until a hush descended over the sports hall, the excitable teenagers and young adults - his team, who were training for the Raymouth Marathon - angry at his decision to take them running outside the premises. Since the faces and similar hobbies of the missing girls had hit the news, barely anyone pounded the streets in the south of England any more, concerned they may be next in line for the mysterious abductor.

"Look, I know you're all worried about being targeted, but if we're all together, and I *mean* that we must stay together. No leaving the stragglers to catch up at any time, we stick by each other's sides."

"My mum told me I was only allowed to come training if we didn't go outside."

Several voices related similar statements and Elliot sighed. He had to admit defeat, and straightened his glasses. "I want you to all jog around the hall ten times. Keisha and Jonnie, can you come here please?"

The two runners strolled over, each pre-guessing what their trainer was about to say. Keisha didn't make eye contact; she couldn't without revealing her crush on the quirky, masculine man. "Dad told me I wasn't to run outside under any circumstances."

"Keisha, there are less than two weeks to go until you run a twenty-six-mile race. How do you expect to complete it if the only training you're doing is a little bit of circuit here and there? Is this race important to you or not?"

"Of course it is, but so is my life and my dad would go ballistic if I went against his orders on this one, trust me."

Elliot didn't bother to hide his irritation and she squirmed, afraid he would think badly of her. He turned to Jonnie. "Looks like you're in the running to win still. Unlike some." A jagged glare at the sensible, torn girl left her under no disillusion of his disappointment. "Are you game?"

"You bet." Jonnie grinned, unused to being the favourite pupil.

But competitiveness was in her blood. "No, wait, I'll text Dad and explain that we'll all be together."

And it was in Jonnie's blood too. "Make sure you tell him there'll only be three of us, and that you'll be the only female."

Elliot left Keisha at the side of the hall and returned to the other eight athletes, alongside Jonnie, who joined in on the fourth lap. A minute later, Keisha's father replied to her message. Furious, he banned her from any outside activity.

Her heart sank. The race meant so much and she knew that limited training within the final two weeks was the kiss of death to her being anywhere near the fastest runners. However, she was a wise girl, aware her father had implemented his rules because he was worried, justifiably, about her safety. Next year would be different.

French and Spencer had expected to be in Raymouth longer, but when a search history on Alice's computer showed she was the only person to have opened the file containing the register for the local marathon, they had nothing left to investigate. Because she supplemented her income from the police force with a bar job, Alice had a solid alibi for all but one of the abductions, and her personnel report showed a perfect track record with no misdemeanours.

However, it had been a long day for both detectives and, after checking with Harner, they made their way to their homes, Spencer to his small, fifth floor apartment and French to the terraced house in Peckham he was temporarily sharing with his colleagues from Southside Police Station.

Almost asleep on his feet, French dropped his suitcase at the bottom of the stairs ready to take up when he went to bed, and traipsed to the kitchen to make a hot drink. The house was quiet, but for various snuffles and snorts behind the closed doors, and he switched the kettle on before slumping on a chair by the melamine table.

Having heard noises downstairs, Jo slipped her robe and slippers on and trotted to the kitchen, but was dismayed to find her boss there. She had hoped it was somebody less cynical and more fun. "Oh, you're back."

French jumped, immediately embarrassed by his reaction to the shock of hearing an unexpected voice. "Jo, what are you doing up? Aren't you on early shifts?"

"I couldn't sleep. I can't switch the bloody investigation off in my mind." She slipped onto a chair beside him and rested against the wall.

"Sounds like you're a detective in the making, it's like that for us all the time. Why do you think there are so many borderline alcoholics on the police force?" Although it was a quip, he had been guilty of the same not so long ago, his recovery a testimony to the dedication of his long-suffering wife, and he wished he could swallow the words back as he scooped hot-chocolate powder into his mug.

She noticed his discomfort. "Not you, though, eh?"

"No, strictly teetotal, me." He squirmed, it was time to change the subject. "Have there been any developments since I've been away?"

"Make me one while you're at it, will you? Um, Guv, please, that is." Jo willed him not to have a go at her; it never took much for him to fly off the handle with anyone, but especially so when she was involved.

"No problem." Jo's eyes widened. Perhaps she was dreaming. "So, go on then, what's been going on back at the Yard?" He chuckled. "I've always wanted to say that."

She checked the clock on the wall. "It's only twelve hours since you left. They've been buzzing away, everybody rushing around with things to do, but if there have been any new leads or whatever, I haven't heard about them." She waited, expecting him to jump down her throat at any moment; he must be exhausted. "How did it go with you? Anything come of the investigation?"

He shook his head wearily and reached for the kettle to finish making the drinks. "No, only one person has accessed the records at the station and she's a civvy whose reputation and conduct are watertight. However this guy's getting information from the register, it isn't through the police computer, so we're back to square one."

Philosophical and upbeat, she shrugged. "I suppose at least it's another avenue checked off, narrowed things down."

"Oh, for fuck's sake." And there was the temper she knew and feared. "Give it a rest with the fucking Mary Poppins attitude, will you. There's your drink. I'm going to bed."

He angrily stomped up the stairs, inconsiderate to the rest of the sleeping team, and Jo reached for her drink, safe in the knowledge that there was nothing she could say in front of her boss that wouldn't rattle him.

She leant against the wall again, eyes closing against the bright fluorescent light, and had almost fallen asleep when a noise disturbed her. She peered along the hall to see Kenneth Boswell hanging his overcoat on the rack by the door and her will to live sank even further. Hoping he wouldn't notice her, she held her breath, but he had already spotted her. "Ellis, I thought you were in bed."

"I couldn't sleep." If she finished her drink quickly, she could get away from him and his nasty sarcasm and unabated hatred. She sipped the chocolate but it was too hot.

"I wish I was in bed." Boswell sagged onto the seat French had just abandoned. "Harner's had me and Barbara going through all the people who've run in the Raymouth Marathon in previous years. There are thousands."

She groaned inwardly, a chat with her archenemy was the last thing she wanted this time of night. "What are you looking for?"

"Nothing in particular, just trying to see if anyone stands out, like somebody with previous, or somebody who's been pissed off in some way, or had an accident at the race. Anything really. I think they're clutching at straws at the moment, there's not much to go on."

"So you didn't find anything?"

"Nothing to speak of. I left poor Barbara asleep at her desk, so god knows when she'll get back. That's if she bothers at all."

Jo was concerned. "That's not like her, she always leaves on time."

He leant closer and lowered his voice. "Between you and me, I think she's taking this case to heart too much, but I can't get anything out of her. Isn't her son quite athletic? Maybe he's due to run, that could be what her problem is."

"That's supposition, Guv, pure gossip. You could have woken her and brought her home, well, here." She expected him to bark a vicious remark, but he smiled, and she marvelled how she had never noticed his lovely eyes. Blushing, she stared at the floor to hide it. "Um, can I get you a hot-chocolate?"

"That's sweet of you, I'd love one." Jo was glad of the task, it would give her cheeks time to return to their normal colour, and she busied herself preparing the drink. Her face had calmed by the time she sat again and her own drink had

103

cooled enough for her to gulp. Eager to end the uncomfortable and strange rendezvous, she trotted back to bed.

Despite having trained for over two hours, which had left her drained, the earlier altercation with Elliot kept replaying in Keisha's mind and she was struggling to sleep. Was her father being too strict? After all, none of the kidnapped girls had been from Raymouth. She was one of the star athletes at Raymouth Sports Club, and she knew that if she kept training intensely, she was a definite contender for a prize, and the sponsorship that would potentially come of it.

Her father had been overprotective since her mother had taken her older sister to America fourteen years before, back to her home and relations, forgetting the family she had destroyed in returning to her own. Did he really have the right to thwart her ambitions over some imagined scenario?

Keisha sipped from the glass of water beside her bed. It wasn't the right time to make decisions; tomorrow, when she had slept properly and had a clear head, she would talk to her father, make him understand how important the race and the accolade of winning were to her. Snug in the comfortable bed, she closed her eyes and allowed dreams of success and acknowledgement to lull her to sleep with a smile on her face.

Chapter 10
Wednesday 25th September

Dick arrived at the neglected building earlier than normal for two reasons: first, it was Sammy Cooper's birthday and he wanted to spend time with her, and secondly, he was scared of another girl dying before he could carry out his big finale.

He headed through the corridors to his room and dished another bowl of poisoned stew to give to his charges with a sense of urgency, desperate to speak to Sammy. Donning his spare protective boiler suit and collecting the breathing apparatus and tank of air, he tapped on the door to her prison. "Sammy, are you awake?"

Inside, she moaned. She hadn't eaten the drugged food, but starvation was taking its toll and she had weakened; sleep was coming easier every day. "Dick, is that you?"

"Did you know it's your birthday today? You're nineteen."

"Oh." She hadn't the strength to care and glanced at her fellow prisoners, peaceful and asleep, wondering if Rhiannon had stopped fighting and succumbed to the mind-numbing drugs.

The flap at the bottom of the door opened and Dick fed a plate holding a single cupcake through. "I bought you a present. Don't worry, there are no drugs in it."

Without a thought for the other girls, her appetite so consuming, she grabbed the cake and stuffed it hungrily into her dry mouth, barely tasting its sweet fluffiness in her desperation. She struggled to swallow and reached to the bucket, scooping water into her mouth, soaking the sponge bolus to help it slip down her throat. "Thank you, thank you so much." Sammy bit again, this time savouring the vanilla flavour, swilling it around her mouth, relishing the texture, the light softness.

"Is anyone else awake?"

"Do you think I'd be eating the cake alone if they were?"

105

"Has the new girl settled down now?" He wondered if she was taking the drugs and behaving like the others.

"She's asleep, that's all I know." Sammy understood what he had meant.

"That cake isn't your only present. I've decided to spare you."

"You mean you're not going to kill me?"

"Yes, you remind me too much of my sister."

"So you're going to let me go?" She barely breathed, the answer so important.

"Yes, but not until the sixth of October." Dick was feeding the hosepipe under the door.

As soon as she heard the hissing, Sammy realised he was gassing the room again and she screamed. "Dick, please, no."

"I'm giving you the bucket you asked for." Sammy dropped to the floor with a groan and there was silence. "You'll be fine, darling, it'll all be over soon. I promise I won't hurt you. I think I love you."

"You are absolutely not running outside, young lady. If you can't train inside the club, then you're not training at all." Ian Hamilton had reached stalemate with his daughter. Usually their close relationship was calm and respectful, but her future in athletics had to come second to her safety.

Keisha knew better than to argue. Once her stubborn father had made his mind up there was no swaying him. If she were to keep training properly, it would have to be in secret and she wasn't sure she was prepared to do that; lying had never come easily. She was confused, caught in a dilemma that seemed to have no benefit to her whatever choice she made. If she ignored her father's wishes, she may be a target to the sick abductor, but if she didn't, she would lose vital training, meaning she wouldn't reach the placing she was aiming for in the race.

The break in hostilities had eased the atmosphere and Ian sighed deeply, knowing how important his decision was to her future career. "I just couldn't bear to lose you. I watched your mother walk away and leave us for good, taking your sister with her, I can't sit and watch you put yourself in danger." He hammered his chest for emphasis. "I couldn't lose you. I *need* you."

Like dust settling, everything fell into place. The race would still happen next year, and what was a year anyway. She would obey her father. It was the least she owed him for having raised her single-handedly. "Dad, you have nothing to worry about. I won't train outdoors, I promise."

Relieved tears filled Ian's eyes and he hugged his daughter, his pride and joy, holding her tightly as if scared to let her go. When the tears subsided, he released his grip and held her by the shoulders. Their eyes locked. "Thank you."

"Come on, Dad, or should I call you my personal chauffeur, you'd better drive me to college."

He playfully mussed her hair, grateful the air was clear between them.

Nancy's first morning at The Daily Review wasn't going as planned, having received an early call from Jonas telling her not to come in. "But I've already prepared my first article. What have I done wrong?"

"No, no, no, Nancy, it's not like that. I want you to stay in Southside because it's so close to Raymouth. I've just sent you a file I was working on yesterday. As you may already know, the police have established a link between the missing girls and the Raymouth Marathon and I want you see what you can find out about the organisers."

"What's the link?"

"All the girls were registered to run this year. I think there may be something in the history of the race that could have led to this current state of affairs. The file is about the Chairwoman, Roberta Robinson. The race was her idea in the first place and she's been the main organiser for eleven years, since the first marathon in two thousand and two. I've documented the information I have on her and I want you to take it from there."

"Write an article about her?"

"No," he waved his hand, "implicate her in the case. Call it a gut feeling, whatever, but I reckon she'll know a lot more than she'll have told the coppers. I'll leave you to it."

"Hold on, Jonas, don't go. What about the article I prepared yesterday?"

"What's it about?"

She mentioned Harner and Penelope De Boucher, but her new boss's interest waned and he became a closed book. "No."

"Why on earth not? Harner's investigating the missing girls, she's a star witness, they're both married yet knocking each other off. How much more of a story can you get than that?"

"We've been bought off. We're on Patrick De Boucher's payroll."

"Her husband? You mean he knows about their affair?"

"He knows about it and pays us to keep it a secret. He's got money coming out of his ears and he's not afraid to use it."

"But if he knows she's being unfaithful, why should he give a damn about her dirty little bonkathon being exposed?"

His tone was firm and austere. "It's a fact that most people are unaware of, but De Boucher owns the newspaper. We dish the dirt on him, he serves out P45's in return."

"Oh, for heaven's sake. Every time I get a good exposé somebody pays the bill to shut me up. What happened to freedom of speech?"

"When that man is paying me enough to live in a luxury apartment overlooking the Thames and own a top of the range sports car, I don't ask questions. Sometimes you have to know when to stop."

"But what if another paper publishes it?"

"If I see anything at all in another newspaper, I swear you will never work as a journalist again."

Unlike her previous boss, Jonas had the power to carry out his threat and she conceded she was beaten. The warning was loud and clear, and her anticipated reverence and glory was, in fact, a slap in the face. "Do you want me to give you the file, nonetheless?"

"Delete it."

She had no intention of doing so. "I'll delete the file and all associated records."

"That's more like it, make sure you do. Now, read what I've sent you and go and find out what the organisers are all about." He cut the call and she rested against the pillows, sighing as she rolled her eyes.

"Problems?" Phil had heard everything.

"They won't touch the affair between Harner and Penelope." It wasn't important to tell him why and he didn't ask. She clambered from the warm covers and sighed again. "I'm working from home, anyway. I'll get the coffee pot going, want one?"

Half an hour later, Nancy had washed and dressed and she checked the detailed email from Jonas. He had clearly spent a lot of time delving into Roberta Robinson's past. One of three children born into an average family in nineteen fifty, her early life had been unremarkable.

She had always been sporty, and dated articles Jonas had uncovered from a local Raymouth newspaper held victorious reports of her athletic career. She had been the pride of her town. She had qualified as a physical education teacher at what was then Raymouth College, now university, in the early seventies, but had deferred finding work for a couple of years to compete in several renowned events.

She had never been an overall winner, but her glory as a local celebrity had shone. Never married, she had ploughed her energy into the pupils at Raymouth Comprehensive, but genuine talent wasn't easy to find. Several students had benefited from her tireless devotion and support during her teaching years, but none had been the jewel she had hoped to find.

Eventually, as the millennium came and went, arthritis had given her no choice but to take early retirement, giving her the time to make her dreams become a reality: to create and control the Raymouth Marathon.

The more Nancy read about the woman, the less credit she gave Jonas's gut instinct, because despite her reputation as a taskmaster who didn't suffer fools, Roberta had always been fair and hardworking. A couple of reports had comments from disgruntled helpers and runners, but they were few.

Roberta Robinson had a clean slate and was highly unlikely to be the link to the abductor. Despite her boss's convictions, she decided not to give the woman any more time; the next committee member on the list looked far more suspicious. She typed 'Elliot Jacobs' into the search bar and waited.

Harner had dragged the team of officers and civilians together for a summary of the ongoing investigation and was as frustrated as everybody else. On one side he had the angry public demanding to know why the abductor and victims hadn't been found, and on the other hand they had few leads to follow up. The girls had disappeared, they had all been registered to run in the same marathon, and that was where the trail ended.

Within the centralised investigation were five teams, each consisting of a detective inspector, a detective sergeant, two detective constables, a police constable and a civilian, and a further nine Met officers manned the desks and phones. The teams were from the towns where the victims had lived, and had been structured this way because their local knowledge, which the Met had no bearing on, may be invaluable.

Monday's press conference had made the public aware of what was going on and how they could avoid subjecting themselves to danger, but the numerous incoming phone calls afterwards hadn't revealed anything of value and had, in fact, wasted time.

Harner suspected his career may be on the line, depending on the outcome of the investigation, especially after narrowly missing early retirement after the mix-up of dates whilst heading the Black Museum Bunch in the hunt for the Kopycat Killer five years before. Unsure how to proceed, the pressure was high.

"As you know, Spencer and French were in Raymouth yesterday heading an internal investigation into the local station. Their inquiries led to nothing, which is a good thing, I suppose; none of us wants to encounter a corrupt police force. However, this also gives us very little to go on as the organisers of the marathon have also come up squeaky clean, and the possibility of the register having been seen by anyone untoward is virtually nil.

"We must be missing something, because obviously the register has been leaked to someone, and that someone now has five girls, who may be dead for all we know. Bearing that in mind, I have asked the heads of each of the visiting teams to give a summary of the missing girls and the circumstances behind their disappearances. Maybe with us all hearing exactly the same details, we can work out who the abductor could be."

"He's lost, isn't he?" Boswell nudged Jo, smiling.

"Without doubt." She hung her head, cheeks flushing, unaccustomed to friendliness from the man who detested her.

"Could we have some quiet, please?" The twittering room silenced. "We'll start with the first victim, Lydia Wilson. Her disappearance was initially handled by Bethnal Green Police Station, so Detective Inspector Forrester, would you mind taking over."

Forrester stepped to the front. "Lydia Wilson, aged seventeen and of Jamaican descent, had arrived back from college at five in the afternoon on Friday twenty-first of June, and a keen runner, like all our victims, she was training for the Raymouth Marathon. She headed out to the Cambridge Heath Leisure Centre about an hour later, where she met with her trainer and four other young runners. For the record, each of these has been interviewed and their alibis are watertight.

"They trained in the gym until quarter past eight, then went for a run on the streets first, then around the circumference of Haggerston Park, before heading back to the sports hall. After a brief cool down, they showered, and the five runners left. The trainer stayed behind to clear up, which has been verified by CCTV.

"The other runners were mostly collected by their parents, but Lydia's mother unfortunately suffers from depression and is unable to leave the house, and she told us that Lydia always came straight home after her daily gym sessions. She was apparently a tower of support to her mother. Mrs Wilson believes Lydia would have taken her normal route home: south on Cambridge Heath Road, west along Bethnal Green Road, and then she would have gone across a park, Weavers Fields, towards her home in Scott Street. Obviously, she never arrived.

"Mrs Wilson waited until midnight before phoning us and was advised to wait until the next morning, when an officer would come and take some details. On Saturday, the visiting officer took a statement, but no alarm was raised at that stage. On Monday twenty-fourth, Lydia was registered on the PNC as officially missing and her details passed to me. We completed all the routine enquiries and raised local involvement with…"

"We don't need to go into fine detail," Harner interrupted, "we're trying to see if there is any other possible link, for example, the way the girls dressed, the areas from which they were taken. We already know the alarm wasn't raised until Sammy Cooper's disappearance."

Forrester had lost his swing and he stuttered, "Guv. Right. Well, that's all then, really."

"What date did she register for the marathon?" French asked.

Forrester shuffled through his notes. "She sent the form, with the fee, on thirtieth of May. It was her birthday and her mother had given the money as a present."

A few more questions were asked and answered and they moved on to the second girl, Sying Cheng. The representative from Brighton Police force, DI Agarwal, took to the stand. "Sying, aged eighteen, had moved from her

112

hometown of Leeds to Brighton during the summer holidays to attend The University of Sussex, studying a Sports Science Degree. She was homesick from the first day, keeping in regular contact with her parents and two siblings, and they had been worried for her.

"Soon after moving, she became a regular at Moulsecoomb Community Leisure Centre, but she was quite a loner - her parents say she was extremely shy - and didn't make any friends. Other members of the gym have remarked that she appeared to be dedicated and organised within her exercise regime. She would swim for half an hour, and then return to the centre roughly an hour later to do cardio and weight training, again alone. It is assumed that she spent the missing hour running as this follows her lifestyle in Leeds before her relocation.

"On the evening of thirtieth of July she went for the run as usual but never returned to the leisure centre. Nobody batted an eyelid there, and her father raised the alarm on Friday, second of August, after becoming concerned about the lack of phone calls home. He first contacted the university, but they advised him to call the police and that's where we came in.

"Although we registered her disappearance on the PNC, we weren't concerned because she had seemed unhappy living in Brighton. We assumed she would either be taking a break or returning home. Somehow it slipped through the net and was never followed up, and we didn't hear back from her parents."

A collective gasp rang out and Boswell couldn't contain himself. "What?"

Agarwal coughed, clearing his throat. "I know. Her father has said he was waiting for us to call him, figuring no call meant nothing had happened, which I suppose was right, but you'd have thought they'd have been going frantic. I know I would have been had it been my daughter."

Harner stood. "So, basically, like Lydia, she'd been training that day, so was wearing sporty clothes, and was snatched in the evening. To further French's earlier question, when did she register for the marathon?"

"In October last year, as soon as they released the application forms after the last one, so a link with the date of registration doesn't seem likely."

No questions came this time and they moved on to Neeraja Sharma, victim three. DI Higgins strode to the front and waited for the room to quieten. "Neeraja Sharma was seventeen at the time of her abduction on the fifth of August. She was a grade A student, leaving school with a bucketful of GCSE's, and was attending East Berkshire College, studying maths, computing and chemistry."

"Quite the egghead, then." The lame attempt at a joke backfired and the officer put his head down, embarrassed.

"She also, as you'll have guessed, was a keen runner, and her father supported her sporting hobby financially. He'd paid for her membership at an exclusive gym in Uxbridge, which he ferried her to every day, and also one of their personal trainers. It seems that money wasn't an issue for the family.

"Mr Sharma dropped his daughter at the gym at six, as he did most weekdays, and the trainer says they did an hour of cardio and weights before going for a run. The course they took was through the streets directly west until they reached Fray's River, then north through Rockingham Recreation Ground and up to Fassnidge Park. On their way back to the gym the trainer and Neeraja stopped at a corner shop. Unfortunately, this was a regular occurrence, which the kidnapper obviously knew, because when the trainer returned with the usual two isotonic drinks, Neeraja wasn't there. Nobody has reported a struggle, despite the local awareness we immediately arranged.

"In contrast to the other girls, Neeraja's disappearance was treated as suspicious from the start and our investigation was thorough. However, without having a witness to her abduction or any other leads to follow up, our inquiries drew a blank. And here we are. Oh, and before you ask, Neeraja's father filled out the application form for the Raymouth

Marathon in January and it was he who paid; no surprise there."

If there was a link between the details so far, it was nothing more than they already knew, and French detailed Sammy Cooper's disappearance from her hometown of Southside, with the officers taking notes and soaking in the details as they had with the three others. The latest team to join the central investigation was from Sevenoaks, and although they hadn't dealt with the Rhiannon Hughes case as she hadn't been reported missing, they had been drafted in to join Operation Bandicoot because of their knowledge of the area.

DI Gipps had far less information to give for Rhiannon as nobody had seemed to care where she was or why at any time. She had been taken into care aged thirteen, just over a year before, and had recently turned fifteen. Everybody who had been questioned had confirmed she was an unpredictable tearaway, and also that she relaxed by running. Nobody knew about her registration for the Raymouth Marathon, nor where she got the money from to pay; several speculated that she might have stolen it. Her registration had been received three weeks before, which bore no correlation to the other girls.

Her mother had been questioned in depth but, an alcoholic, she'd not had much to say, except that Rhiannon had been a handful who had no respect for the law, and there was every possibility she had run away, which she had threatened on many an occasion. However, the police included her with the other missing girls due to the eyewitness to her abduction.

As the room cleared, the team still had barely anything to go on, yet hoped they would find whatever they were missing before another girl was taken against her will.

Chapter 11
Wednesday Lunchtime

"Are you taking the drugs as well, now?" Sammy was furious with Rhiannon when she awakened from her long sleep.

Rhiannon pushed herself up, grasping at her pounding head with a grimace. "Free drugs versus being awake in this nightmare; what do you think?"

"You saw what it did to Lydia. You don't want to end up like that, do you?"

"No, but I don't want to be freaking out like you because you're living through every disgusting moment. There was a major investigation started after you went missing, so if they're looking for you, they'll find me too, won't they?"

"They'll obviously be looking for you too, though."

Rhiannon snorted, "I doubt anyone's even noticed I'm not there."

"Don't say things like that, of course someone will have reported you missing."

Rhiannon's eyes were blank, an empty void, as she glared at her cellmate. "Nobody gives a shit. My old man's in prison, my mum's off her head with booze and smack all the time, and my little sister was taken into care when she was five; I haven't seen her since. I asked them to put me into care too, but they waited until I was thirteen before they actually did, and I can promise you that nobody gives a shit when you're in care."

Sammy resisted the urge to cuddle Rhiannon, who had made it clear she wasn't a tactile person. "That's terrible, I'm so sorry."

"I'm not. You come into the world alone and you die alone. I don't need anybody."

"Everyone needs somebody."

"You can't want or need something you've never had." Rhiannon scanned the room now the bleariness was clearing from her eyes. "Where's all the shit gone?"

"There's a bucket over there, he said he was going to get one for us. I guess he must have cleaned up when he brought it in."

"We've been upgraded to five-star luxury then." The irony ended the interchange and they sat, neither with anything to say, and when the warning door sounded it was a welcome reprieve. Sammy put a finger to her lips to hush Rhiannon and waited for him to reach the door to feed the latest batch of poisoned stew under the hatch. "Dick?"

"I said too much last time. Why don't you ever sleep?"

"You know I won't take the drugs; they've already killed Lydia. Thanks for the bucket, by the way." She scanned the clean floor. "It's so much nicer in here now you've given it a scrub."

"You're welcome. I never realised young girls could make such a mess."

"Be fair, Dick, we had nowhere else to go. Do you fancy a chat?"

"I already told you, I've said too much already."

Sammy glanced at Rhiannon, unsure where to take the conversation, and the girl mouthed 'plan' back to her. "You've said you're not going to kill me; why do you have to kill the others?"

"I don't have to, it'll just make things a lot easier for me, and make much more of a statement when I avenge my sister."

"Does she know you're doing this for her?"

He chuckled at the thought of his gentle, kind hearted, loving sister; Bubby was such a sweet woman. "Of course she doesn't, this is all a surprise for her. A gift, if you like."

"Why would she want four dead girls as a gift, well, three if you don't kill me."

"Four, I have to replace Lydia. It's not about you girls though, it's a statement that will raise the issue of the way she was treated by certain other people."

Sammy had no idea what he was talking about, but it was irrelevant anyway. Her job was to persuade him not to kill her

117

new friends and if possible encourage him not to go through with whatever plan he had concocted and set them free. Preferably unharmed. "I think you should tell your sister. I think it would come as quite a shock to her if you don't."

"No, she thinks I can't do anything right and I want to prove to her that I can."

"I still think you should tell her, but obviously that's your choice. I think it would be fairer. Does she give you the drugs to give us?"

"No, I steal them from... Oh, you're good, aren't you? That's why I like you, you're very clever."

"So is Neeraja, she's the brain box of the four of us. Anyway, why do you need five girls? And why are we all different races? I don't get it."

"For the rings, of course, they represent the world. I'll call them the rings of death. They'll be a form of art. They'll take pictures, and they'll be in newspapers and on the telly all around the world."

Rhiannon had listened to the conversation with disgust and couldn't keep quiet any longer. "So all you want is your fifteen minutes of fame, really, you deranged fucking psycho?"

Dick was shocked. "Who's that? I don't recognise your voice."

Rhiannon injected a heavy dose of sarcasm into her voice. "Rhiannon Hughes; remember me? Tall, ginger, general pain in the arse."

This time he shouted. "You should have told me she was awake, Sammy, I only wanted to talk to you."

"You should have asked her if I was awake then, shouldn't you. Don't shove the blame onto her shoulders, you're the one who fucked up."

And now it was roared. "Now you know, Sammy, why the others have to die."

His stamping footsteps receded and the warning door slammed, leaving them in silence. After a while, Sammy spat, "Thanks for helping me gain his trust, moron."

"Fuck off."

Dick had intended to take things one step at a time, despite the sixth of October nearing, but that slag - mouthy bitch, Rhiannon - had put him in a foul mood and he felt reckless. After he had locked the run-down building, he drove the short distance to Raymouth Sports Club, where he had seen Lydia's replacement the night before. She had been dropped off and collected by a man in a car, so if he was going to snatch her, he would have to be quick and dive in at the first opportunity.

He parked under the oak tree again to avoid being noticed and, inconspicuous in the beaten, old Range Rover, watched discreetly from behind a newspaper. A while later Elliot came out, followed by a group of young adults.

Dick's eyes were drawn to the only black girl in the crowd and he started the engine, watching her movements keenly. She waved to her friends, and he was about to accelerate towards her when another car pulled up outside the building and she climbed in. He thumped the steering wheel in frustration, squinting to see the coloured driver, who he assumed was her father. She was definitely the one, but if her dear-daddy was her door-to-door chauffeur, he needed to find her alone somehow.

When the car park had cleared, he drove home, bought a four pack of beer from the shop beside his house, and went upstairs to his study where he set to work. Sinking the first can, ready chilled, he opened the second. He knew from hearsay that Elliot's team were training mostly indoors, so the girl couldn't be taken like the others had. He had to find a way of abducting her from inside the building.

She was petite, but too big to fit into even his largest holdall, and drugging her and carrying her from the building in his arms would bring questions. He didn't know her name or where she lived. It was a quandary, but he would find a way.

It hadn't taken Nancy long to find details of Elliot's life. He worked at Raymouth Leisure Centre during the day and trained pupils privately at a sports hall in the north of town in the evenings. He was a busy man, but traceable. "Are you Elliot Jacobs?"

Elliot gave the older woman a once over before replying. "Depends who's asking."

Nancy smiled and introduced herself, fluffing over the fact she was investigating him for her new role as crime reporter for The Daily Review. "I'm just doing a small story for the sports pages of the Southside Express and I heard you are coaching a team to run in the Raymouth Marathon."

"Well, in that case, do you fancy a drink? There's a café over the swimming pool and they tell me the coffee's just about okay."

Nancy nodded and followed him up the stairs to the noisy cafeteria, which doubled as a social centre. "I'll get these, Elliot. How do you take yours?"

"I'll have a mineral water please. I try to avoid caffeine if I can." He sat at the only empty table, moving the dirty crockery to one side and wiping the sticky surface with a serviette. Nancy soon returned with his drink and a black coffee for herself and slipped onto the seat opposite him. "So, what do you want to know?"

"Well, with the marathon coming up, I wanted to know what role you play in the organisation, I mean, I know you're on the committee."

"We all do a little bit of everything, the seven of us work really well together, but the one thing that's solely my responsibility is the register."

She had to play dumb or her cover wouldn't be believable. "Register?"

"Yes, I receive and process the applications."

"How many people are due to run this year?"

"We've got nearly six thousand now, it's the most successful year so far. The event's really growing."

"It's a shame it's surrounded by such controversy this year." Needling in, bit by bit.

Elliot was disgusted. "*That* is no reflection on the race. It's not our fault some psycho is picking off the young women. The event is still as clean and wholesome as it always was. I just hope they find that sicko soon, and, of course, those poor missing girls."

Nancy had hit a nerve and intended to run with it. "Yes, it's awful, isn't it? But, of course, it is your responsibility in a way because the leaked personal information must have come from the register. Whoever this man is, for I assume he's a man, he's had access to those details, so there must be some link with a committee member."

Elliot sat up straight, vexed; public relations had never been his strong point. "Our privacy controls are airtight. There's certainly been no leak from me and I fully trust every single member on the board. It's the police you should be looking at, not us."

"Oh?" Now she had a bite and it sounded wonderfully newsworthy; Jonas was going to be pleased.

"After the Boston Marathon bombings earlier this year, the police asked us to copy them the register every week. I complied, and I must add that all seven of us have assisted the police with everything they've asked for. If you want to find a leak, look at the boys in blue."

Elliot became a closed book and Nancy figured it would only antagonise him further if she said any more on the subject, so she finished the interview with a few meaningless questions about Elliot Jacobs and his role in the committee - trash that would never be seen in print - to appease him, keep him on side.

The next person to interview on her list of committee members was Lily Jenkins, but not before she told Jonas about the police having access to the register.

Ian Hamilton was in trouble with his employer for taking time away from his middle-management job to ferry his daughter to and from college. He had arrived two hours late that morning, Keisha having had a late start, and had been hauled in front of the boss to be reprimanded. He was told in no uncertain terms that he wouldn't have a job to come back to if it happened again, despite offering to work from home as a compromise.

"Come on, Mark, you know how dangerous it is out there at the moment. Keisha's registered to run in the marathon and she's the same age as the missing girls. She's a prime target."

"My hands are tied, Ian, I'm sorry. The order has come from above. This is the third day this has happened, and you know how bad business is at the moment, what with this goddamned recession. We need all hands on deck and if you can't commit to that then, well."

"Mark, I've been here over ten years, have you ever known me to slack at any time - ever - before? You know I'm a hard worker, that's how I've risen through the ranks."

Just the messenger, Mark was fed up and didn't have time for the meaningless conversation; an order was an order. "Yes, but you're about to tumble back down the ranks if you don't do what you're being asked to do."

"Don't you have a soul? That's my daughter. They're going to find that guy soon, according to the newspapers the coppers are working round the clock to find those girls and whoever it is who has them; it'll probably all be over by the weekend. This week, that's all I'm asking for. I need to keep my baby girl safe."

"And what if he hasn't been caught by next Monday, eh? You'll be doing the same thing next week, then the week after, and all the while this company is hanging by a thread. We are *that*," he held his fingers close together, "close to going into receivership, we need you to be putting in overtime, like the rest of us - who also have daughters at home - and the meeting tonight, despite being out of hours, is compulsory. Which includes you."

Ian's head sank and he mumbled his agreement reluctantly.

"Why don't you just get someone else to drive Keisha? She must have friends whose parents drive them in. I just can't see the problem."

Ian sighed. If he wanted to keep his job, he would have to do just that, although instinct told him he should be protecting his child, not someone he had never met. "I've got no choice, have I?" Laced with bitterness and conformity.

"No." Mark shook his head in emphasis.

Ian checked his watch; Keisha was due to finish at four and was expecting him, which left two hours to find someone willing to collect her. With very few friends in the area, that would be a chore. He headed back to his desk and texted Keisha, asking her to find someone from her college for that afternoon. They could talk about it later to come up with a better solution.

Lily Jenkins hadn't been an easy person to locate, she seemed to be on every committee that existed, but Nancy had caught her teenager, Karen, after school in front of their house and the girl had directed her to Tildsley Road Sewing Club, held at the local community centre.

The woman in charge directed Nancy to Lily, who politely agreed to come outside for a chat.

Nancy introduced herself and told Lily the same story she had told Elliot earlier, that she was doing a story for the Southside Express about the marathon. "I'm not sure how much I can help, to be honest. I'm on the committee, but I'm on lots of committees. I spread myself too thin, really."

Easing in, building confidence, Nancy smiled affably. "I heard that the race has more applicants than ever before. Has that come about through advertising, or word of mouth, or..."

"Totally word of mouth. Raymouth is such a pretty place. It's a town, so there's plenty to do, but once you get to the cliffs, there's stunning scenery on one side and the ocean on the other. You can see for miles on a good day. I think that's why people want to do the marathon here. They get a bit of everything."

"Thanks." Nancy scribbled in her notebook, only the shorthand wasn't what Lily was saying but her demeanour; her boring story was irrelevant. "Why did you become involved with the marathon committee?"

"I love sports, all sports, but I particularly love athletics. I was good when I was younger, but then I had an accident, so any ambitions I had were wiped out."

"Oh, what happened?"

"Nothing much, I was silly, in the wrong place at the wrong time. I was running cross-country with my class, got too close to the edge of the cliff, lost my footing and fell. I broke my back in two places and there's a small amount of damage to my brain. But I'm alive, I was lucky. At least I can put my efforts into seeing others achieve their dreams instead."

"That's a very kind spirit you've got there."

Lily shrugged. "It's all I can do. I lost everything I'd ever known that day, but as soon as I accepted that life was going to be - had to be - different, I found I could put my energies to good use. I'm not a spiteful person, I don't see the point."

Nancy felt it was time to dig deeper and change the subject. She leant towards the innocuous woman, white-blonde and fragile, her spine twisted and disabled. "Have you found that the marathon being linked to the cases of those missing girls has had an adverse effect on its reputation?"

"The police have told me I'm not to talk about it."

Bastards. "Of course, I understand." She zipped her mouth shut with her hand. "Count the subject changed. What about Elliot Jacobs and Roberta Robinson?"

"Well, I've known Roberta for years, she used to teach me and we kept in contact. In fact, it was she who suggested I join the committee. And Elliot, I went to school with him, we used to train together. Mum didn't mind me running with him because he wasn't a threat." She laughed, humble, gentle.

"What do you mean?" Having met him, Nancy knew what she meant. Every man turned his head when she walked in a room, yet he hadn't batted an eyelid. Without doubt he was homosexual.

"Well, he's gay as they come, isn't he? You'd never know it to look at him, all beefy and manly, but he's never been interested in women, and believe me, a fair few girls in my year tried their luck with him, all to no avail." She chuckled at the memory. "But he's very private. I've never known him to have a boyfriend either."

They soon said their goodbyes and Nancy returned to her car. Something about the angelic Lily didn't fit and she determined to do some more digging. In the meantime, there were five more committee members to see.

Keisha was a popular girl, but her friends weren't interested in running and although she had easily found a lift home from college, she struggled to find someone to take her to the sports hall at six for her training. Her father had told her explicitly that if no lift was available, she wasn't to leave the house. She felt he was being paranoid, but understood why, and had already accepted she wasn't going to be one of the forerunners of the marathon this year. It was a shame, but the risks were too high.

Worried it would sound like an excuse to see him, aware he suspected her schoolgirl crush, she phoned her trainer. "Hi, Elliot, it's me. I know it's a big ask, but is there any chance of a lift to the gym tonight, because Dad can't take me."

"You're in Westlands Avenue, aren't you?"

"Number twenty-seven."

"That's no problem, it's on my way. Is five-thirty okay? It's just I'll have to get the equipment out."

"That's fine, and thank you, I really didn't want to miss training. See you later." She hung up and fell back in with her friends as they strolled towards the final lesson of the day. She settled behind a desk, wondering why she had chosen to study French, and resigned herself to ninety minutes of tedium.

When the bell finally sounded she was first from her desk.

Her friend's mother was pleasant, offering a lift any time she needed, and Keisha was grateful. She said goodbye and let herself into her modest house. After a couple of crackers with cheese to keep her energy levels up, she changed into her loud, pink tracksuit. Although it had seemed she would have plenty of time when the arrangements had been made, the journey home had been through heavy traffic, mid-town roadworks halting the flow, and she hurriedly grabbed her shower bag and checked her hair before darting outside to wait for her transport. She was just in time.

"Hi, Elliot, thanks again for the lift."

"No problem." He pulled into the stream of traffic, rush hour in full force. "What's up with your dad then, he always brings you in?"

"Work. The company he works for is in trouble and they're holding a crisis meeting or something like that."

"Oh dear, that doesn't sound good. Oh well, you know you can trust me. I'd rather give you a lift and have you training than have you miss out. I've got high hopes for you, you know that."

He winked at her and she blushed, staring through the window to avoid him noticing. They had never had a conversation before, he was simply a trainer who happened to figure in her daydreams. "What do you mean?"

"Do you have any idea how good you are, Keisha? You're one of the best runners I've ever trained. With hard work now there's a real chance you could be competing nationwide and you have the unusual talent of being able to run both short and long distance with ease. That's a gift."

She was embarrassed and tittered lightly. "No one, well, no one except Dad has ever said that before. Do you really think so?"

The traffic had cleared and Elliot sped up, enjoying giving the pep talk as he drove. "Yes, I do. In fact, I was going to have a word with you this weekend about it, you and your dad."

She grinned widely. "Oh, don't make me wait until then, I'm all excited now. Tell me, please."

He grinned back. "Do you promise to keep it to yourself for now, because the details haven't been finalised?"

"Yes, what is it?"

"I've been asked by a friend to put my two best runners forward for a sponsorship and I've chosen you and Jonnie." They had reached the car park and he drove neatly into a space before cutting the engine. He pulled the handbrake and turned to face Keisha, who was speechless, beaming from ear to ear. "An anonymous businessman has offered to pay for two promising athletes to be entered into competitions across the UK, all expenses paid, with a view to competing in the two thousand and sixteen Olympics."

"Never!" Goggle-eyed, she lost her reserve and hugged him, pulling away as soon as she restrained her abandon, but he held her closer and leant down to kiss her. Shocked, she kissed back, savouring the long-awaited moment. All too quickly it was over and both were uncomfortable. They got out of the car and Elliot locked it.

Somebody had to break the ice or the tension would interfere with training, and neither wanted that. "I meant what I said, by the way."

"You really think I'm that good?"

He laughed as they marched towards the sports centre, bags over shoulders. "Enough fishing for compliments already. Anyway, don't get too excited because nobody's signed on the dotted line yet, and I need to speak to your dad because you're still a minor. But if it goes ahead, you and Jonnie are first in line."

She desperately wanted to ask: *and the kiss?* But, inexperienced and young, she didn't want to speak out of line.

As they pushed their way through the double doors, neither had noticed the blue Range Rover parked at the far side, sheltered by the branches of the oak tree. Dick laid the binoculars on the passenger seat and prepared for a long wait.

Chapter 12
Wednesday Evening

Barker was working late to catch up on paperwork when Carl burst into the room, excitable and out of breath. "A body's been found in the River Ray, I was there when Julie took the call."

Barker closed the file he was working on and stood, shrugging his jacket on. "Let's go."

Dusk had fallen outside, the sky red for the second night running, and the coldness bit Barker as he rushed to his car, closely followed by Carl. They made their way through the streets to the remote area on the northern outskirts of town and drove as close to the scene as possible, walking the final fifty yards. Betty and Neil, blankets covering their shoulders to comfort them after the shock of their find, were with the two officers who had first responded to the call. "How did you get here so quickly?" Barker was genuinely surprised.

"We were just around the corner when the call went out so we came straight here."

Barker, scared of water, but more scared to admit it, took a few steps towards the riverbank, his head becoming woozy as he got closer, breaking into a light sweat. He loved living on the south coast but it had its downfalls and the River Ray was one of them. The body was face down, but air trapped in the jacket of the tracksuit kept it afloat. "How long until the rest of the crew get here?"

"Give me a chance, Guv, I only just put the request in." Carl had spoken to a colleague on the radio during the short drive and had been assured a forensic team would arrive soon to start the investigation. "Do you think it's one of the missing girls?"

"How on earth would I know?" Incredulous, Barker backed away from the river, his butterfly tummy easing with the safety of solid ground beneath his feet. "You can't see anything, the body's under water."

"Okay, if we have to be pedantic about it, I shall emphasise my question: do *you* think it's one of the missing girls?"

"I wasn't being pedantic. I was simply saying that you cannot tell the sex, colour, or anything of the body at this current moment in time."

"Well, isn't it your job to go and find out?" Carl dragged a hand through his spiky hair, regardless that it was immaculate already.

Barker regarded the choppy river from the corner of his eye and shuddered. "No, it needs to be photographed before anyone touches it." Quick thinking.

"I touched it with a stick. I was trying to find out what it was."

Barker turned to the man who had discovered the body. "And you are?"

"Neil Atkins." He held out his hand and the two men shook a greeting. "We saw the blue material from over there," he pointed to a walkway that ran through the field, "and came to see what it was. I wasn't sure so I got a stick and poked it, and…" He clasped his stomach, paling. "It doesn't look human." Betty put her arm around her husband, hugging him and feeling the same repulsion, the glimpse of the bloated, mottled, sunken-eyed face seared into her memory.

Gradually more vehicles arrived, the first a forensic photographer who, dressed in a white coverall and slip-on shoe covers, went straight to work. A couple of paramedics treated the elderly couple for shock, checking their blood pressure and heart rates to ensure the stress of the find hadn't been too great for them.

Finally, a car took them home, neither feeling able to drive after the horrific discovery, leaving only officers at the scene, now with a white tent erected by the waterside to shield the body once it was removed from the water and crime tape sealing off the surrounding area.

The pathologist arrived an hour later and described the body and its position to his dictaphone, before signalling it could be removed onto land. Barker stood but made no advance towards the riverside, instead calling, "What have you got so far?"

Fenwick chuckled as he approached the detective. "Still suffering from aquaphobia, are you? Isn't it about time you did something about that?"

"Aquaphobia, eh?" Carl loved finding new information to taunt his boss with. "A phobia of water. I hope that doesn't affect your washing habits, I mean, you do pong a bit sometimes."

"No I do not, and you can keep it quiet, I'm warning you. I don't want to be teased relentlessly for the next six months."

"As if I'd do such a thing."

Fenwick reached them and shook Barker's hand. "We have a young adult female of Afro-Caribbean descent, judging by her skin colour and facial structure. She's been in water roughly twenty-four hours, but until I've looked at her properly..."

"You can't give me anything officially, I know. Was there anything on the body, any ID?"

"Nothing on first examination, no."

"Injuries? Cause of death?"

"Nothing obvious, but I suspect - and I emphasise *suspect* - that she was dead before she was put in the river as there's no obvious foaming in her mouth and nostrils, but it could have been washed away, the river's quite fast with this wind. The PM will determine the cause of death accurately. What are you thinking?"

"Those missing girls, obviously, what else?"

"One was black - sorry, coloured - wasn't she?"

"Yes, that's what worries me. If that poor girl is Lydia Wilson, then the abductor has just upped his game. We'll be hunting a killer."

Fenwick patted Barker on the back, friendly and reassuring. "Don't jump the gun, old mate, at this stage the girl could be anyone. But let the Met know anyway. It has been centralised in London, hasn't it?"

"Yes, Operation Bandicoot, and you're right, I should let them know."

Keisha tried her father's number but the call went straight to voicemail and she hung up. "Problems?" Elliot was packing the sports equipment they had used that evening into the small storeroom.

"No, not really, I was just seeing if Dad had finished work but he's not answering."

"I could give you a lift home if you like, you know you can trust me."

She smiled gratefully, heart speeding, and began to help clear up. "Thanks."

"Look, about earlier, you know, the kiss." She gazed at him, holding her breath. He took her hand and stroked it gently. "I meant that too."

Outside, Dick had watched the young athletes leave the building and go home, but was certain he had not seen the black girl leave, nor the car that had collected her the day before. Nervous, he drove closer to the entrance to wait. Soon the doors opened and the trainer, followed by the girl, came out. Elliot locked the door behind him while she strolled towards his car. "Shit. Wait there a second, Keisha, I left my car keys on the hook. I'll be right back."

It was a gift; it was meant to happen. The sky was dark, giving him cover, the girl he wanted was on her own, and he had the engine running. Without a second thought, Dick squeezed the accelerator, screeching towards her. He jumped from the seat, throwing the door wide and ran to her with a ready-prepared chloroform soaked rag.

Initially rooted to the spot when the vehicle raced towards her, Keisha's common sense kicked in and she ran, this time in a race for her life. Never before had her speed been so vital. He grasped her, tackling her to the ground, and

131

she smelt an odd, pungent vapour before darkness clouded her.

Nancy gasped the fresh air as she left the house. The meeting with Graham Henderson had been horrendous. The old man, with weasel eyes and a half-mast trouser zip, was slimy, revolting, and she likened him to Jabba the Hutt. He had found lewd insinuation in every word she had uttered and his slavering was disturbing. To ice the cake, his house stank of wet dogs mixed with stale cigar smoke and she had struggled to breathe the whole time she was there.

She had planned to see four committee members that day, but after Graham she'd had enough, missing the one Jonas had been so interested in, Roberta Robinson. Instead of going straight home, she headed in the opposite direction, needing some fresh air and scenery.

After passing the last few houses on the edge of town, she parked in a layby, the hill giving her a wonderful view of the countryside, and pulled her mobile from her bag. She called her husband to ask him to do a little research for her, and then her boss. "I've seen three of the committee members, there are just four left to do."

"What did you make of Roberta?" Jonas was tired and it showed in his voice.

"Um, she's one of the four I didn't see, but before you tell me off, one of the others, Elliot Jacobs, is far more interesting. My money's on him. My husband has started checking out his past so hopefully I'll have something for you tomorrow."

Although he replied something about Roberta Robinson, Nancy's concentration was affected by a commotion in the distance, a couple of uniformed officers guarding a white tent and two police cars. She cut the call - she could explain later - and re-started the engine, heading towards the intriguing action.

She drove as close as possible and walked to the men guarding the tent. Realising telling the truth would get her nothing, she flashed her credit card pouch momentarily. "DI Bray, Southside. Can you brief me, shorthand version please?"

"Ma'am, the body was found earlier in the river and we suspect it may be one of the missing girls."

Nancy struggled to control a beaming grin. Her wish to have her first day at The Daily Review go with a bang had been granted. She gleaned as much information as the clueless officer could give her and waited until the body had been taken to the morgue, before heading home to write the article.

"I was just too late, he was speeding off as I came out. There was nothing I could do. I tried, God help me, I tried." Once again Elliot broke down, sobbing. His moment of forgetfulness had put his star runner and potential girlfriend in devastating danger. Why had he left his keys in the building? If Keisha died - talented, beautiful, unique - it would be his fault.

Barker had been alerted immediately and had left the body on the riverbank to attend the scene of the latest kidnap. Elliot Jacobs was under suspicion, but would have to be a fine actor to put on such a believable display of desolation. "Carl, get someone to let the guys on Operation Bandicoot know. Tell them we'll update them with everything we find. We also need forensics down here pronto; the abductor may have left something."

He followed Elliot into the leisure complex and they sat in the kitchen while waiting for the crew to arrive. "Elliot, you say it was a large vehicle, do you have any idea of the model?"

"Not really, I'm not one of those blokes who's into cars and football. Maybe a Range Rover, or a Land Rover, something like that. It was dark-blue and quite tatty."

"Carl, get cars out there looking for a dark-blue four-wheel drive. I want all patrols out there, and someone on the A21 checking everyone leaving town." He returned to Elliot. "Can you remember anything about the number plate, anything at all?"

Elliot squeezed his eyes shut, fishing for an answer, but nothing came. "God, please let her be okay."

Now Barker was commanding. "Pull yourself together, will you, you can take your time to fall apart after we've found her. Tell me, what exactly did you see?"

Elliot breathed slowly, calming himself. "I'd forgotten my car keys, so I left her outside while I went to get them. I was gone a minute at most, I swear. It all happened so quickly."

"So when you came out, what did you see?"

"At first I didn't notice anything. I don't usually give the kids a lift home so nothing seemed out of the ordinary. But then there was a slam and a squealing noise and I saw the car up there, and it suddenly shot off, hurtling round the car park before going up Tildsley Road, up there. I looked around, everywhere, realising I hadn't seen Keisha, but she wasn't there."

"So you didn't actually see Keisha in the car?"

"No, but I know she was in it." He removed his glasses and fat pools tumbled down his cheeks, guilty tears of irresponsibility.

Barker considered the melodrama suspiciously. "How?"

"Because she's not fucking here, is she?"

Dick drove into the yard, but instead of leaving his Range Rover beside the back entrance as usual, he hid it under the cover of a corrugated iron shelter away the road. Curled on the passenger seat, the girl moaned and he placed the chloroformed rag over her nose. He would have to work quickly.

Darting to the passenger side, he tugged her limp body from the seat, dropping her to the ground ungracefully, before using a grey blanket from the boot to cover the back of the car. Swiftly checking the yard, he took Keisha's hands and dragged her to the building, unlocked the door and brought her inside. He secured the door and stopped, safe, breathing deeply, adrenaline swamping him. "That was close," he whispered with relief.

After calming himself, Dick hauled Keisha through the corridors to the centre of the building, the private place that had been his second home for the past three months. The room had originally been a laboratory, which was perfect for his purposes, and he washed his hands in the cold water, orange with rust from the pipes. He unwrapped a syringe and punctured a small vial of ketamine. Tapping out the air, he plunged the needle directly into a vein inside Keisha's elbow, issuing the drug slowly.

Pouring a mug of tea from the flask he had prepared earlier, he relaxed.

When Harner heard the news that not only had a body been found, but another girl abducted, he instructed a team headed by Spencer to visit Raymouth immediately and not to expect any sleep that night. It was critical they found the girl as soon as possible, else they may be dragging her body from the River Ray too. Without waiting for the other officers to gather, a colleague drove Spencer at lightning speed, blue lights flashing and sirens blaring, and he spent the entire journey on the phone to staff at the Raymouth Police being updated with anything and everything so he could hit the ground running when he arrived.

Roadblocks had been set up on all major routes out of Raymouth and every officer available searched for a dark-blue four-wheel drive or a witness who had seen one. Amidst the confusion and panic, Spencer, wide-awake with the thrill of the unfolding events, ran into the familiar building. "I'm here to see DCI Barker." He flashed his badge at the desk sergeant, who phoned the incident room.

Moments later, a constable whisked him upstairs to the bustling activity. Barker beckoned him over. "Good to see you again, Gordon, shame about the circumstances."

They shook hands. "What have you got for me?"

"Fenwick's doing the post-mortem…"

"No, the dead girl can wait, she's going nowhere. My priority is with the girl who's been snatched."

Barker grimaced, compassion for the youngster enhanced by thoughts of his own children. "There have been no suspicious, dark-blue Range Rovers leaving the town. He's still here somewhere."

"And you've got everyone searching for him?"

"Of course I bloody have."

"Hey, mate, I have to ask. I'm not criticising, I'm on your side. What about the geezer who saw the car, has he given you anything?"

"He's in shock. I think he was quite attached to Keisha. He's been blubbing a lot. He said he went inside the building for no more than a minute to fetch his keys and when he came out the blue vehicle was speeding away. It headed north, but there's a five exit roundabout up the road from the sports hall so we've no idea what direction the abductor took from there."

"And how do you know he's not fabricating this as a cover for himself?"

"What?" Barker was stunned.

"He disables the girl - no one else was around, remember - and hides her, tied up or whatever, then fabricates the story of a kidnap before his eyes to cover his own arse. We can't forget that this is the guy who has full access to the marathon's register."

Barker shook his head. "No, he's too upset for that. I don't doubt for a second that what he's saying is the truth."

"Even so, I want him detained here for as long as possible, and if he wants to go at any stage I want to know about it, because I'd want him tailed with the possibility he might lead us to the girl. What's her name again?"

"Keisha Hamilton."

"What do you know about her?"

"Not a lot just yet, we're trying to get hold of her father. Elliot told us she's sixteen, from an American-Jamaican family, well, there's just her and her father. Mother left, or something."

"Could it be mother who snatched her?"

Barker's mouth hung open, staring at his friend and colleague. "Where do you even get these ideas from?"

"We have to cover every possibility, not make assumptions. Things aren't always what they seem and you may be too close in this case."

A howling from the stairwell rattled through the room, piercing and pained, and Barker looked at Spencer. "I think they've found her father."

Carl drew the short straw and was sent to babysit the hysterical Mr Hamilton to enable Barker and Spencer to coordinate their plans. They headed for the relative quiet of the room they had used the last time Spencer had been in Raymouth. "I can't hear myself think out there."

"Yes, the father seems a little too overwrought if you ask me."

Again, Barker was stunned. "You know, it really shows that you haven't had kids, you heartless bastard. I suppose you're going to suggest next that it was him who concocted an elaborate plan to kidnap his own daughter."

Spencer sighed. He had worked on worse cases and the outcome wasn't always what they had expected. He had learned to think laterally and trust no one. "So, back to the sports centre, were there any cameras focused on the entrance that may have recorded what happened?"

"Yes, one directly above the doorway and another in the car park. I have officers looking at the footage now."

"What about eyewitnesses? A leisure centre's bound to have plenty of people milling around, has anyone come forward?"

"It's not that kind of place, you want Raymouth Leisure Centre for that kind of thing. No, it's literally just a sports hall next to a football field on the edge of town. The only people who use it are a couple of running clubs, two local football teams and I believe a rugby club trains there too. Other than that, it's barely used."

Spencer withdrew his laptop from his bag. "Are you okay if I work in here, I won't be able to concentrate with all that wailing going on out there."

Barker wondered if he knew his old friend at all. He and Spencer had known each other from childhood, had been schoolmates in Mill Hill, then college, and both had attended the same police-training centre. Only then had their paths separated, with Spencer joining the Met and Barker heading for the south, living with his grandmother as a rookie and eventually marrying and having a family as he rose through the ranks on the force. He regarded Spencer; whatever the Met police had made him, he wasn't sure he liked it.

Dick changed into his boiler suit and hooked the air tank onto his back, taking the tank of fluothane and the short hosepipe through the warning door. He returned for Keisha, leaving her unconscious on the floor. He attached the pipe to the canister and pushed the end under the door.

"Dick, what are you… oh no, not again. Please don't, it leaves me with the most hideous headache and…" Sammy's words stopped and she slumped to the floor; he wasn't in the mood to talk. The evening had been so exhilaratingly scary, he needed to digest everything that had happened before he spoke to anybody. And he wanted the newest prisoner locked away safely, unable to contemplate losing her after the risks he had taken to collect her.

Once certain the occupants of the windowless room were asleep, he dragged Keisha into the room. Dick rested briefly to view his victims. They were perfect, an array of races, five sleeping beauties who, together, would shock the world. After the hiccup of Lydia's demise, he finally had his five multi-coloured angels. And now it had gone midnight, only ten days were left before they would finally be free in a display of their eternal glory.

Chapter 13
Thursday 26th September

Drenched from the short walk from his car, Harner trotted towards the incident room, annoyed. He signalled to French, dropping his newspaper on the desk. "Come here."

"Morning, Guv. What's up?"

"You know Raymouth pretty well, don't you?"

"I do, in fact I worked here briefly before I moved to Southside. Why?"

Harner was surprised, sure the latest developments would be on everybody's lips by now. "You haven't heard then?"

Harner detailed the events of the previous evening and French's stomach churned. "Shit. What do you want me to do?"

"Spencer went down there last night, he's working closely with DCI Barker, and I want you to join them. The reports that have come back so far suggest that the car involved - a dark-blue Range Rover, supposedly fairly old, although the CCTV wasn't clear enough to make out the number plate - hasn't passed the roadblocks they've set up on all major routes out of Raymouth. That means the killer - we can call him a killer now, because Lydia didn't drown, there was no water in her lungs - is still there. Spencer is leading the team and they have everybody out looking for the car and obviously the latest girl."

"Okay, shall I get someone to drive me or should I take the train?"

Harner stroked his chin. "Hmm, get a driver, I think, another officer down there will probably be helpful."

"Two questions: what was the abducted girl's name; and do we know how Lydia died?"

"Ultimately a heart attack, but there was nothing on her body, apart from signs of malnutrition, to show she'd been mistreated. We've sent tissue samples to toxicology so hopefully they'll get a move on and give us some answers. Oh, and the latest girl is a Keisha Hamilton, again a keen runner and registered to run the Raymouth Marathon. But the kidnap was different this time, it was less calculated and far more risky. I think our man's getting brave and that's when he's going to start making mistakes."

"I'll contact Spencer before I leave and get him to send me as much detail as possible so I'm fully prepared."

Harner dragged his copy of The Daily Review forward, scanning the detail he had read several times already. "How are they even getting this information?"

French squinted at the headlines and shrugged. "You know how these things work, Guv, some little reporter somewhere with too much time on his or her hands. I'm sure the press department will take care of it, minimise any damage. Anyway, I'll get a copy and read it on the train."

"Take this one, I've had enough shit for one day."

Keisha opened her eyes, unsure where she was or how she got there. Her head was sore, giddy and thudding and she groaned. She pushed herself up a little, frowning, and jumped when she saw she wasn't alone.

Swiftly, terrified, she crawled away from the four filthy and skinny girls, and her heart leaped when she realised two had been featured in the newspapers: Sammy Cooper and Rhiannon Hughes. "Oh my God, no."

Sying shuffled closer and laid a hand on the new girl's shoulder. "It's okay, we're not going to hurt you."

"What date was it when you were taken?" Rhiannon had no empathy for the girl; in self-protection against the difficult life she had endured she'd become selfish.

"You're the missing girls, does that mean…" It was too awful to contemplate and tears brimmed, wishing she were in her strong father's arms, sheltered from harm, from the dangers and cruelty of the world.

Once healthily vain, Sying hadn't a clue about her appearance nowadays, it was unimportant in their predicament, and it upset her when the new girl pulled away from her welcoming arms, fearful and wary. "I'm just trying to let you know you're not alone, we've all been where you are, we understand how it feels."

"You look so… What has he done to you all? Who is he, anyway? Do you know?"

"What was the date? Have I suddenly become invisible or something?" Impatient, Rhiannon, still strong enough to stand without staggering, began to pace back and forth.

"I don't know, it was a Wednesday, I think. Yes, Wednesday the twenty-fifth."

"Of September?"

Warily. "Yes."

"Just checking." Rhiannon threw herself on the floor away from the others, tutting and murmuring.

Sammy gasped. "I'd forgotten it was my birthday yesterday. And he gave me a cake. Jesus, the days seem like years. So, it must be the twenty-sixth now, because it seems that whatever drug he gives you when he kidnaps you keeps you asleep for a while, and he does his abducting in the evenings. That means I've been here for seven days. A whole week."

"I can't even be bothered to work out how long I've been here. I just wish we could get out." Slurring, Sying had difficulty staying awake, her weakness and malnutrition so severe.

Keisha pointed to the sulky redhead in the corner, who picked at her fingers, bored. "So that's Rhiannon? I read she was pretty streetwise. And I know you're Sammy Cooper, you've been in the papers pretty much every day since he got you."

"At least that means they're still looking for us." Sammy had wondered time and again during the long hours she had been awake, un-drugged, while the others slept their tortuous imprisonment away. "How did he get you?"

Keisha's hand went to her head, trying to remember what wasn't there. "I really don't know. I know my dad told me not to go out alone and I didn't, I got my trainer to pick me up."

"You're a runner too? Registered for the Raymouth Marathon by any chance?"

"Yes, I fit all the criteria," she realised aloud and recalled her father's concerns, worries she had thought were paranoid. If only they had been. "Elliot had given me some good news."

"Elliot?"

"My trainer. I think it was a sponsorship or something, my mind is pretty fuzzy. Then I was outside... That's right, I was outside the sports hall, Elliot had gone back in for something. I saw this big car coming at me. I didn't see the driver but I started running. That's all I remember, it's all blank until just now when I woke up."

"He gives us some kind of drug to keep us asleep, he puts it in the food. I don't know what it is. And sometimes he blows gas into the room to knock us all out, and that really gives you a headache afterwards. Like the one I've got now."

"Does he," she quietened, the question so personal, "does he, like, touch you, you know?"

"Not unless he does it when we're out cold, but I've never felt like I've been violated in any way. In fact, when we've spoken, he seems to actually care for me in a perverse kind of way." Sammy related her special relationship with their captor, their chats, that he had promised he wouldn't kill her, and Keisha shuddered.

"He plans to kill us?" She was more scared than she had ever been.

"I wish he'd bloody hurry it up, I'm fucking sick and tired of being locked in this disgusting hole." Rhiannon was the most realistic having spent a lifetime fending off trouble and hardship.

"You don't mean that." Neeraja was ignorant to how privileged her life had been compared to the girl who hadn't even been reported missing.

"Yes I do, I fucking well do. It was shit on the outside, it's shit in here, and when it stops being shit in here - that's if

142

they find us before he does whatever it is he intends to do to us in here - it'll just go back to being shit out there."

Sammy, her green eyes sunken and dull, the once bright and happy spark gone, leant towards Keisha, who recoiled, still unable to accept that she was now one of *them*. "Don't worry about her, she's kind of a glass half-empty type of girl. Look, I still feel that somehow I can swing things round with Dick if I keep talking to him, but I can't help you lot if you're sparko all the time. What's your name, new girl?"

"Keisha. Keisha Hamilton."

"Keisha, please don't eat the food, because if you do you'll sleep for hours, and if I get him to let me go, I can hardly bring you all with me if you're drugged zombies."

"Of course I won't have any, as if I'd put drugs in my body." Keisha shook her head, repulsed by the idea.

"Yeah, well that's what I said to Little Miss Perfect over there when I came in, but I'll tell you what, you'll be so fucking bored you'll want to eat your own foot for a little bit of excitement."

"Oh, shut up, Rhiannon, I might get bored but at least I'm trying to find a way out of this prison rather than give up like you lot have." Sammy couldn't understand why they weren't fighting back.

Silence fell over the room and Keisha was lost in her own world, trying to come to terms with the horror life had thrown at her. But then, "Hold on. Weren't there five girls taken? Wasn't there a black girl? I can't remember her name."

"That was Lydia." Quiet and sad. "She died. He didn't kill her, she just died. I reckon it was the drugs that killed her, she had too much."

Two fellow captives had friendly arms around her shoulders but Keisha felt more alone than she would have thought possible. Tears sprung to her eyes, glistening until they escaped and rolled down her cheeks onto the cold floor.

Jo couldn't believe her luck, and she couldn't understand why her boss was being nice to her for once. At twenty-three, she had only been able to afford tatty old cars and driving a BMW, one of the Metropolitan Police's pool cars, was unbelievable. So smooth, so much power.

French had barked a few statements about their reason for heading south at her and she had not taken much in, but the details became clearer hearing his endless phone calls on the journey.

The traffic had been fairly heavy, stop and start on two occasions, but the closer they got to the coast, the freer the roads had become and now they were only a couple of miles from Raymouth. Jo glanced at the dashboard and noticed the tank was low. "We need to get fuel. There's a petrol station up there, shall I pull in?"

French, engrossed in the details he had been given about the previous night's events, grunted in reply. She drove onto the forecourt and tried to get his attention again. "I've pulled up at a pump."

"Good." Jo remained in the driver's seat and eventually he registered her presence. "Well, go and fill her up then, what are you waiting for?"

"I can't." Embarrassed.

"Can't? You mean they don't even teach you how to fill a fucking car up nowadays? Not that they should have to, it's such a simple fucking process."

"Guv, I can't afford to, I don't have the money."

"You can claim it back on expenses, what's your problem?"

"No, Guv, I physically haven't got the money to pay."

"Oh, for fuck's sake." French shoved the door wide and stomped from the car, which was now blocked front and back by other vehicles. "And you've pulled up on the wrong side of the pump. Bloody women drivers." He pulled the hose as far as it would reach and with some manipulation managed to slip the nozzle into the tank. "Bloody women," he muttered under his breath.

Jo was used to being in the wrong with her boss, always rubbing him the wrong way, and she ignored his rudeness, devouring the scenery, the hills in the background, the beauty of the British landscape. The only blot was the grey, murky industrial estate, silent and eerie in its disuse, and Jo focused on the eyesore while waiting for French to finish refuelling.

Presently he climbed onto the back seat once more and Jo started the engine, gleeful at the gentle purr. She pulled out of the garage and back onto the main road. "That's a real bastardisation of the view over there, isn't it?"

"Huh?" Swamped in data and details again.

"That industrial estate over there, it really ruins the view." With no acknowledgement, she cleared her mind and enjoyed the final part of the drive in the executive car.

Dick had spent the night in his room, deep in the heart of the run-down factory, aware it would be dangerous to use the Range Rover now. The former industrial estate, a shadow of its one time bustling productiveness, was roughly two miles from the nearest house on the outskirts of Raymouth, which was a fair way to walk. But he would have to do it soon, unless another car magically appeared out of the blue.

Once he had calmed down from the risky business of snatching the new girl in front of Elliot's eyes the previous evening, he had returned to the car to work out what to do with it. The police would search the estate at some stage and he wanted no trace of it showing. Somehow he would have to move the car to the River Ray without being noticed and hope the spot he chose was deep enough to swallow it from view. And suspicion. Abducting the girl so recklessly had been exciting, an immense adrenaline rush, but the culmination of his plan wasn't for ten days and the police were firmly on his tail. Messing up now was not an option.

However, with the car currently concealed thoroughly from the road, the most pressing problem was food; the last batch of stew was finished and the girls would be hungry. He needed to buy the ingredients, prepare another pot at home and somehow get it back. If he stole a car they would be on the lookout for it soon enough. The only solution had to be

Bubby's Mercedes, but not only would she never agree to him borrowing it, she was always using it to attend some committee or other, so taking it would be tricky.

Snapping back to reality, Dick took a multipack of chocolate bars from a drawer and went through the warning door, striding towards the hidden room. "Is anyone awake?"

"We all are," Sammy offered.

"Yeah, bloody oversight on your part. Where's our drugs? I don't like being normal." Rhiannon's voice grated on him; he hated the sarcastic bitch.

"I haven't got any food to give you except this. Sorry." He pushed the bars of chocolate under the door and Sammy grasped the packet hungrily, tearing the wrapper and throwing a bar each to her cellmates. "My car's broken down so I'm going to have to walk. I won't be able to give you anything else until late this evening."

"For fuck's sake, talk about shooting from the hip. So we're going to be locked in here, wide awake, all bloody day?"

"I'm sorry, but things are really risky out here, they nearly caught me last... Talking of last night, how's the new girl?"

The girls exchanged glances; something was different. Waving at Keisha, Sammy put her finger to her lips. "She's okay. A bit shocked and scared, but I've told her you're kind and that you won't hurt us."

"You said that? I mean I know I am, but most people look for the worst in me. My sister tells me I'm useless at everything, just like Mum and Dad used to."

"Well, you know you're not, because you've got us all and that was planned, wasn't it?" Sammy hated buoying him up in a way that seemed destructive to herself but her instinct told her it was the right thing to do. She glared at the other girls, a warning not to interfere.

The smile sounded in his voice. "I've been planning this for sixteen years since Bubby..."

He was lost again and Sammy thought quickly. "That's your sister, right?"

"Yes."

"What happened to her?"

"They hurt her. Those jealous, thieving bastards hurt her. Cunts."

"Dick, it's okay, just tell me. Keep calm."

"Yeah, Dick, just tell us how it's somehow our fault that your sister had something happen to her sixteen years ago. I mean, we were all just innocent babies back then, so we're to blame, right?"

Sammy growled angrily at Rhiannon, who smirked. He erupted on the other side of the door, bellowing, "I'm going to make your fucking death so fucking painful, Rhiannon Hughes. You're a snidey fucking bitch, just like Roberta..." He stopped abruptly and a few moments passed. "Fuck you. I'm glad you'll be starving all day and I'm glad you'll be awake through it. You're just a bunch of fucking selfish lowlifes, the fucking lot of you."

He stomped from the cell and the warning door slammed, leaving them alone in the horror once more. Sammy glowered at Rhiannon, furious. "You just can't help yourself, can you?"

Barker put the phone down, beaten. "What's up?" Spencer had heard the difficult conversation.

"That was the Mayor's office, they're demanding we take the roadblocks down before tomorrow because of the expected weekend exodus to the coast. God forbid that a few little tourists might have their holiday plans disrupted because some darned girls got themselves abducted. Sheesh."

French had overheard and approached with his coffee. "In all fairness, I think if the roadblocks were going to stop him they would have done so by now. The bloke's not going to use that car again, not unless he's completely stupid, and if he's in a different car they won't be stopping him anyway."

"It's a good point," Spencer conceded. "How's the search for the car going?"

French and Jo had arrived at lunchtime and, knowing the area, had been put in charge of the search for the four-wheel drive. "I've been over the CCTV footage several times and it's definitely a Range Rover. We've tried to enhance the number plate but it's just not clear enough, not even to get an idea of the structure. That's the problem with the old security systems: if they'd had one of the newer ones there wouldn't be a problem.

"Anyway, Jo's been on to the DVLA and there are four dark-blue Range Rovers registered in the area. I've got a list of the names if anyone wants to take a look?"

"Do any of the owners have previous?"

"Two have been done for speeding but that's as dangerous as they get."

"I take it you've got someone checking them out, all the same?"

"Of course, the first three are clean, they've got alibis that have checked out, and Bill's on his way to the fourth as we speak; he had a bit of trouble finding him."

Dick guessed the police would run a check on Range Rovers in the area, so it came as no surprise when they pulled up outside. He opened the door with a friendly grin, welcoming the constable into his home, and the delicious aroma of stew tickled hungry Bill's taste buds. Stomach growling, he asked the man for his car's registration certificate. "Take a seat and I'll get it for you. It's upstairs in my study."

"No problem, sir." Bill remained standing, nosily inspecting the photos on the shelves, his books, the clean and tidy state of the house. He called up the stairs. "You live here alone?"

"Yes." Logbook in hand, Dick trotted down. "I've never been married, was never that lucky. I bought this place a couple of years ago after my parents died, used my inheritance money."

"Sorry to hear about your parents. What is it that you do, job-wise?"

He was under the spotlight and a lie was necessary. "Oh, engineering. Boring stuff."

The policeman nodded. "The documents look fine. Thanks for your time, and I'm sorry I had to bother you." Bill opened the front door and stepped onto the block-paved driveway. Turning back, he said, "Just out of interest, where is your car?"

Without hesitation. "I had to leave it in London last night. There was a bit of a do and I had a few too many so I took the train home."

Already suspicious from the man's overt friendliness, Bill's brow furrowed. "Could you tell me exactly where it is in London so we can check it out?"

"Oh, right. I can give you the general area but not exactly where." Dick was struggling now. "You see, I got a bit confused by a one-way system so I ended up parking in car park, then I walked, using my smartphone to direct me to the venue."

"Then tell me the venue's name, sir, and I'll have the surrounding area checked." Bill may have lost his hair and grown long teeth since he had joined the force, but he could still spot a lie.

Dick smiled, glancing at The Daily Review that lay open on the telephone table beside the door, displaying an article about the missing girls. A full-page advert for the O2 in London on the adjacent page triggered his imagination. "Well, I know it shows my age, but I was at a Fleetwood Mac concert in the O2 Arena."

Bill had also noticed the advert. "Do you have the ticket stub or anything to prove you were there?"

"I can go and check the pockets of the jeans I wore, if you like?" Sweat beaded on Dick's back, although he appeared assured and confident.

"I'd be very grateful."

Dick's heart sunk, having assumed the officer wouldn't bother. He headed for his bedroom upstairs and stood, scuffling his feet on the spot for a minute to sound busy. "No,

I don't think I have. I must have thrown it away." He came down, nervous to find the policeman inside again and snooping through a pile of paperwork on the dining table. "I'm sorry, officer, but are you looking for something?"

"Sorry, sir, force of habit." Bill returned to the door, ready to leave. "I can't help myself." He smiled and was gone.

Now another arduous task had been added to the hundred-and-one things he already had to do that day and Dick immediately turned the hob off. Somehow he would have to get the Range Rover, unseen, to London, ready for when the police followed up their enquiry.

Chapter 14
Thursday Noon

"Bubby?" She always read to the children at the nursery a few doors down - walking instead of taking her car - on Thursday afternoons, so Dick was sure she would be out. He closed the door of his sister's house quietly and took a picture from the sideboard, a framed memory of him with his Bubby, radiant at a local charity event, tucking it into the bag he had brought. She wouldn't notice it missing.

In the kitchen, he found a pen in a drawer and rifled through the recycling bin to find a used envelope to write on: *'Hey sis, hope you don't mind but I've borrowed your car. Mine was stolen last night and I've got an important meeting to get to. I'll have it back soon. xxx'*

Having not had the chance to finish the stew, he raided the cupboards; the girls would be starving and he couldn't risk another death. He gathered a few carrier bags of food together, tins mainly, from the larder and grabbed a can-opener from the drawer. He had already decided to move the plan forward, because he couldn't fend the police off for ten days now they were suspicious. Would tonight be possible? He had a lot to arrange, but maybe.

Finally, he took the keys to Bubby's Mercedes A160, chosen for its high seats because they made it easier for his sister to climb in and out, and had a last, lingering sweep across the room; it would probably be a long time before he saw it again. If ever.

The first stop of the lengthy journey ahead was the industrial estate to swap cars. He drove the Mercedes as far forward as possible under the corrugated iron roof and took the grey blanket from the Range Rover, throwing it over the rear of Bubby's white car to conceal it. Reversing his own car from its hiding place, he took the back exit from the industrial estate onto a track through a field to avoid the roadblock on the A21, and drove along narrow lanes until he was far enough from the town to brave the open road.

An hour later he reached the M25 and the traffic became heavier. Without time to waste, he took the first exit he came to and headed northwest through Orpington and Chislehurst, Blackheath and into Greenwich. The sat-nav told him he was just over three miles from the O2, which seemed a believable distance, so he left the car at Kidbrooke Railway Station and went inside to catch a southbound train.

Soon he was on the Underground travelling to London Bridge, and from there took a train directly to Raymouth. After a lot of messing about, his alibi was at least provable to some extent, and that should buy him time.

Dick rested back on the seat, overwhelmed with relief that he was finally on his way back to his girls, and he drained a can of Coke he had bought at the station. It had been a long day, yet there was still so much to do.

Nancy had just parked outside a small terraced house, the garden neat and well cared for, when her mobile rang. Answering, she heard her husband's voice. "I think you'd better take a look at the news. There have been some big developments on the missing girls."

"Like?" Sure she was ahead of the police, Nancy wasn't too concerned.

"Another girl was abducted last night, this time from Raymouth. She's a black lass named Keisha Hamilton, and as you've probably already guessed, she was due to run the Raymouth Marathon."

"What the fuck? And I've been messing about interviewing people who are less interesting than a blasted shoelace."

"There's more. They've confirmed that the body found in the river was Lydia Wilson."

"I thought it would be. Leave it with me, Phil, I'm about to go into someone's house so I'll see if they'll let me watch the news."

Nancy gave Albert the same cock and bull story she had fed the other committee members, having spent the morning with the fourth and fifth, and he happily let her through. She went through the preliminary rubbish faster than before, and couldn't wait any longer. "I know it's cheeky, but my colleague has just told me there's been some developments in the missing girls' investigation. My brother's daughter is friendly with one of them so I'm following it keenly, is there any chance we could watch the news channel for a minute?"

With help from the more technical reporter, Albert found the channel and turned the volume up. "I'm interested too, it's such an…"

"Shush!"

Hearing the newsreader telling her things she should have already known had she been a half-decent journalist, Nancy berated herself for wasting time with the daft old committee members, do-gooders with self-righteous airs and graces. Without saying goodbye, she rushed through the door, considering how to play catch-up with the case. Jonas had hired her because she was good, and now she had to prove it. Her first stop was Raymouth Police Station. As none of the staff knew her, she would blag her way through somehow and get another meaty story to send to her boss that evening.

Bill had tried to tell Barker his suspicions about the registered owner of the fourth Range Rover, but they had fallen on deaf ears, which came as no surprise. He had been a policeman for thirty-five years but hadn't risen through the ranks by choice. Policing the streets the old-school way was what he had wanted as a bright, enthusiastic child, and what he still enjoyed now. This latest investigation, though, was the highlight of his career so far. The hustling and bustling, uniforms and plain-clothed dashing this way and that, collecting information, sifting it, digesting it through the eyes of a possible killer.

When Barker, true to his name, had barked at him to go away, he had accepted his lowly place on the force and followed his intuition. A simple internet check showed that Fleetwood Mac had been playing, but unless the car was found, Bill believed the alibi to be false. He redialled the number in London. "Has anyone located the Range Rover yet?"

"No, we've had patrols looking for it but nobody's radioed anything through."

That was enough for Bill. He strode to Barker - deep in discussion with Spencer - and waited patiently, not wanting to interrupt. Eventually his presence registered and Barker stared at him, annoyed. "What, Bill?"

"I don't want to be out of place, or tread on your toes, or any…"

"Get to the point, Old Bill." Barker demanded, and Spencer sniggered like a girl at the nickname.

He had heard it all before. "Sorry, sir, it's just the owner of the fourth Range Rover, you know I went to see him earlier, well his alibi doesn't really check out."

Bill had been in the force forever, the same job, day to day, never wanting to better himself or challenge things. He had no ambition and Barker, like everyone else at Raymouth Police Station, merely saw him as a piece of furniture that had always been there. "What's the problem with it?"

"Thing is, the event he said he was at last night happened, although there's no proof he was there, and they haven't found the Range Rover."

Barker humoured him. "And who's been looking for it?"

"I spoke to a woman called Barbara, I think she's one of the secretaries. She arranged for the search."

Spencer moved closer. "Barbara on the Bandicoot team?" Bill nodded. "She's one of the seven from Southside brought in to help with the investigation. She's okay, is Barbara."

"Well, tell her to keep looking." Barker was about to return to his conversation but stalled. "Hasn't the guy told you where he parked it?"

"He said he couldn't remember, said he'd got lost in the one-way system and just parked somewhere and walked."

"That's always possible in London, bloody one-way systems are a nightmare if you're not used to them." Spencer could just about remember the days when he could travel through the City with a logical mind and always end up where he had planned to be.

"Okay, Bill, just keep trying, I'm sure it will turn up somewhere." Barker had finished with the old man.

"Just one thing, how did he intend to collect his car if he can't remember where he parked it?" Spencer hadn't.

"Good point, Gordon. Bill, go back and see the guy, just so we can rule him out. We don't want to be wasting valuable time following up some silly old man who's lost his memory."

"He's not old, sir, he's mid-thirties by the looks of him."

"Okay." Barker was dismissive, but Spencer's suspicions were raised.

Bill headed back to his desk, dejected and useless, and called Barbara again to ask if the vehicle had been found. It hadn't. Nobody was listening, but he informed his colleagues all the same: "I'll go and see the owner of the Range Rover again, then."

The computer beeped and Barker opened the email. It was from Fenwick and held the results of the toxicology tests. He scrolled through to the conclusion and called Spencer and French over. "The likely cause of Lydia's heart attack was the high level of ketamine in her blood. I'm not sure how close that comes to murder, but it's a good start."

"It's manslaughter at least if she didn't administer the drug herself, although I know plenty of idiots who use it as a recreational drug. Dickheads." Living in London had hardened Spencer to junkies; they were everywhere. "What's that at the bottom of the email?"

French hadn't read through properly and he focused on the screen. "Hmm. Bizarrely, it's about the clothes she was wearing, the blue tracksuit. He says it's not a good fit and looks brand new." He leant across to Jo. "Find the statements from Lydia's mother and trainer, see if they mention what she was wearing when they last saw her."

155

Having familiarised herself with the computer system in London, Jo was now learning the antiqued one, in comparison, used by the Raymouth team, and it didn't help that two detective inspectors and one chief watched over her shoulder; she was nervous. With relief she eventually found Cantrice's heartfelt statement. "Her mother said she was wearing a taupe, LA Gear tracksuit, says it was Lydia's favourite."

Spencer mulled his thoughts out loud. "So whoever drugged her also changed her clothes. But she was missing for over three months so it doesn't really come as a surprise. In all honesty, if she'd been wearing the same kit for that long it would probably have welded itself to her body. It's not such a big deal really."

Jo had searched for the trainer's statement during Spencer's musing. "Yep, the trainer says the same thing. A beige trackie that she often wore, and it was definitely LA Gear." She stood and regarded the pictures of Lydia on the whiteboard, in life and death, and bullet points about her case. "I don't know much about these things, but the thing is, everyone in the world knows I'm poor, so I've never been able to afford to buy the posh labels, I get my clothes at either charity shops or the supermarket if they're on offer."

"Very good, very good." Spencer shook his head, rolling his eyes. "Very resourceful."

Jo was indignant, his rudeness unnecessary and patronising. "My point, if you'll do me the honour of listening for a second, is that I think I know where that tracksuit, the blue one, is sold. I was looking at something similar the other day, but in orange."

Annoyed, Spencer pursed his lips. "Good, I'm sure you'll look very nice in it, but please can we continue investigating Lydia's death now, rather than her dress sense."

Barker had been proven right about the man he had, until now, always admired: Gordon Spencer was a pompous, despicable, impatient and arrogant prig. He missed, however, the irony in his treatment of aging Old Bill. "Where are you going with this, Jo? It is Jo, isn't it?"

"Yes, sir. I was just saying, if he bought it from Bestco in Raymouth they'll probably have CCTV footage."

Spencer winced under Barker's glare and shamefacedly asked Jo - nicely - to contact the store immediately.

Bill had returned to Watford Street to speak to the owner of the Range Rover, but wasn't surprised to find nobody in. If the owner had been telling the truth and left his car in London, he was probably picking it up, so Bill wasn't too concerned. He stopped at a petrol station to buy a bar of chocolate and headed back to the station. Again to nobody, he mentioned the visit had been a waste of time and sat at his desk, invisible.

His phone rang. "Hello, Bill speaking."

"Hi, it's Barbara. Just to let you know that the Range Rover's been found. It wasn't very close to the Arena, three miles away in fact, but it's there."

"Three miles. Oh, well thanks for letting me know, I guess he's off the hook."

Bill put the phone down, angry with himself. For a wonderful, brief time he had thought he was on to something, but no, of course not. That was why he was a mere constable and those surrounding him were detectives. He was just a silly old man - Old Bill - and all he was good for was helping the public with mundane problems and telling people their loved ones had died - a job always left to him due to his kind and empathetic manner. He continued working like a good little boy and resolved never to listen to his hunches again.

Half the chocolate bar later, Jo tagged him on the arm. "Bill, can you come with me? There's a lead to follow, we need to go to Bestco."

Jo explained about the tracksuit on the short journey to the retail park at the edge of town, that the superstore had invited her to take a look at their CCTV footage. "They've run a list of the tracksuits sold and who to - if they used a

BestcoCard, that is; they get a lot of detail about their customers from the purchases they make. They're also locating the security tapes at the times of purchase for the last three days, which is as far back as they keep them at that store."

The next half hour passed with pleasantries and introductions, and finally Bill and Jo watched the tapes. The two women of the four people to have purchased the same style and colour tracksuit in the past three days were quickly ruled out; both were elderly ladies who had probably bought the outfit as a gift for their daughters or granddaughters.

The third video interested Bill. "That's Elliot Jacobs, he's well known in the town."

"I know that name, I've heard it before." Jo watched the toned man, handsome in his spectacles in an awkward way, and tried to place the tiny amount of face visible under the baseball cap.

"He's on the marathon committee and he's well known in the sports world, one of the best trainers round here, they say. I've no idea why he'd be buying women's clothing though, rumour has it he's never had a girlfriend in his life."

"Gay?"

"Who knows. From what I remember, he's in charge of the register for the marathon, so he's under suspicion already, especially as he was present when Keisha was last seen."

"Interesting." Jo smiled at the store manager. "Can we take the tapes with us, I think my boss will want to see them."

French, Spencer and Barker watched the video with interest and French, impressed with her keen eye, thanked Jo. He had seen her potential from the start and adopted a 'treat them mean' policy to keep her on her toes; if she didn't break under pressure, there was a future for her as a detective.

"Bring him in?" Spencer had already tried and tested the man.

"No, I know Elliot and find it difficult to believe he's involved with something like this." Barker had met him a couple of times after minor incidents at the leisure centre.

Spencer rolled his eyes. "He works with young girls and controls the marathon register, he *says* that Keisha was snatched from under his eyes, and now he's on videotape shown buying the very same tracksuit that our dead girl was found in. Come on, Jez, be realistic. This guy has guilty coming out of his ears."

Reluctant. "I'll bring him in, but only if you leave the interview to me. Elliot's a gentle soul, really he is, and I know how to get the best results from him. Jo, go and pick him up."

She glanced at the old man beside her. He had seemed downtrodden during their trip and she was keen to include him. "I'll take Bill with me, just in case the suspect gets violent or something."

Barker laughed. "What, so he can defend you with a walking stick?"

Ignoring her superior, she and Bill returned to the car, the engine still warm from the previous journey. They were about to climb in when Nancy screeched into the car park and ran over breathlessly. "Jo Ellis, my best forever friend, what are you doing here?"

"None of your business." Jo cocked her head to the side, annoyed with the intrusion.

"Oh, please don't bear grudges, it's so unladylike. I've just seen the news, what can you tell me about the latest abduction?"

Bill loved helping members of the public. "Quite horrible…"

"Don't talk to her, Bill, she's press. Sod off, Nancy, I'm not saying anything." She slammed the door and Bill shrugged an apology before climbing in. Leaving Nancy standing, he drove through town to Raymouth Leisure Centre, where Elliot usually worked during the day.

They found him inside leading a group of disabled children, smiling and clapping, happy and fun. "Can we have a word, please?"

Annoyed, he glanced at the clock on the wall. "These kids spend all week looking forward to my session, at least give them their last ten minutes for heaven's sake."

The officers sat in the reception area and Jo was fidgety. "He's the prime suspect in a murder enquiry, well, manslaughter or whatever. Shouldn't we be dragging him straight out of there?"

"You watch too many crime programs, young lady. Firstly, he brought a tracksuit, big deal. And secondly, he's got a fantastic reputation around here, he's a local hero. If we ruin that then, before I know it, I'll be dusting myself down when they boot me physically out of the force. They've been trying to for years. Anyway, he's not the guy, simple as, he's one of life's good guys."

"The goodies are often the ones with the dirtiest, darkest secrets, Bill, you know that."

"I don't know him personally, but I know his parents and they're the nicest people you could ever imagine."

"Being nice doesn't mean you can't have a psychopath as a child. You never know what goes on behind closed doors."

"A psychopath doesn't give his free time away to teach disabled children how to skip."

"A psychopath who's sexually motivated often loves to work with children. John Wayne Gacy is a good example of that."

"Tom Wayne who? Anyway, from what I've read of Keisha Hamilton, she was his star pupil. It says in his statement he was putting her and a young lad forward for a scholarship and he'd be paid to train them. Why would he kidnap somebody who could be of such financial advantage to him?"

Jo chuckled. "Okay, I can't think of a quick retort, you win that set."

They had enjoyed the debate, an interesting interlude to the day, but Elliot came through and they accepted it was over. "Right, I finished a few minutes early just for you. Well, not just for you, because I'm as worried about Keisha as anybody and I'm obviously full of guilt."

"Are you?"

Jo was a terrier with a bone and Elliot was stunned. "Of course I am. What is this? Am I a suspect?"

Bill glanced around to ensure nobody could hear. "We wondered if you could come down to the station. It shouldn't take long."

"I *am* a suspect. I swear on my life, my mother's life, whatever you want, I had nothing to do with her abduction, apart from seeing the tail end of it."

Jo knew she should leave the interrogation to her superiors back at the station but she was on a roll. "Maybe, but can you explain how come you were in Bestco on the day that another girl's body was dumped, buying the tracksuit that her body was dressed in when she was found."

"What?" Confused, Elliot obediently followed the officers to the patrol car, stopping once to ask the father of one of the disabled children - a man he had known a long time and trusted - to lock the hall and put a note on the door with his apologies, stating any further lessons of the day were cancelled.

Chapter 15
Thursday Afternoon

Although pleased for the peace and quiet, the chug of the train relaxing, Dick was eager to get back to the girls. They'd only had a paltry chocolate bar each since the evening before and he felt guilty they'd had no drugs. It was painfully clear to him how much the girls - apart from his Sammy - relied on them to while away the dark days. He passed the time by watching the scenery through the window, and as the train pulled into Raymouth station, he was first to the door.

He took the bus to the northernmost point of town and jumped off. It would take half an hour or so to walk to the industrial estate. Every now and then he scanned the surrounding fields him to ensure nobody was following and soon reached the scarcely used road that led to the old factory where Fubarre and Sons Ltd had once thrived.

His first job was to remove the back seats from the Mercedes he had borrowed from his sister without permission. It was nowhere near as big as his Range Rover and getting the five girls into the back would be a struggle, especially as they would be dead weights from the drugs he was about to feed them.

It was problematic at first. Not being his own car, he didn't know where the release buttons were, but he managed to contain his frustration. Next, he took the carrier bags of food he had stolen from Bubby's larder and fridge and unlocked the building to let himself in, securing the door behind him. Once he had reached his room, he opened six cans of stewed steak, poured them into a dish and mixed in a couple of vials of ketamine.

Opening the warning door, his welcome was unprecedented. "Where the fuck have you been, you filthy bastard. We're starving in here and I've never been so bored in my whole fucking life, and that's saying something."

"Shut up, Rhiannon." Sammy clambered to the door to ensure her captor could hear her. "Dick, we've been worried. We thought you weren't coming back."

"I'm sorry, I had to go to London. It's a long story." Dick was pleased to hear Sammy was awake. Something about her - her tone, her gentle voice - made his stomach flutter when she spoke to him. He slipped the large bowl of drug-laced meat under the door and the girls dived on it, birds catching their prey, noisily scoffing the stew. "You're not eating, are you, Sammy?"

"You know I never do."

"What about the black girl?"

She paused. "That's what confused me earlier, but I've worked it out. You've admitted that you trailed us for weeks before you grabbed us, and we know you must have got our details from the register for the Raymouth Marathon, so how come you don't know the new girl's name?"

"You're calling me useless, aren't you?" Angry and belittled.

"No, I'm just wondering why, really. Please don't be annoyed, I wasn't calling you useless at all. We've already been through that."

He was quiet and Neeraja, Sying and Rhiannon weren't interested, hungrily scooping handfuls of cold gravy containing very little meat into their mouths. Keisha watched, listened, unsure whether to follow the crowd or stand out bravely like Sammy. "Please, Dick, don't tell me if you don't want to, just tell me about your day or something else."

"Lydia wasn't meant to die, I never planned for that. When she did I had to replace her with another black girl and I can't see the register any more, not without rousing suspicion. The thing is, they're on to me, the police. I knew Elliot was training a team for the marathon so I took a chance and grabbed the only black girl. She had to be black."

"Why? We're all different races, why is that?"

"It's got to be fair, I'd hate to be accused of racism. What is her name, anyway?"

"I'm Keisha, Keisha Hamilton." She had decided to be brave.

"Hello, Keisha, are you eating?"

"No, I've chosen not to."

"I'm glad, it will give Sammy some company. She's being very tough; it must be hard. It won't be long now; I've got to bring everything forward. They know about my car and it won't be long before somebody makes the connection and they come to get me. I can't go home now. This is it, I'm here now until the end."

The girls now found the conversation more interesting than the tasteless food, despite being groggy and lightheaded from the ketamine seeping into their bloodstreams, and the five girls focused on the door. With a tremble in her voice, Sammy said, "What's going to happen now?"

"You won't feel a thing, I promise. I'll knock you out with the fluothane, the gas, then I'll give you a good dose of ketamine before I put you in the car. You won't feel a thing."

"I thought you said you couldn't drive your car?" Rhiannon, for the first time, was terrified, but her mind was still intact.

"I've borrowed my sister's car. It's a Mercedes, so you'll be travelling in style for your final journey."

"No final journey, Dick, please."

"Don't worry, Sammy, I was directing that at the mouthy bitch in there. Just like fucking Roberta, she is, selfish and pathetic. You're safe, Sammy, and I'm not sure I want to - even can - kill the others, but it's going to be pure pleasure when I slice that fucking slag's throat."

Rhiannon's jaw thrust forward, defiant. If her time had come, it had come. Tough shit on her, but there wasn't much this side of death anyway.

A minute passed in silence and they could only assume Dick was still there on the other side of the door to their prison. Gradually Neeraja, Rhiannon and Sying succumbed to the effects of the drug, slumping where they sat, away from the fear and squalor their conscious minds registered.

164

"Sammy?"

She had been crying, her throat raspy and nose full. "Yes." *Sniff.*

"No tears, sweetheart, I promise you won't die."

"Are you scared? I know I am." *Sniff.* Oddly, she wished she could hug him; he sounded so childlike and vulnerable.

"I am, actually. I'm not scared of being caught, not really, because if they come after me I've got the perfect place to go, up in Manchester where they'll never find me. I just don't want to be - can't be - caught before I can display what I've been working on for so long."

"You never have told me what happened to your sister."

He exhaled loudly, choosing his words carefully. "Bubby, my dearest, sweetest, little sister. She was a promising athlete when we were growing up - I'm four years older than her. Everything we did, our entire family - not just my parents and me, but aunts, uncles, grandparents - everybody's existence revolved around her future career. It's all I can remember, Bubby entering competitions, winning trophies here, medals there, newspaper articles and photos. Everything was about Bubby's talent."

"That must have been hard, didn't you get jealous?"

"Of course not, it was all about Bubby. I've always been useless no matter what I do. But she had a true talent from such an early age, who would I be to stand in the way of that?"

"So what happened? Was she in an accident?"

"When she started high school my parents explained to the staff that she was gifted at sports and begged them to do everything they could to encourage and assist her, like when she had to take time off for competitions, that kind of thing. It wasn't a big ask, not for somebody with such potential. Well, from day one her sports teacher, Roberta, made things difficult. It was clear she hated her - jealousy, that's what it was - and she put Bubby down so badly, insulting her, belittling and humiliating her, that finally Bubby's spirit cracked. Her fight had gone."

"What happened?"

"We tried as a family to perk her up, whatever we could. We complimented her abilities, over-enthused when she won something, really bigged her up, and eventually Mum got fed up and took control of the situation herself, sick and tired of complaining to deaf ears. She took a second job to pay for Bubby to go to a sports academy, a place where they would see her potential and boost her confidence.

"She was due to start after the summer holidays when she'd turned fourteen. Anyway, it came out in conversation - it wasn't a secret, after all - and Roberta was furious, saying she wanted to be the one who brought stardom to the town, said it would benefit the school."

Keisha found some courage at last. "Are you talking about Roberta Robinson?"

"Who's that?"

"It's Keisha, the new girl. It's just if you are, then she did much the same thing to my sister, brought her down, stole her confidence. That's why my mum took Adanna with her when she went back to America, so she would have the chances she needed without a jealous teacher putting her down."

"Keisha, you've just bought yourself your life. I feel sorry for you and your family, I didn't realise Bubby wasn't the only one."

She was almost scared to speak aloud for fear of jinxing things. "You're not going to kill me?"

"No."

Inside the cell, the two girls smiled at each other. Sammy patted Keisha's hand and continued, "So what happened then? Your sister had a place at a sports academy, then what?"

"It was the final week of school before the summer holidays and everyone was in high spirits. The weather was gorgeous and everybody was looking forward to six weeks by the beach, bumming around. I know I was, I'd just left college and was about to enrol in the army, so I was going to make the most of the time off.

"On the dreadful day, and for no reason that ever came to light, Roberta insisted her class, including Bubby, went on a

166

cross-country trek. It wasn't part of the curriculum and she'd never done it before. Raymouth High - it's a Comprehensive now - isn't far from the coast, so they took the road along the beach and climbed the footpath to the cliffs. She let the rest of the class run ahead, but called Bubby back. She can't remember what for, Bubby has little short term memory as a result of Roberta's viciousness.

"Well, the next thing anyone knew, and Roberta swore it was an accident, was that Bubby had fallen over the edge. They all ran over and saw she had landed on a ledge, which was lucky, I suppose, because at least she lived.

"Air rescue came and hoisted her into a helicopter, and they rushed her to Raymouth General, where it was touch and go to save her. She survived and her brain, thankfully, was almost as good as new, apart from memory problems, but her back was broken and she's never been able to run again."

"I've heard about that, you're talking about Lily Jenkins, aren't you? I know her through running and I've heard the story about her accident. It's terrible."

"It wasn't an accident. Roberta Robinson pushed her, I'm one hundred percent certain about that and now it's time to show her just how fucking much she destroyed our family that day. I've got to leave you for now, there's so much to do yet."

"Please stay, I'm enjoying our chat." Sammy really was, it was informative.

"Don't worry, either of you, you're both going to live and I'm pleased about that."

Elliot attended the police station voluntarily. He was under suspicion and for good reason, but the time they were wasting on ruling him out should be spent looking for Keisha. Nancy approached as they entered the reception area and Elliot hung his head in shame.

"Go away, Nancy." Jo wondered if the reporter was stalking her as she led the suspect inside.

But Nancy had what she wanted already. Elliot's arrest triggered an idea for her next article, to name and shame him, and she started typing on her laptop immediately. Jonas would be happy.

Settling in the interview room, Elliot felt like crying, the thought of the girl he adored in the hands of a madman, a man who had just killed another black girl. He would help in any way he could, anything to bring Keisha home, safe and unharmed. However, his lifelong friendship with Lily would be over if he told the coppers his suspicions. He had to see her first.

The interview was gruelling and he tired of the implied accusation that he was a murderer. He wasn't capable, didn't have whatever it was that made humans kill each other in him. Elliot didn't possess a cruel streak; he was a nurturer. Just one that liked younger girls. He explained his secret, that he and Keisha had been about to start a relationship - at least that's how he had read their shared kiss - and that he had bought the tracksuit the previous Monday as a present for her birthday.

Spencer checked the records; Keisha would be turning seventeen the next day. "So if she's over sixteen, the legal age of consent, why the cloak and dagger business about the relationship?"

Barker was fuming; they had agreed he would be in charge of the interview, but his domineering friend was running the show. He could now see it was a habit of a lifetime. Why had he not noticed before?

"I've always liked younger girls, call it a curse, if you like. Keisha isn't the first of my students I've had extra-curricular activities with, if you get what I mean. I was caught once, back when I was nineteen. I'd been given a work placement within my studies at university and got involved with a young girl - she was thirteen - and when my boss found out she went ballistic. I was told in no uncertain terms not to come back. That was in Birmingham, I went to university there.

"Anyway, that had blown up in my face so badly, I told myself I'd never let anyone know my penchant for younger girls again."

"But Keisha's not so young. Have your preferences changed?"

"You must have seen a picture of her, she's cute, like a little cherub. She certainly doesn't look her age."

Spencer had noticed. "Did her family know?"

Elliot laughed. "Her dad's the strictest guy I've ever known. His wife left with Keisha's older sister fourteen years ago, they went back to America and Ian never got over it. He treats Keisha with kid gloves, barely lets her out of his sight. If he knew she was behaving like a normal teenager does, you know, actually wanting sex, I think he'd have a heart attack on the spot and die. Keisha's his everything. But she needs time away from him and his controlling ways, and I intend to help her with that."

"Was it serious with Keisha?"

Elliot was quiet for once, eyes focused on nothing as he reflected. "We only kissed for the first time yesterday, give me a chance."

"So you just want to fuck her and chuck her?" Barker cringed at Spencer's crude terminology.

"It's not like that, we've been friendly for years and it was obvious she had a crush on me. Maybe I did - do - love her. I'd never hurt her, that's for sure."

"But you don't disagree that it's a huge coincidence that you bought a tracksuit that ended up on a dead girl, whose body was dumped in the river."

"It can't be the same one, the one I bought is still in the boot of my car. I was going to take it home and wrap it, but I was so busy I kept forgetting. Then Keisha was abducted and I was down here giving statements, and then it was work as normal this morning."

"And that's something else that confuses me: if a loved one of mine was abducted from under my eyes, the last thing

I'd be doing would be working as usual. What's that all about?"

"If I don't keep my mind off it all, that I may never see Keisha alive again… I'd go stark raving mad." Elliot's heart physically hurt. Why had he realised he loved Keisha too late? Was it too late? Was she going to be found in the river too, with none of her joyous vitality left. A discarded body?

"Where's your car?"

"It's outside the leisure centre, where you picked me up."

"So if I get someone to take you back there, you're going to be able to open the boot and show us the tracksuit you bought, complete with the bag it was put into at the supermarket?"

"Yes."

Spencer turned to Barker, higher in rank but being treated like a lackey. "Get someone to take him back." He whispered, not wanting Elliot to hear his shame. "And I think we'd better take a look at the video of the last person to buy that tracksuit."

"You know it's possible the killer didn't buy the outfit at the Raymouth branch of Bestco?"

"Of course I do." Spencer considered life would be so much easier if Elliot had been the man they were looking for.

"Before we look at the video, can we just rerun the one of Elliot?"

"Why?" Barker didn't see the point; the man was clearly innocent.

"He's coming across as completely believable, but the other things fit into place with him, all the evidence is against him. Maybe he bought two tracksuits."

"He has nothing to do with the Range Rover and the CCTV footage shows it racing away with him on the kerb."

"No, it doesn't. It shows the car driving away, but the entrance to the hall is out of view. There's nothing to say Elliot wasn't the driver."

"But he called the abduction in straight away."

Bill was setting up the video machine, there but invisible. He tried to attract attention to let the two officers know it was ready, but to them he didn't exist, a cool breeze they enjoyed the benefits of without noticing. Spencer continued, "He could have drugged her, staged the kidnap, then hidden her. Who knows? We've got to keep our eyes and ears open, as far as we know the five girls are still alive."

Fed up with the victimisation of the man he knew and believed, and of his old friend's arrogance, Barker growled, "Let's just watch the tape. Bill, is it ready?" And before Bill could nod a reply, "Good."

The tape played and Spencer leant forward, scrutinising it keenly. "He takes one off the rack, puts it back, takes another. Checks the size. Stop the tape."

"What have you seen?"

"Bill, get Jo to look at the post-mortem report to see what size tracksuit Lydia was wearing. And get whoever's looking at the tracksuit that's supposed to be in Elliot's car to first ask him the size, then check he's telling the truth."

"You're determined to pin this on Elliot, aren't you?"

"No, I believe him, I just want to make absolutely sure he's innocent. Right, play the tape again."

The screen remained the same and Barker glanced around, confused. "Where's Old Bill gone?"

Shaking his head, Spencer leaned towards the machine and pressed play. "So he puts the second tracksuit in the basket and goes out of view. Keep watching, I want to see if he comes back."

"Enough." Barker stopped the machine and changed the card, grasping the remote control. "Elliot Jacobs is not the man, okay. Let's see the fourth video." They watched for a moment. "It's a man, can we get a closer look at his face… oh, I forgot, Bill's not here."

Barker checked the date on the card holder. "He bought it on Monday; that would fit with her body being dumped Monday night. Gordon, he's the one. Can we get a look at the

CCTV of the car park, see what car the guy goes to? I'll bet you anything it's a dark-blue Range Rover."

He hastened to the door and Spencer followed. "I'll get Jo straight onto it seeing as she was there before. I'm sure she said they only kept the tapes for three days so we might be too late."

"Then I want all their tapes brought in as evidence. I do not want them saving over these. Carl," he waited for the effeminate officer to acknowledge him across the room, "can you get someone to enhance that picture in there, the one that's on the screen? I want to get the best possible close-up of the guy who's buying the tracksuit."

Ian Hamilton had been climbing the walls, unable to do anything to bring his beloved daughter back. He had arrived back from work the night before at ten-thirty. The meeting had been arduous, discussing job losses and redundancies, a restructure of the business, a possible takeover. Things that were no longer relevant in his deep despair.

He had barely taken his jacket off before the police hammered on the door, wanting to know everything about the last time he had seen his daughter. He had cried wretchedly throughout the interview at the station, his heart in physical agony as it broke in two. His job had been to ensure Keisha was safe from harm and he had screwed up.

In short bursts between overwhelming, guilty sobs, he had explained that he'd insisted his daughter had a lift to and from training, and she had told him of Elliot's offer. He'd been pleased, Elliot Jacobs was such a nice man and he trusted him.

They had told him to wait at home, would inform him if anything new came to light, but now the evening was descending and his baby was out there, lost and scared. He couldn't stay home any longer. Shaking with grief, he drove to the station.

"Guv, I've got Keisha Hamilton's father here in reception, he wants to know what's going on."

Ian paced, waiting for a response, and the desk sergeant assured him DI French would be down in a minute. He sat, unashamed of the tears that wouldn't stop. Soon he realised someone had joined him and was trying to get his attention. "Are you okay?"

Nancy recognised the man from the news report earlier and laid a hand softly on his, willing him to talk, to give her details the newspaper could print now the article she had prepared about Elliot was redundant after his release, albeit with two officers by his side. "It's Mr Hamilton, isn't it, Keisha's dad?" She hoped she had remembered the name correctly.

"Yes, my daughter. She's the one."

"What happened?" Five minutes later he had poured out his misplaced contrition and she had the well-rounded skeleton of a front page article; Elliot Jacobs could wait. She gave Ian her mobile number and he promised to call when he knew more, grateful for her sympathy.

"That was Jo, she's seen the footage of the car park and is bringing it in. It's our man, he got into a dark-blue Range Rover after buying the tracksuit. Who was it that visited the guy with the dodgy alibi?"

Bill raised his hand, vying for attention. "It was me, Guv."

Barker was surprised but covered it quickly. "Didn't I hear they found the vehicle in London?"

"Yes, it was left in Kidbrooke Railway Station car park. That's about three miles..."

"Didn't you say he parked up because he was lost in a one-way system?" Spencer was familiar with most parts of London due to living and working there and knew Kidbrooke station like the back of his hand.

"Yes, he said the Fleetwood Mac concert was due to start and he didn't want to be late."

"But the station's not on a one-way system, I'm sure. And if you're late for a gig and you've parked at a train station, wouldn't you just take the tube rather than walk?"

"I thought that when they told me where they'd found it." *Careful, Bill,* he told himself, *remember your hunches are worthless.* "It also had a parking ticket on it, I thought that was odd too."

Spencer jumped into Barker's shoes again, taking control. "Get on the blower to the Met, I want the car taken straight to forensics. If he's had the girls in it there'll be evidence. Bill, what's the name of our man?"

He had memorised it, having suspected him from the moment he had laid eyes on him. "Charles Fubarre."

"I want everything," Spencer shouted, "everything there is on this Charles Fubarre. Get to work, we've got our guy. What's the address?"

"Twenty-one Watford Street."

"Come on, Jez, let's get him."

They raced to the door and Bill called after them, "I've already tried but he's not there." But his words blended into the background noise as officers ran this way and that, phone calls made, computer files accessed. The manhunt, the search for the missing girls, was finally progressing.

The plain-clothed detectives ran through the reception area and Ian Hamilton tried to grab their attention, but their hurry was too great. Holding his hands out in confusion he strode to the front desk. "I thought someone was coming to see me? I've been waiting over half an hour."

The desk sergeant hadn't heard on the grapevine what the urgent exodus was about and pacified Ian, dialling the incident room to catch up on events. "Sir, Detective Inspector French *will* be here in a minute, apparently there have been some developments."

Nancy was instantly by Ian's side, her dictaphone discreetly waiting. Ian began to sob again, frightened, hopeful, pleased - an array of emotions, none of which made sense. "Have they found her?"

"I don't know, sir."

"Have they found out who the kidnapper is?"

He glared, one eyebrow raised. "I don't know, Nancy."

"Is there a body?" She was excitable, oblivious to her tactlessness.

The desk sergeant stood straight and crossed his arms to hammer his point home. "When somebody tells me what's going on, I will tell you, but in the meantime," under his breath, "*shut the fuck up.*"

"Mr Hamilton?" French hurried through the door and Ian nodded. "Can you come with me, please?"

"I'm his friend, I'll come with him." Nancy took Ian's arm.

"Nancy Blaine. My, you get around, don't you? We haven't anything to give you bloody reporters, but when we do we'll be sure to let you know. Through the press desk."

Nancy woefully recognised French from her trips to Southside police station when Sammy Cooper had first gone missing and she kicked herself. What the hell was he doing there? She had no choice but to sit again, waiting - hoping - for a lucky break.

They hurried to an interview room. "Mr Hamilton, can I call you Ian?"

"Call me what you like, just give me good news." Inside he was praying.

"Have you ever seen a dark-blue Range Rover hanging around your house, or the college, the sports hall - anywhere?"

"No, not that I can think of. Why?"

"Do you know a man named Charles Fubarre?"

"Is that the name of the bastard who's got my little girl?" Ian hadn't sat as directed, too fuelled with emotion to be still.

"Ian, you've got to calm down, you'll not help anyone like that."

"No." His temper was fraying with urgency. "I've never heard that name before. Have you got him? Do you know where Keisha is? Is she okay?"

With Ian's current hyperactivity, French realised they wouldn't get anything of worth from him, and he sat, sorry for the distraught man. "All we have is a name, Ian, that's all. We're doing our utter best to find him and your daughter." And remembering the vulture in the waiting room, "Can you stay in this room for now? That woman downstairs is from the press and it's imperative we keep details away from the media at the moment. If the suspect knows we're on to him the results could be disastrous."

A light bulb sprung in Ian's head. "They can help, the newspapers. If they release his name somebody will come forward and lead you to my daughter. To all of the girls."

French saw no point beating around the bush; the truth was harsh, but the man was a loose cannon. "Or he may just kill his captives, knowing he's about to get brought in. Ian, I strictly forbid you to talk to the press." Standing, stretching straight to click his tired spine into place. "I'll send someone in with drinks, what would you like?"

"Coffee. Strong coffee. I need to stay awake." As French left the room, Ian sent a text to Nancy. He didn't care what they said, he wanted his beloved daughter found.

Chapter 16
Thursday Evening

The afternoon had been hectic, so much to prepare and in so little time. He had placed a box of vials in the car, along with a couple of syringes - he had nearly run out, having been away from work for over a week, so the girls would have to share - and had packed a length of rope, a knife and some cans of energy drink to keep him going. The only thing left to do before he carried out his plan was to give the girls some food and he emptied two tins of corned beef into a bowl, mashing them up, mixing in a can of chopped tomatoes and two of the vials of ketamine he had kept back.

His mobile buzzed and he threw the empty tomato tin across the room, furious at the intrusion. "What?"

"Charley, are you okay?"

"Sorry, Bubby, I didn't mean to snap."

"For God's sake, I wish you'd stop calling me that, I grew out of that nickname when I was a toddler. Why the stroppy mood anyway?"

"Sorry, Lily, it's just I'm just in the middle of something and it's getting to me. It's a logistical nightmare."

Sarcastic. "Oh, well sorry for disturbing you, but I was wondering when you were bringing my car back? You know, the one you took without asking. I'm supposed to be at a meeting tomorrow morning and I can't find a lift."

He thought quickly. "It won't be tonight, I'm in London. On business," he added as an afterthought.

She sighed, uptight. "Charles, you work as a cleaner in a veterinary surgery, you don't do business in London. What's going on? Are you in some kind of trouble?"

"No, not at all." He tried to sound bright but the strain was apparent.

"Charley, what is going on? If you won't tell me, then I want my car back right away. In fact, I'll report it stolen to the police if you…"

"No." Lily had never tolerated shouting and he swore under his breath. "No, don't do that. Please, Lily, I'll have your car back tomorrow morning…"

"Don't you bloody swear at me, Charles Fubarre. How dare you, you worthless piece of tripe. You were always a bad penny, always in trouble. You used to drive Mum and Dad crazy, they wished they'd never had you."

He kept calm during her tirade, having heard the taunts time and again over the years, that he was useless, pathetic. Tonight he would show his sister he was a capable and valuable member of society, she would see she had got it wrong all these years. "I will have the car back tomorrow. Don't call the police."

He hoped he had sounded threatening but, "I'm calling them…"

"If you call them I'll kill you, Bubby, I swear I will."

"Sticks and stones, you idiot." She cut the call and he threw the mobile to join the dented tomato can.

Seething, he took the dish through the warning door, hoping Sammy wasn't awake; he didn't feel like talking. "Dick, what's going on? I heard some crashes."

"I've been packing. We're moving on tonight."

"Where are we going?" Sammy stared at Rhiannon, silencing her.

"I won't hurt you." He posted the dinner underneath the door and Neeraja and Sying reached across, but Sammy slapped their hands, mouthing, *'No!'*

"I know you won't, Dick, you promised me and I believe you. So does Keisha. Where are you taking us?"

"Sammy, please stop asking questions." His head was bursting with hastily arranged plans and he had to concentrate. Plus, the threat of the police. If his sister called them, it would ruin everything. He needed quiet, time to think properly. "Please don't make me angry with you, you've got to let me get this right."

"You're scaring me though."

"Sammy, I'm warning you: enough now. Eat that food, all of you, because it's the last you'll get for a while."

He stomped off and once the warning door closed, Sammy addressed her fellow captives. "Whatever you do, don't touch the food tonight. If he's moving us, he could be planning to kill us."

"But he said he wouldn't, not me and you, anyway."

Rhiannon grunted, bored with life. "So naïve, aren't you? Trust my luck to be locked away with a bunch of sad muppets, he could at least have given me a group of girls with a bit of spunk in them."

"Oh, shut up complaining, Rhiannon, that's all you ever do."

"Yeah, maybe so, Sammy Squeaky-Clean, but if you'd had to put up with the shit I've had to…"

"Yeah, we get it, alright. You had a bad childhood, you were in a children's home, mummy and daddy didn't love you, nobody loves you. We get it, and I'm sure we're all sorry for you, but for God's sake, stop bitching about it. Right now the only thing that's even remotely important is that we've been kidnapped. We don't know what Dick's capable of and he's intending to do something tonight. If you're blotto on drugs, then that's up to you, because I'm past caring about you, but the others are nice girls and if I can somehow help us all to make it out of here, then that's what I'll do." She breathed deeply, her rant over. "Now, let's try again. Keisha, are you with me?"

"Yes."

"Neeraja?"

"Yes."

"Sying?"

"Yes."

"You can do what you want, Rhiannon, because I officially no longer care."

The constables who had escorted Elliot back to the sports hall had been satisfied with the tracksuit in the boot of his car, and despite Spencer's ongoing concern that he was too smooth, there was nothing they could pin on him. But as he drove from the sports hall - there had been no point opening it for the final hour - he felt the need to talk to somebody about the Range Rover, someone who could handle the truth that only he knew. He pulled up outside Roberta's house. She had only recently moved into the faceless estate and it was the first time he had seen her new home.

She welcomed him in, bustling about, serving tea and biscuits before covering her dinner with cling film and placing it in the microwave to eat later. Her tasks were finally done and she sat with Elliot in the lounge. "I'm sorry about that, a woman's work and all that. What did you want to see me about?

"Oh, I don't know, everything's getting too much. This missing girls thing, they've had me down at the police station for ages."

"Why?"

"All the evidence is adding up against me. I haven't got anything to do with it, by the way. I know people are suspecting me."

"You need to clear your name. Did you ever let anyone see the register? I won't have a go at you if you did, it's just, if you're covering for someone?"

Elliot was annoyed; even his old friend and former teacher had suspicions. "Of course I'm not. Nobody saw that register. I emailed it to the police, and you all saw it when you wanted. However this idiot got hold of the details, it wasn't through me." He noticed Roberta was unsettled at his outburst and calmed himself. "Roberta, I haven't done anything, I swear. But I do have something to tell you that may come as a shock."

Roberta took her tea from the table and sipped. "Go on." Weary, she wasn't sure how much more she could take at her age. This was such a mess.

"The last girl to be abducted, Keisha Hamilton - you've met her once - we were on the point of starting a relationship."

"Is that all? You had me worried there."

"Really? I thought you'd blow your top."

"Is that why you were putting her forward for the scholarship? You get her where she wants and she scratches your back with a bit of you-know-what."

"No." Maybe it had been once, but he had gone and fallen for her. "She's a bloody good runner, she's amazing. You saw her on the track, didn't you?"

"The black one who looked about twelve? Mind you, all youngsters look like they're twelve to me nowadays."

"Yes, she looks young for her age. Have you seen the reports on the telly? She was snatched pretty much right before my eyes."

"Nobody could have missed it, it's all over the news. So why are you telling me this?"

Elliot hung his head, aware that what he was about to reveal could cause insurmountable problems for the committee and, in turn, the future of the Raymouth Marathon. "I recognised the Range Rover."

"And you're telling me like it's a bad thing? Surely you're the police's favourite... That's not all, is it? Who?"

"I might be wrong, but I think it was the one that Lily's brother drives."

She gasped, her head reeling. "So the police are looking for him then?"

"I didn't tell them."

She almost spat her tea out, shocked. "Why on earth not?"

"Can't you see the position I'm in here? If I go spouting accusations, naming names, you know how weak Lily is. I didn't want to do anything that may upset her without knowing for sure."

"Your girlfriend is abducted in front of you by a man who's already killed someone, a man who has kidnapped five other girls, and you're worried about treading on people's toes? Elliot, you have to tell them, in fact," she leant over the arm of the sofa and grasped the phone from its holder, "if you don't, I will."

"No." Elliot laid his hand on hers, pushing the phone onto the table. "Would you come with me to speak to Lily?"

"I don't know. It's late, I really need my sleep nowadays, I'm getting older…"

"Please, Roberta, if she has a fit and I'm the cause… I just think the news should come from people she knows, rather than some gruff old copper who doesn't know her health history. Anyway, there's every possibility it wasn't his car, just one that looks like it, and she'll say something like 'oh, yeah, my brother was with me last night'. Please."

Tight lipped, she bustled about the room, straightening cushions, neatening paperwork on the table. Eventually, "Okay, but then I think you should take this to the police, they need to know. Charles Fubarre, eh, who'd have thought, nasty little waste of space."

"Don't hang him without a trial." Forceful. "As I said, it's possible it was a completely different car and driver."

Nancy received the text from Ian Hamilton and called her husband, telling him the suspect's name. He in turn called Raoul, who let Jonas know. They wouldn't print speculation, but Nancy was an excellent investigative journalist and they trusted her to find enough truth behind the man who had been named to prepare a ground-breaking article for the next day.

She ordered a black coffee in a nearby fast-food restaurant and set her laptop on a table to access their WiFi; going home would waste valuable time. She typed 'Charles Fubar Raymouth' into the search engine and scanned the list of results, but there was nothing of note, so she tried again, this time without the town. Still nothing.

It would be a free for all for the newspapers if the police arrested him and Nancy was impatient. She dialled her husband. "Have you managed to get a background check yet?"

"As we speak. Are you sure that his surname is spelt F-U-B-A-R?"

"That's what Ian sent through in the message, but I suppose he could have got it wrong. I strongly suspect he shouldn't have given me the information."

"The reason I ask is that I've found a Charles Fubarre, that's A-double-R-E, on the Raymouth electoral roll."

"Go for it." She typed the new spelling onto her laptop.

"I thought you'd say that so I already have."

"You're a wizard, Phil."

"He lives alone at twenty-one, Watford Street, works at Arndale Veterinary Surgery as a cleaner, single, no kids that I can find, no criminal history at all, no debts except a small mortgage, and no CCJs. Parents are dead, but he has a sister, Lily, and a niece. Pretty insipid for a possible murderer, eh?"

Nancy typed the information onto her computer so nothing would be forgotten and looked at the data curiously. "No, he doesn't sound anything other than ordinary. Maybe I was wrong, maybe Ian texted it for some other reason. I bloody hope not, that'll blow my story out the window."

"Why don't you go and see Ian Hamilton again?"

Nancy glanced at the time: five past nine. The restaurant was on a steep hill and the views were tremendous; she gazed through the window, deliberating. The sky was dark now, the sun long gone, and the wind had picked up, blustery, teasing the sea. "It's late, but I think I'll try out Watford Street, see if I can talk to this Charles Fubarre."

"No, Nancy, I forbid it. He might be a murderer and I don't want you taking that risk."

"But…"

"No buts on this one, promise me that you won't go and see him. Anything else, but not that. Please, you're all I've got, babe, I can't let anything happen to you."

"Phil?" He had never spoken like that before, regardless of the risky situations she was often in, whether through work or the adverse allergic reactions. Phil was strong and independent; she didn't like the sudden neediness. "Is there something you haven't told me about his past?"

"No, I've told you everything, I just think you should leave that bit to the police. Talk to his sister, his neighbours, whoever, but stay away from him."

Perplexed, Nancy agreed, assuring her husband that although she would be home late, depending on what she found out, she would be in time to send something to Jonas for tomorrow's edition of The Daily Review.

She ended the call and closed the laptop, draining the strong coffee. She would drive to Watford Street despite her promise to Phil; what he didn't know couldn't hurt him.

Dick pulled the PVC boiler suit over his clothes, trapping the sticky and uncomfortable warmth, and took a kidney dish containing two vials of ketamine and a single syringe from the side. He had already left the breathing apparatus, hose and tank of fluothane beside the door to the girls' room.

He suspected they were all awake as the noises were different to usual, but only Sammy spoke. He blanked her questions, ordering her to eat the food. "Dick, please talk to me."

She wasn't sweet and lovable any more, but plaintive and annoying. He ignored her, attaching one end of the hose to the gas tank, setting the other end by the door. "Dick, please tell me what you're going to do with us. I'm so scared."

Fitting the breathing apparatus over his head, he turned the switch and inhaled through the mouthpiece. "Dick, please."

He couldn't bear the irritation any longer and dragged the mask to one side. "Shut the fuck up, will you." Pushing the hose under the door, Dick turned the tank of fluothane on and in seconds heard the regular breathing of unconscious bodies. He unlocked and unbolted the door for the final time and brought the kidney dish through, filling the syringe with the colourless liquid. He gave each girl a high dose to ensure they remained comatose while he prepared them.

Neeraja was first and he located a vein in her inner elbow, pushing the needle through her skin, withdrawing slightly to ensure he had pierced the blood vessel, and injected the drug. Next was Rhiannon, then Keisha and Sying. He looked at Sammy, so beautiful. Why had he lost his temper with her? He felt so guilty now. Kissing her gently on the forehead - a father, not a lover - he filled the syringe once more and injected her, discarding the empty container.

Already built-up in their systems, the drug should keep them either unconscious or in a dreamlike state for several hours. There was a possibility they could wake, but he would add to their dose as and when rather than risk killing them early. However, this meant he had to work swiftly.

One by one he dragged the limp bodies to his room. He gratefully removed the clammy overalls, before taking five differently coloured dresses from a carrier bag. He used the hose that had washed Lydia to clean the girls, removing as much of the sick and sewage as possible, taking care not to wet their hair too much.

First he dressed Neeraja, a cool blue to contrast with her coffee skin. Sying's yellow dress enhanced her ochre skin-tone and shone beautifully against her long, black hair. He dressed Keisha in a red that made her chocolate skin glow, and was filled with pride to clothe whippet-like Sammy in the black dress, which set off her emerald eyes and complimented her blonde hair.

He passionately detested the last girl, who reminded him so much of Roberta Robinson in both looks and personality. He manipulated the green dress onto her lithe body, marvelling at how remarkable the auburn-haired youngster looked. A face so lovely with the mind and persona of a sewer rat. He hated her, wanted to disfigure her, and he took the carving knife he had sharpened earlier from the side. Mustering courage, he passed it over Rhiannon's face, trails of red trickling from the superficial wounds and soaking into the material.

Adrenaline forced the tiredness of the hectic day aside, after bounding the girls' wrists and ankles, he took them to his sister's car, administering another dose of ketamine once they were securely tied inside.

Finally, his job in the former premises of his great-great-grandfather's once industrious factory was done.

The dark windows and curtains wide open suggested nobody was home, but Nancy tried the doorbell several times all the same. It was no surprise he was out; if he had the girls, he would be busy wherever he was holding them. Unless they were in the house.

Having peered through the windows and seen nothing remarkable, she headed for her car. Across the street, a man wheeled his recycling bin to the kerbside and Nancy trotted over. "Excuse me, I'm trying to find the man who lives across the road, Charles Fubarre."

The man left the bin by the gate. "Sorry, love, can't help you."

"Do you know anything about him?"

"Who are you?"

"I'm his sister, Lily, you see, we're a bit estranged and I was hoping…"

"No you're not. Lily's blonde and you're a brunette, for a start."

"You know her?"

"Everybody knows her. She's a gem, she is, spends all her time on some committee or other, always helping people. Who are you?"

"Do you know where she lives?"

He sighed, bored. "Depends who you are."

"Okay, you've got me. I'm a reporter, I work for The Daily Review and I need to speak to Charles about a story I'm preparing for tomorrow."

"Oh?" Wondering why the national press wanted to speak to his neighbour, his curiosity overcame his hostility. "Why don't you come in for a drink?" And before she could answer, "It's okay, my wife's indoors. I'm not some deranged criminal."

Nancy hadn't considered the possibility but his remark disconcerted her. She tentatively stepped inside, relaxing when she heard a woman's voice. "Stan, did you put all the bins out?"

"We've got a visitor, Margaret. Come on in, love, make yourself comfortable." He showed her to the living room and indicated a seat next to his overweight wife. "She's a reporter from the Daily Mirror."

"Review. The Daily Review."

"Sorry, love. She wants to know all about Charles across the road."

Margaret tutted her distaste. "Funny one, he is, barely talks to anybody. You know, I can't get out much, not with my back and ankles, but the few times I've seen him in person, not through the window, I always watch through the window, have to because I can't get out..."

"So the few times you've seen him?"

"Yes, keeps himself to himself, he does. Says hello, but that's all you'll get from him. Is he in trouble?"

"No, no, nothing like that. I'm, er, I'm doing an article about what it's like to be related to Lily, er..."

"His sister, Lily Jenkins, that's who she's on about, love."

"Oh, that Lily's such a lovely girl, such a shame about her back. I can really sympathise, what with my back and all."

Nancy burned the name into her memory. "Yes, she doesn't know yet, so please don't say anything to anybody, but she's been nominated for an award for all her good work with," she waited, hoping they would fill in the gaps.

"On every committee going, she is. Disabled and handicapped children, sports societies, church groups, sewing clubs; you name it, she does it. An angel, is Lily, an angel."

Margaret laid her plump wrists on her vast lap, proud for knowing everything there was to know.

"Do you know where she lives?"

Stan sucked his breath and crossed his arms. "Hold on a mo, if you're doing an article about this award or whatever, and it's a secret, then why would you want to speak to her?"

Nancy chuckled affably as she lied. "I don't, I just wondered if Charles would be there. We want to run the story tomorrow and it's getting late, so if I don't find him soon he won't be included, and that might seriously damage Lily's chances of winning the award."

"Well, we don't want that, do we. She's in Beaumont Road. Go to the bottom of the street and take a left. Will we get a mention, me and Margaret?"

"Obviously, yes, I've written your names here, Stan and Margaret." She briefly flashed a blank scrap of paper in the hope they were both myopic. "I'll make sure your helpfulness is noted. What number Beaumont Road?"

Chapter 17
Late Thursday Evening

Elliot and Roberta had been parked by the kerb outside Lily's house for what seemed like hours, but her car wasn't there and it was past ten in the evening. Roberta yawned constantly, usually asleep by this hour, and Elliot was nervous and tetchy. She yawned again. "Can't this wait for tomorrow? It's so late."

"I'm sure she's got a meeting and they usually end by ten. Give it another quarter of an hour."

Roberta closed her eyes; she was too old for this kind of thing. Presently a figure came up the road, silhouetted by the streetlight, with an awkward gait. "Here she is, and she's walking; that's unlike her. I wonder where her Merc is." He greeted her, asking the question.

"My brother borrowed it. What are you doing here, anyway? And Roberta too. Is she okay?"

"I think she's asleep. Can we come in and talk to you for a while, it's important."

"I suppose so."

Labouring against her twisted hip, Lily hobbled up the path and unlocked the front door, while Elliot woke Roberta, helping her from the car. They sat in Lily's lounge, waiting for her to settle after her busy day. "Where's Karen?"

"She goes to youth club on Thursday nights, she'll be home soon."

"You let her out on her own with that abductor guy out there, are you crazy?"

Elliot had never understood why Roberta was always so hard on Lily and he patted his friend's arm reassuringly. Lily smiled weakly at him. "She's fine, Roberta, her dad takes her there and back, you know he helps out when he can."

"Oh, that old sod who left you high and dry, up the duff and without a future."

"It was a mutual decision; I've told you that so many times. I knew he wasn't my Mr Right when I fell pregnant and we agreed to share her care. Why don't you listen?"

"You never say anything interesting enough to make me."

Elliot winced, wishing the two women could get on - that everybody everywhere could get on - and changed the subject to avoid the brewing argument. "We're actually here to see you about your brother."

"Oh, for heaven's sake, what's that useless lump gone and done now?"

"Does he still drive that ancient Range Rover?"

"That old heap, yes. I've told him a million times he'd save so much money if he got rid of that pile of junk, but will he listen?"

Elliot braced himself. "Then I think it was him who abducted Keisha."

A hammering on the door broke the stupefied silence and, dazed, Lily twisted from her orthopaedic chair. She opened the door to a woman she recognised, but unsure from where. Tired and upset, she immediately put her defences up. "Have you seen the time?"

"I'm sorry, I know it's late, but I'm doing an article for…"

"Now I remember where I've seen you. No reporters, I'm not interested. Please go away."

"It's about your brother."

"No," she raised her voice, not wanting to hear anything about Charles ever again, "go away." She tried to slam the door, but Nancy had put her foot in the way. "Please, you can't do this. Not now. Just go away."

Elliot came to his friend's defence, his arm across her shoulders reassuringly. "Go and sit down, Lily, I'll deal with this." She followed orders gratefully and Elliot hushed his voice. "Nancy Blaine, what are you doing here?"

"I have - from a very good source, I assure you - been told that Lily's brother, Charles Fubarre, has something to do with the missing girls."

"Shit. Who said that?"

"I can't say, but I do need to talk to Lily."

With a sigh, he stood aside for Nancy to enter and briefly checked outside to see if anybody had witnessed the revelation before closing the door. "Please let me do the talking, though. Lily's so fragile, and she has epilepsy, so I don't want her upset too much. What am I saying, of course she's going to be upset, but you know what I mean?"

"She has no idea?"

"I don't think so. Come on."

Lily had settled back on her chair, leaning on the side with her head rested on her hand. Although tired, Roberta forced herself to stay awake, eyes wide, eager to hear the latest developments; she had always known that Lily's hopeless rogue of a brother would end up in trouble. Elliot sat on the edge of the sofa and leant towards his friend, taking her free hand gently. "Lily, I'm sorry about this, but I think Charles really is in trouble."

Lily would normally crack a joke when she heard her brother's name in the same sentence as trouble, but not today. A dark cloud hung over the room and she waited patiently while Elliot gathered the strength to continue. "You probably know I was with Keisha when she was snatched yesterday."

"I heard someone say something like that."

"The car that she was dragged into, it was a dark-blue Range Rover."

Lily waved her hand, dismissive. "Everybody and their dog has a dark-blue Range Rover."

"Not with an official Raymouth Marathon sticker on the back window," Roberta added.

Lily's face crumpled. "Oh, God no. I gave him that. He was so pleased."

"You really had no clue? No clue at all?" Elliot stroked her hand, desperately willing her strength.

"I know that he doesn't fit in well, you know, into society. I know he's a loner. But why would he want Keisha?"

"We think - and the police do too, that's my source for his name - that it's not just Keisha. We think he's the man who's taken all the girls." Nancy had broken her promise not to speak.

Lily shook her head slowly from side to side, shaking the unwanted words away. "No, he's an oddball, but he wouldn't hurt anyone."

"We had to tell you before the police turn up. I haven't told them that I thought it was his car, I didn't want to say a word without letting you know first. I wanted to be with you, make sure you're okay."

Tears rolled down Lily's cheeks, dripping onto her frilly white blouse. "Well I'm not okay, not in the slightest."

"What do we do? What do you want to do, Lily?"

"How much do the police know?"

Nancy held her mobile up needlessly. "All I was given was his name, nothing else."

"And what's your interest in the case, anyway? Who are you really?"

There was no point in lying, not this time. "I was going to prepare a story for The Daily Review for tomorrow morning, naming him."

Lily turned and twisted in her seat and eventually managed to swivel up, standing with her hand on the small of her back, discomfort etched on her face. She shuffled from the room, leaving Roberta, Elliot and Nancy perplexed.

Nancy shrugged in question, but Elliot shook his head. "I need to get the story for my boss, it'll be so good," she stopped herself from saying 'for my career', aware of how selfish it would sound, and filled the gap, "to have those girls safe again."

"We play this however Lily wants to play it, the decisions rest with her. She's so fragile, I don't want to risk anything happening to her because of this stupid situation."

"Do you know him? Charles Fubarre."

"Not really. I've seen his car, and Lily talks about him a lot, but I wouldn't know him to look at."

They silenced as Lily returned, carrying a tray with four glasses of pale yellow liquid, which she laid on the table. "I've brought us a glass of chardonnay each. It's a nice one, bit of an aftertaste, but…"

Nancy raised a hand. "Not for me, I don't like to drink while I'm preparing an article."

"Well," Roberta took a glass, sipping, "I won't say no."

Lily twisted onto her seat, eyeing the reporter sternly. "You're not working on an article. We're talking about my brother here and he's not a story. If what he's being accused of is true, then he needs help. He needs me. You're not writing anything, you're going to have a glass of wine and we can sit back, relaxed, and think about where to go from here."

Annoyed, Nancy snatched a drink from the tray and knocked it back. "I am still working. The public needs to know what's going on. It's my job, and from the sound of things, your brother is a dangerous man."

Lily laughed and Elliot gazed at her, bemused. "Go on then, do your thing."

Nancy uncrossed her legs and tried to get up, but sagged feebly back onto the seat, eyelids drooping and tired. Her words were slurred. "Maybe in a minute. I'll just sit for a minute."

Elliot glanced at Roberta, who had fallen asleep, and jumped up, grasped Lily by the arm and dragged her to the door. He whispered, angry. "You've bloody drugged them. What have you done?"

"They'll be fine, I ground a few Diazepam tablets into the drinks."

"What about mine? Is mine drugged too?"

Lily's eyes dropped to the carpet, avoiding his furious glare. "They all were. I couldn't guarantee the reporter would take the right one."

"So you would happily have drugged me? Me, your best friend for over twenty years. And poor old Roberta. How could you, Lily, I thought I could trust you."

"And I know I can trust you, and that's why I would have stopped you if you'd made a move to drink it. You wouldn't have anyway, because you rarely drink. I know you won't go running to the police, no matter what. You've protected him so far and I'm grateful for that, but what that selfish cow was planning to do would have destroyed Charley; he's such a sweet-hearted man. I want to find him myself before this goes too far."

"How can you? You have no idea where he is."

"Not yet, no, but I've texted him, asked him to call me as soon as possible. He never ignores me, he's good like that, so I'm sure I'll hear from him soon. In the meantime, I can't have that witch over there sensationalising my family for her own gain."

Barker and Spencer hadn't expected Charles to be at home, that would have been too easy, but they also didn't know where to look next. All patrols had been furnished with his details and, in the police station, the photo that had been emailed by the DVLA before closing for the evening was being circulated. In the meantime, they had tried Lily Jenkins's house, but she had also been out.

French had been instructed to arrange an urgent warrant to search Charles's house, and once permission had been obtained to force entry, he arrived with four uniformed officers to help Barker and Spencer, but apart from a large pot of stew - far too much for one man - that was cooling on the cooker, nothing seemed out of the ordinary.

They finally returned to the station with nothing more than when they had left, and Barker sent Carl to see if Lily had arrived back yet. It was late - nearing midnight - and Barker was frustrated, feeling that unless they found the suspect, they had nothing further to do, yet he knew he would not be able to sleep if he returned home.

The incident room was quiet, but officers were working overtime on the streets searching for Charles Fubarre. Spencer, Barker and French sat apart from each other, lost in their own worlds, ruminating the details hopelessly.

Spencer finally broke the silence. "What are we going to do? We can't just sit here wasting time."

"I've got every available officer out there looking for him, what more can I do?"

A phone trilled and French answered, listening, before calling out, "There's a light on in the sister's house. Carl wants to know whether he should bring her in, or if you want to go and see her."

Spencer was, again, in charge. "Bring her in."

"No." Barker pulled rank. "I'm bored to smithereens in here, let's go out and see her. At least we won't be sitting here doing nothing and feeling useless."

They trotted down the stairs, tugging their jackets on, and French offered to drive the pool car he had used to attend the house search. The roads were empty due to the late hour and they soon drew up outside Lily's house.

Inside, Lily and Elliot heard the car pull up and guessed it would be the police. "What are you going to do now? Ignore them?"

"No, I want to know what they have on my brother. You let them in though, my back's so painful, what with not having had the chance to lie down and stretch it."

Wide-eyed, Elliot gestured wildly to Nancy and Roberta's snoring bodies. "What about them? They'll throw the book at you if they find out you drugged them."

A hammering at the front door made their plight urgent. "Leave Roberta there, she's always falling asleep nowadays, and take Nancy to my bedroom. It's through there." Lily pointed to the room Elliot had assumed was a dining room; she slept downstairs to avoid using the stairs at night, scared of falling on her regular trips to the toilet. Elliot hoisted the sleeping reporter over his shoulder and hastily carried her to the room. The rapping came again, harder.

Elliot quietly shut the door, raced the tray to the kitchen to tip the spiked wine down the sink, immersing the glasses in water, and dashed to the front door, straightening his clothes before opening it.

"We meet again, Elliot." Spencer still didn't trust the man. "We need to speak to Lily, is she in?"

He moved aside and they followed him to the lounge, greeting Lily, who didn't stand. "Do you know why we're here, Miss Jenkins?"

"No, is there a problem?"

"Are you sure? You see, normally when three detectives turn up at somebody's door at midnight, people tend to worry about why we're here, but you kind of look like you were expecting us."

"I've seen police cars swarming the streets and I know that a girl who was registered to run in the marathon was snatched yesterday, it's a no-brainer that you may turn up." Lily smiled. "Are you close to getting the girls? You must be on to something."

"We're closing in. We have a name."

"Oh? Anyone I might know?"

Barker knew Lily's favourable reputation - that she was intelligent and astute - and didn't believe a word; he was not a man to be patronised. "Where is Charles?"

"He's in London. He had some business to do there, we spoke earlier this evening."

"Do you know where exactly?"

"No, that's all he said. Why?"

"We have reason to believe he may be involved with the girls who have gone missing, his Range Rover has been positively identified as being the one used when Keisha Hamilton was abducted. Talking of which, Mr Jacobs, do you know Charles Fubarre, Lily's brother?"

"I know of him, I've heard his name, but I haven't seen him in person for years."

"So you've definitely not seen the car he drives?"

"No."

Lily coughed to regain their attention. "But why do you think Charley might have anything to do with these girls. He's never been in trouble before, he's a good, upstanding citizen. Why on earth would you suspect him of hurting anybody?" Lily noticed a movement from the corner of her eye and snarled, "What are you doing?"

Spencer stopped by the door to Lily's bedroom. "I'm just having a look around. You've got nothing to hide, have you?"

"My friend is asleep in there and I don't want her woken up."

Barker and Spencer shared a glance, and Spencer burst through the door. "Charles Fubarre, I'm arresting you on susp... oh, ma'am, I'm sorry." He switched the light on to reveal Nancy, sleeping fast on the double bed. "I'm sorry about that. It's late, I guess this case is getting to me."

French had moved to the doorway and glanced inside. "Nancy Blaine. That bloody woman gets everywhere." He moved closer and pushed her shoulder, gently at first, then harder. He leant down to check her breathing and found, to his concern, that her face and lips were swollen. "I think she's in anaphylactic shock." Lifting her up, checking her eyes, shaking her. "What has she had?"

Lily had wriggled from her chair, her back aching and painful, and reached the doorway, crossing her arms. "She wasn't feeling well and asked to lie down. I sent her through and she's been there about half an hour, snoring like a trooper. I guess she's exhausted herself."

French was urgent. "Get an ambulance. I've known of Nancy for years, unfortunately, and it's well known that she has a severe allergy to lactose. Quick, one of you look through her bag, I know she carries an EpiPen. It should ease her symptoms."

Barker coughed for attention as he shook Roberta's shoulder. "I think it may be more than a lactose allergy, I think drugs may be involved."

"What?" French came to the door and regarded Roberta, shoulders sinking.

"Lily, what have you given them, the hospital will need to know?"

"Sleeping tablets, okay, and nowhere near enough to kill them, just knock them out. The reporter was going to run a story on my brother and I couldn't let that happen."

Barker rifled through Nancy's shoulder bag and handed the EpiPen to French, who injected through her trousers into her gluteus maximus, massaging the area gently with his fingers. "Nancy, wake up."

"She won't wake for hours, I gave her a good dose."

"If she wakes at all, you stupid woman. Some tablets contain lactose and I'll bet the ones you gave her did."

Lily hung her head and Barker stepped behind the disabled woman, slamming a handcuff over her wrist. "Lily Jenkins, I'm arresting you on suspicion of administering a drug without permission…" He continued with the caution; once she was in custody he could question her at leisure about her brother.

As Barker led Lily to the car outside, French chucked the keys to Spencer. "You take them back. I'll wait here for the paramedics. It'll give me a chance to talk to Elliot; he knows more than he's letting on."

"I'm glad someone's taking my suspicions about that worm seriously."

"I don't think he's involved at all, but he would cover for Lily if she asked him to, it's clear he adores her, and I think she'd do anything to protect her brother."

Spencer harrumphed. "He's got something to do with it, I'm telling you."

"Whatever." French closed the door and returned to Elliot. "What did she give Nancy and Roberta? The ambulance will be here soon and they'll need to know."

Elliot reluctantly admitted that Diazepam had been put in the wine, and his insistence that he didn't know how many tablets were used pointed the finger directly at Lily.

Presently the paramedics took Nancy and Roberta away and French prepared a mug of tea each for himself and Elliot. They sat, regarding each other for a while and eventually French spoke. "I think you should tell me exactly what's going on."

Sighing heavily, Elliot leaned forward in the seat. "Lily's got nothing to do with it, she's a good person. I know she put

198

the sleeping tablets in the drinks and that she shouldn't have, but she was scared and acted irrationally. You need to understand the dynamics of her relationship with Charles, that way you just might understand why she feels the need to protect him. You see, although Charles is the older one, she's had to mother him since their parents died because he's so childlike. It wasn't always that way."

Elliot explained that, at the age of fourteen, Lily had fallen from a cliff and been badly injured. Although she swore she couldn't remember the events that led up to the accident, Charles had had other ideas and had kicked up a fuss, telling everyone that Roberta Robinson was a jealous teacher who had pushed her star pupil deliberately in an envious rage. "I was there, Lily and I were classmates as well as friends, and I saw nothing untoward, but Charles had this bee in his bonnet and wouldn't let go.

"At the time, he'd just left college having flunked most of his exams. Lily told me that, growing up, he'd wanted to be a vet, but academia wasn't for him, so he'd enrolled in the Army and spent quite a few years in service, his last placement in Iraq. Soon after, he was retired for medical reasons - that was in two thousand and four - and he started his current job at Arndale vets, working as a cleaner. Shortly afterwards, their parents died in a car crash, and this was when Lily became the stronger of the two, and she has been ever since.

"There really has been no reason to suspect he had any involvement with the missing girls. Lily would have told me if she'd known something was going on, we tell each other most things. I didn't tell you that I thought the Range Rover may have been Charles's because I wanted to see Lily first; I've seen her epilepsy in action and, if I can help it, I never want to see her go through that again. It takes so much out of her, leaves her in agony for a long time after."

"So, back to the question Detective Barker asked earlier: do you know Charles Fubarre?"

"I've seen him, okay, I remember him when we were growing up. I used to send a lot of time at Lily's house. You want my honest opinion? I don't think he's all there. He went doolally when she had the accident. He'd always been her big, protective brother, but something seemed different. It was like he latched onto her, scared that if he let her out of his sight, something would happen and he'd lose her. Of course, when their parents died he got ten times worse.

"She keeps him at arm's length and treats him like a child, and I don't mean that in a bad way; she has to, because he just seems incapable of coping."

"So you thought it was his Range Rover when Keisha was taken."

"I suspected, the Raymouth Marathon sticker on the back was too much of a coincidence. But truthfully, I don't understand why he would take the girls. He's gentle, Lily's always saying how soppy he is around the animals at work. He's got some kind of a screw loose but I can't see him harming anybody, or anything. That girl, the black girl who was found in the River Raymouth, I don't believe for a second that he killed her."

"He didn't deliberately kill her, but she died of a drug overdose and we believe he fed her those drugs. Just like his little sister did to Nancy and Roberta - the tendency to poison people must run in the family. Can you think of anywhere that Charles might be, somewhere he could imprison the girls?"

"All I know is what Lily said, that he's in London on business, although I don't know if it's true or not. I can't see what business there would be for a cleaner in London, but I have to take Lily's word for it."

"The Range Rover has been found in London so it's possible that it's true."

"Look, Lily doesn't need to be in trouble. I know she shouldn't have drugged Roberta and Nancy, but finding Charles may be involved in all of this has come as an awful shock, she's not in her right mind."

"I can see that and I can't imagine that Barker will go ahead with the charge, he's probably just brought her in to interview her thoroughly about Charles's whereabouts. I wouldn't worry about that. But we *do* need to worry about those poor girls who are possibly - probably - under his control." He stopped abruptly, his brow furrowed. "If Keisha's your girlfriend, why are you not concerned about her welfare? You seem a little too calm."

"Charles is obviously troubled, but he's not a murderer. I don't feel Keisha's in danger, I really don't."

On the table, Lily's mobile buzzed and the two men glanced at each other. French opened the text. "It's from Charles, it says: 'Meet me at the quay at three a.m. Important. Got a surprise. I'm not useless after all'."

He typed a short reply and Elliot asked, "What have you said?"

"None of your business." The young man was wounded and French was ashamed by his curtness. "Look, I know this is tough for you. Please, if you think of anything at all that might help us find those girls, let me know this time. Whatever you may say, I believe that Charles is not only unbalanced, but also dangerous."

French dialled a number on his own phone, pocketing Lily's. "Carl, transfer me to Barker, and then come and collect me from Lily Jenkins' house."

Chapter 18
Early Hours, Friday 27th September

It had been a struggle to get the five girls into the back of the small, upright Mercedes. With the rear seats removed, the freshly drugged girls fitted in below window level, and Charles had covered them with the blanket he had used to conceal the car from the road. It was time, and he was thrilled and terrified in equal measure.

After sending the text to Lily's phone, he had placed his mobile in the tray between the front seats and started the engine, shaking with nerves, but before he could pull away a reply came back. Pleased for the brief reprieve, he took it and read: 'Where are you?"

He would have understood a 'bugger off', or her telling him not to text so late at night, but 'where are you'? He guessed the police had got to Lily, because the response was absolutely not something she would have said, and it dawned on him that his sister may not see his carefully planned work. He would go ahead with the plan anyway; somebody would show her the pictures if she couldn't be there in person.

Clutch down, he eased the gearstick into reverse and steered the car from its hiding place. He drove carefully from the former industrial estate and headed towards the remote cliffs to the west of the town, an area he had visited many times while plotting this very night's spectacle. Despite being heavily populated on a summer's day by locals and tourists alike, the perfect spot was always deserted at night.

He passed several police patrols during the drive, both walking and cruising in marked cars, and he remained confident at the wheel to avoid giving them reason to stop him. His heart a beating drum, he drove up a steep, winding lane that led to the stunning picnic area and was disconcerted to see a tiny car parked a way back from the cliff edge. Leaving the engine running he stopped to take a closer look, but in the darkness could see nothing and assumed the car was abandoned for whatever reason. His plan could go ahead.

Charles returned to the driver's seat and drove close to the sheer drop to the choppy sea below, reversing precariously into position. He stepped from the car and slowly scanned the horizon and car park, ensuring there were no witnesses to hamper his plans at the eleventh hour.

The tree he would use as an anchor was close by and he opened the boot, removing both the rope and the guide he had sketched months before showing how and where to secure the girls without causing them harm when they dropped. He tied the rope around the tree securely; it would have to hold a significant weight.

He gently carried Sammy's limp body to the edge and laid her on the grass, tenderly stroking her hair into place, the blonde lengths frizzing slightly in the salty air. "I won't hurt you, Sammy, I promise. I love you."

Next he collected Neeraja, droopy and drugged, eyes open but unseeing. Pulling her arms and legs behind her to meet, he tied rope around her ankles and wrists tightly, doubling the knot for extra security; if the girls slipped from their bondage to the rocks below it would not only ruin the display, but hurt them, and he didn't want that - bar Rhiannon, she could die for all he cared.

Finished with the Indian girl, he took Keisha from the car.

"I'm not saying anything." Lily refused to cooperate; it was her job to protect her hapless brother.

Spencer growled, annoyed, but Barker was more patient. "Unless that reporter doesn't recover from the overdose you gave her, I don't intend to take the charges against you any further, but please, Lily, it's not about your brother now, it's about those five girls. They're out there somewhere, and they'll be terrified. If not worse, after all, we don't even know if they're still alive."

"They'll be alive, Charley's not a killer."

"Have you any idea where he may be holding them?"

Lily looked at her nails, fiddling, picking at the skin, and winced as a spasm ran along her spine. "I'm due for my painkillers, is this going to take long?"

"Probably not if you cooperate. Where would Charles hide the girls?"

Another jolt of pain ran through her back, but her need for painkillers wasn't enough to stop her hindering the police. "Try his house."

Spencer barked, "Obviously we have, and there's no sign of them there."

"Then I have no idea."

"You know, I've had enough of this." Spencer strode to the door, angry. "For the tape, Detective Inspector Spencer is leaving the room." The door slammed behind him and Barker put his head in his hands.

"He's a bit of an arse, isn't he? It's no wonder people don't like the police."

"He's a London boy, born and bred; everyone's harder there. I know, I was born in Mill Hill, but I moved south twenty years ago and that's where I intend to stay. The pace of life is so much slower and I like that." His elaboration was gaining her trust.

"Look, there is somewhere that he could be, but I doubt it. If you do find him, please be kind, because he's not a bad person, he's just troubled. I don't understand why he's taken those girls, but I don't think he'd mistreat them. Promise me?"

"Where?" She hung her head, a traitor, and a tear rolled silently down her cheek. "Please, Lily, I want those girls back. One has already died, and whereas we don't think he deliberately set out to kill her - it was a drug overdose - he was probably the one who gave her the drugs that caused her death. That could happen, could already have happened, to the other five he still has. Please, you're protecting him, but who's protecting them?"

Spencer returned with French, who held Lily's mobile up. "There was a text from Charles asking you to meet him at the quay at three in the morning."

"Shit." Barker had a dreadful suspicion that whatever Charles was up to, and however quickly they found him, it would be too late for the girls. "Get officers to the quay and see if he's already there. Lily, I'm begging you, not for me, not for us, but for the girls."

She was forlorn. "He's really doing something, isn't he?"

"Yes."

Taking a deep breath, Lily betrayed her brother. "My great-great-grandfather owned a factory in the Ruins."

"The Ruins? You mean the derelict industrial estate on the northern outskirts of town?" Barker had never known any of the abandoned buildings to be active; they should have been knocked down years ago.

"Yes, the company was called, imaginatively, Fubarre and Sons Limited. Charley was obsessed with its history as a youngster, he used to spend a lot of time there, but then Dad banned him from going, said it was unsafe. I never heard that Charley had gone there again, but it wouldn't surprise me if he did."

Spencer ran from the room, shouting, "I'll go; you worry about the quay."

Barker took Lily's hand, staring deep into her eyes, and his own filled with gratitude. "Thank you, Lily, you've done the right thing."

The five girls were tied securely, the tight ropes linking their bodies together in the design Charles had fixated on for so long. He had added extra rope to Sammy, Neeraja and Keisha to attach to the anchoring rope, which was wrapped around the tree that grew on the cliff edge. He was determined not to hurt Sammy, would be unable to live with himself if anything happened to her, despite supposing he would never see her again after letting her body fall. As the final girl due to go over, she would be the first they hauled to safety when they found his display.

In contrast, he hated Rhiannon and her mouthy way, her cockiness and lack of finesse, and wanted to mutilate her, remove the snarling face from the body. Using the knife he had cut the rope with, he hovered over her, alive yet incapacitated, steeling himself to perform out of character.

Slicing into her skin, already scratched from his attack in the factory, he cut her cheeks, lips, eyes. Gouging, carving. Remembering her taunts, her brash manner and common-as-muck voice. Fuelled by fierce anger, the body below him was Roberta Robinson now. He hacked, shredding her, ribbons of flesh hanging where the scowl had been.

Rhiannon remained silent, unconscious.

He kicked her body to the edge of the cliff - she would be the first to drop - and took Sying, the colour of her dress deciding her place in the display. Next, he placed Keisha, Neeraja and Sammy as close to the drop as possible without tipping Rhiannon and Sying over before he was ready.

Glancing around again, focusing on the abandoned car for a little longer, he breathed deeply. He was ready.

Inside her car, Jill opened her eyes, surprised to see night had fallen, the autumn temperature markedly dropped. She glanced around, trying to remember what had happened, and soon chuckled as the memories drifted back.

She had taken the meandering lane hours earlier to spend the sunny afternoon in the sea breeze, as she often did to sleep better at night. However, when she had returned to find her brand new Smart car blocked in, she hadn't for the life of her been able to work out how to put the gearstick into reverse.

She had messed about for a while, trying anything that came to mind, and had eventually decided to wait - do some Sudoku puzzles to waste time - until the driver of the car returned and moved it.

And here she was. She must have fallen asleep and slept through the rest of the day. She laughed again at her silliness.

Jill brought the key from the door pocket and plugged it into the ignition, but noticed a movement from the corner of her eye. A white Mercedes was parked by the cliff edge with a pile of rubbish beside it. A dark figure was silhouetted by the moon. Indignant - Jill cared deeply for the environment and did everything in her power to assist planet Earth to survive - she watched, determined to report the fly-tipper.

Charles intended to push Rhiannon gently, but his desire to hurt the revolting girl returned and he kicked her hard.

Too hard. Bigger and heavier than the other girls, her body plummeted and a sickening crack rang out. The ropes that linked the girls strained, and suddenly all five had fallen before Charles had a chance to hold them back. A cacophony of bones breaking, joints snapping, muscles tearing, and the anchoring tree bent dangerously towards the sea.

With horror, Charles leaned over the edge to survey the display and realised too late that his design was flawed: Sammy's body had taken the full weight of the other girls and her spine had snapped in half.

"*Sammy!*" He desperately waited for her to respond, anxious and panicked, but there was no reply; she had taken her final breath. He wanted to drop to his knees in grief, sob until every tear had run dry, but he had to get away. As far away as possible. Away from the victims, the girls he had murdered. Away from everything he knew.

Aghast, Jill squinted to make out the number plate of the car to report the driver to the council the next morning. She scribbled it - what she could make out - on a scrap of paper. Not wanting his anger at being witnessed to be directed at her, she waited for the man to drive off and followed at a safe distance, bubbling with fury at the man's shoddiness.

Spencer had taken three officers with him to the industrial estate where Fubarre and Sons Ltd had once been a booming business and they had found a door at the back of the building wide open, a padlock hanging from a hook. He raced inside, holding his torch in front of him, searching left and right, shining it into the empty, dust-filled rooms, with office and factory equipment left as it probably had been for the past century.

Carl hurried ahead, focusing on the floor. "There's fresh mud in this corridor, I'm going to follow it."

Batons not far from their hands, anticipating trouble, they trotted through the blackness, the trail illuminated by Carl's flashlight, and passed through door after door until they reached a large area. They stopped, shining their torches around the room. It was clear it had recently been occupied. Braver, having seen the room was uninhabited, two officers went to the left to investigate, while Spencer and Carl searched the right.

They came to a door further along - the warning door - which Spencer tentatively pushed open, the squeal of unoiled hinges grating their ears. He shone his torch through to a further corridor and called back to the other officers, "We're going in here. I can smell excrement. I think the girls might be in there."

At the end of the corridor, they found the room it led to was also empty and their shoulders sagged. A bucket in the corner reeked of sewage and closer inspection showed the contents weren't too old; no maggots thrived in the faeces. But they were playing catch-up, with Charles definitely in the lead. Spencer took his radio and called the scene through to the control room, urging them to tell Barker and arrange backup and a forensics team immediately.

Spencer punched the wall, a childish gesture that hurt his knuckles, brimming with frustration that the suspect was still ahead of them. Carl patted him on the back, attempting to be friendly and understanding, but Spencer screwed his face up in disgust. "Get off me, you fucking bum-bashing pervert."

"Fuck off yourself, you homophobic idiot, I've got far better taste than to hit on a wrinkled old turtle like you."

Spencer puffed his chest to prove his masculinity, while Carl glared at him, challenging another reference to his sex life. Eventually, Carl pointed to the bucket. "Anyway, the fact that there's shit in the bucket shows he didn't kill them outright, and there's no blood, so we might just get those girls alive."

"If we can find him. I'm going back to the station. I'll leave you in charge for now, because if we haven't got him before the meeting he's arranged with his sister, I want to be the first let loose on him."

Charles drove like the wind, away from Raymouth, away from the girls, away from his life. And from the murders. He had guessed from the text that the police had Lily and he felt desperate for her, knowing she would be scared, but he couldn't wait around. Only his sister would understand why he had arranged the girls in that particular location and he wished he could be there when she saw what he had done for her. She would hug him, thank him, tell him he wasn't useless after all.

It couldn't happen though, he couldn't be there for that wondrous moment, for the praise and glory, because nobody would see things the way he intended, and life as he knew it in his hometown of Raymouth was over forever.

Panicking, he had to get to the other factory in Manchester, but how - he didn't know the roads.

He took a deep breath, heading north towards London; he would find the haven somehow.

After the revelation about her brother's possible hiding place, Lily had fruitfully given the detectives an in-depth account of Charles, his job, personality, manner and, most importantly, what he was likely to do next.

Barker had arranged for the quayside to be surrounded by officers, instructing them to stay out of sight at all times to ensure Charles didn't become suspicious when he arrived. He glanced at his watch - half past two - and called French. "Has that taxi arrived yet?"

"It's waiting outside. The driver's in the canteen, says you can use it all you want."

"Of course he said that, he's getting paid double time for this. Right, come on Lily, let's go."

Lily's steps were laboured and painful. She'd not had painkillers for over four hours, and without having lain straight for such a long time, her spine grumbled angrily. "What exactly did the text say?"

"Just that he wanted to meet you at three, it said something about him having a surprise for you and that you wouldn't think he was useless after all."

Her stomach churned to match the agony in her back. "This is for me? This whole thing is for me? I don't understand, he doesn't have to prove anything to me."

"I don't know what's going on in his mind, only he can answer that when we take him in. My officer texted him back to ask where he was, but so far there's not been a reply."

Lily smiled as she climbed into the back of the taxi that Barker was about to drive to the meeting point; she knew her brother too well. He would have realised that her mobile was in the wrong hands, because she would have insulted him for suggesting they meet at such an ungodly hour. She felt sorry for the girls, but she also wanted her brother to be free, and he would never be again if he were caught for the kidnappings.

When they arrived at the quay, Lily painfully shuffled to the bench she had always shared with her brother before. It was their place, a beauty spot with a scenic, unhindered view of the cliffs. Confident he wouldn't turn up, she settled down to wait for nothing.

Rhiannon's head pounded, her mouth dry and cracking, and her face felt as if it were on fire. Her back was bent unnaturally, her ankles and wrists tied tightly together, and the pain in her joints was intolerable. She heaved her body against the discomfort. High and fuzzy from the drugs, she couldn't work out where she was, but felt a cold wind that tasted salty battering her body.

Everything felt different, the pain, the location, the freshness of the air, and she mustered some energy, but it was hard. Daggers of pain rifled through her body with every movement and eventually it was too much to bear. She succumbed to the overwhelming sleepiness.

Sying was stronger, her body more supple and not as heavy, and although her lungs felt like they had been crushed against her ribs, she managed a whispered 'help' to whoever would listen. But the wind took it away and she received no reply. She moved as far as the constraints would allow, but couldn't raise her head. All she could make out in the moonlight was air beneath her and the choppy sea a distance below, crashing against the jagged, treacherous rocks. The weight of her body pulled her shoulders from their sockets, the agony unimaginable, and however hard she tried, she couldn't pull herself up against the force of gravity.

"Dick?" A hopeless wish, but she wanted him to give her more drugs, anything to combat the searing pain that hammered her broken body. She didn't care where she was or why, but having to tolerate the pain was too much. She had no choice but to give up her fight. Her head fell forward once more and she desperately willed sleep to visit.

Chapter 19
Friday: 4.30 a.m.

Spencer returned to the station to find a scribbled note from Barker telling him he had gone to the quay in the hope Charles would be there to meet with his sister. Spencer suspected it was pointless, although necessary. He had changed his mind from earlier - said with macho bravado after queer Carl had dared to touch him - and abandoned any thoughts of attending the covert operation.

Instead he sat by his desk, exhausted from the long day that had become night and now the early hours of the morning. He took an energy drink from the drawer to add to the two he'd already had. With a forensics team on its way to the industrial estate to examine the building that had recently housed the girls, and French and Barker at the quay, he felt unable to do anything more than wait patiently for news. Laying his head on his arms, the desk cold against his forehead, he closed his eyes.

It felt like he had only slept for a moment when a commotion woke him and he raised his head. Barker was leading Lily, shrunken and wincing in pain, to his office, and French was behind. "Please," Lily could only tolerate so much, "if you're going to keep me here any longer, I need my medication."

Barker stopped and looked back at the woman he had only ever known to be disabled, and caught Spencer's eye. "Give her house phone a call, see if Elliot's still there. Either he can bring the medicine in, or we can send a car round to collect it. Come on, Lily, come in here and sit down."

Following orders, Spencer woke the computer screen up to find the number and addressed French while waiting for the details, "I'm guessing Charley-boy was a no show at the quay."

"Did you really think he would?" French, equally drained, sagged onto a seat and slipped his shoes off. "I think Lily knew he wouldn't, too. I'm not completely convinced of her innocence in this debacle at all."

"What did you get from Elliot after we left?"

"Nothing that would help us find Charles. Barker told me you'd been to an old factory. How did that go?"

"He's had the girls there, forensics will have arrived by now, but there's no trace of him - or them. He's taken them somewhere and we're still clueless." Spencer punched a number onto his handset. "Oh, Elliot, I'm glad you're still there. It's DI Spencer, I was with you earlier."

French left Spencer to his call and tapped on Barker's open door. "What now, Guv?"

"That depends on what more Lily can tell me about her brother." He directed the statement at the woman.

Wincing with pain and speaking through gritted teeth, Lily managed, "I honestly can't tell you anything, I had no idea he was doing any of this."

"But you pointed us to the factory, and we know the girls have been kept prisoner there now. Surely he must have a favourite place to go to, somewhere he feels is important."

"We've just wasted an hour waiting there. If you'd not texted him back, he probably would have gone." She was tetchy with pain.

Barker considered the paracetamol in his drawer, but supposed it wouldn't touch the agony she was in. "The thing is, he's been doing this for a long time. The first girl was abducted over three months ago, and to move them now means he's fulfilling whatever plan he had when he took them in the first place. I think those girls are in danger, more than ever. Lily, you may be the only person who can help them now."

Irritable in her suffering, Lily screwed her face, vehement. "I've done every sodding thing you wanted me to. I sat on the beachside - freezing and in pain - for ages, I've answered every question you've asked, but I have no answers to give you. I'm completely stunned to find out Charley's involved with this, I'd never have thought him capable."

She twisted, grimacing, and placed a hand on her back. "I'll continue to help, and gladly once the painkillers have kicked in, but I can't tell you where he is because I simply can't think of a place that bears any significance to him, apart from the old factory and our seat. Now, please, I need some rest and I desperately need some pain relief."

The journey had been smooth with barely any traffic, bar the usual overnight lorries and insomniac car drivers, and having taken the A12 from the M25, Charles had stuck to the road through Colchester, then Ipswich, Lowestoft and Great Yarmouth, where the road had ended. He had entered the wilderness of the Norfolk Broads and knew nothing of the area, not being a well-travelled man, but realised it wasn't Manchester and was probably nowhere near. However, the area was peaceful and he liked the space and privacy of the winding, narrow roads.

Finally, he found a remote spot - one of many - and drove onto the grass verge, killing the engine. Comfortable he had escaped unseen and not been followed, he closed his eyes to the tiredness that burgeoned.

The dreams that swiftly engulfed him were based on reality, visions of the Olympic rings he had made of five girls. Although he had not seen the full effect of the display from the top of the cliff, he was sure the result he had wanted had been achieved. Now he just had to wait for the photos to appear in the newspapers. In his sleep he smiled, but pleasure turned to a grimace as the dream became a nightmare: he had killed Sammy.

Sammy, his sweetheart. He had cherished her, loved her. Killed her. The horror woke him, glistening with sweat, and he cried, sobbing like a baby at his broken promise to let her live. Her back had snapped, he had heard it before seeing it, and every tear hammered guilt into him. Why had he kicked Rhiannon so harshly? Sammy would still be alive if she had been gently lowered over the side.

Angry, he rechecked the message on his mobile that he was sure was from the police, not his sister. 'Where are you?' As if he would be stupid enough to let them know.

Lobbing the phone - his only link to the police -through the open window, he started the engine and drove away without a clue where he was heading. His life in Raymouth troubled him as he steered through the roads. Had it been worth it?

He had held a prisoner for over three months, adding new girls when the opportunity came. He had cooked their meals and carried out the gut-wrenching task of scrubbing their foul mess. He had risked being caught every time he had stolen drugs from his employer, which would have stopped everything there and then; thankfully their stock control system was useless. It had been a ghastly few weeks, yet despite his best efforts to produce the perfect display, he had failed. Once a failure, always a failure.

The unwanted thoughts taunted him and he couldn't honestly give a positive answer to the initial question. It would have been brilliant had the plan worked, but it hadn't.

The sun inched above the horizon behind him and Charles drove past a sign for North Walsham. He slowed, searching for a newsagent, and soon parked behind a white van, the back doors wide open. A deliveryman took heavy bundles of daily newspapers to the porch that shielded the locked door of the shop, and Charles waited patiently until he had dropped his load and driven away. Checking nobody was around, he cut the plastic binding that held the tabloids and broadsheets, taking one paper from each pile.

He threw them onto the passenger seat and sped away, and was soon back on the remote roads that ran alongside the waterways. He drove for a couple of miles, the lanes narrowing further, and when he was safe from prying eyes, he stopped and grasped the first paper.

And the second. And third, and fourth, and fifth. "The bastards haven't released it." He thumped the papers, the dashboard, steering wheel, in frustration; his display hadn't even registered as national news.

No, he conceded through frightened, worthless tears. It hadn't been worth it.

Trev Hollins had been on his trawler for hours, dragging fish to their deaths in the large net that he towed behind, and by five in the morning he had a boat full. He steered the vessel north, returning to his hometown of Raymouth. He and his three employees were used to working nights, but they never ceased to enjoy the trip home, back to their families after the catch had been sold to local restaurants, cafés and fish shops.

The sun rose slowly in the sky, a ball of intense orange that reddened at the edges, and gradually it lit the darkness enough to reveal the beginnings of a beautiful day. Trev navigated, steering through the calm sea, while his two sons and lifelong friend sorted through the catch, discarding prey that had no commercial value.

A flash of colour at the top of a white cliff drew Trev's eye as they passed and he raised his binoculars to magnify the sight that seemed out of place. Body tensing, he shouted to his fellow fishermen to come and look. "It looks like five girls hanging off the cliff edge to me."

Trev's son, Graham, reached the helm first and surveyed the area his father pointed to through the binoculars. "What? They look a bit like the Olympic rings, the colours of the... oh, my God, they are girls and the colours are their dresses. It must be some gymnastic display or something."

His brother snatched the binoculars and confirmed what Graham had seen, and Will took a look through curiosity. "Move the boat closer, Trev, I'm not sure that they're gymnasts at all, they'd have to be pretty bendy to get in those positions. Probably just shop dummies."

Trev chugged towards the spectacle, and as they neared, the ruddy colour drained from Will's face. "It is five girls and I think they're dead. I'm going to radio the coastguard, have someone else check this out. Stop the boat, Trev, I'm not leaving here until I've seen those girls getting help."

"But what about the catch? We need to get to shore without it spoiling."

"Trev, I'll pay you personally for whatever you lose today. This," he gestured to the cliff, "is a once in a lifetime event and I can't wait to see the drama unfold. I'll eat my fish dinners to this story for years to come." To secure the memory, he took his mobile phone from his pocket and took a few photographs of the display.

Barker had stayed awake, despite French and Spencer sleeping uncomfortably at their desks, and had questioned Lily - more comfortable since Elliot had brought her painkillers - in detail about her brother. Finally, he called an officer to take her home. He sifted through the information but still had nothing to go on.

The forensic team had confirmed that the girls had been at the factory until recently, but there was no indication of where Charles Fubarre could be taking them, or what for. Vials of ketamine were strewn everywhere at the factory, but that was in the past and Barker was acutely conscious that the girls were in danger.

He was worn out, yet knew he couldn't give in to the sleep that threatened. He didn't care how long he had to stay awake, as long as he was there when whatever news he was waiting for came.

The phone on his desk rang and he wearily answered. "A call has just come in from the coastguard, some fisherman reckons that five girls are dangling from a tree over the edge of the cliffs to the west of town. He said he'd normally have checked it out before saying anything, but because of the missing girls…"

"He's done the right thing, tell him to wait for me."

"It's too late, Guv, he was heading straight out."

"Shit. Do you know exactly where this spot is?" The control room operator gave him the latitude and longitude she had been given and he cut the call, grabbing his jacket as he raced into the incident room to wake Spencer and French, who followed him to his car. The journey was unhindered, with little traffic on the roads as dawn became morning, and

217

when they reached the local beauty spot high on the cliffs they jumped from the car and waved to the coastguard, whose boat bobbed on the gentle waves, close enough to confirm the display was definitely five girls, but far enough out to sea to avoid hitting any underwater rocks.

Barker trotted to the edge and lay down, leaning his head over, ignoring the wooziness from his fear of water. He scanned the cliff from left to right and saw colourful material billowing in the breeze. "Over there, under that tree. The tree is holding them up."

Spencer and French reached the anchor before Barker and they tugged on the ropes. "No, don't, you don't want to risk hurting them any more. There's a rescue helicopter on its way."

"We can't wait for that. We might be able to save them." Determined, Spencer tugged again at the rope, but the weight was too much for one man. A helicopter neared and he screwed his eyes against the sun, hand shielding his face.

Barker beckoned the vessel to land, but the pilot hovered on the coastal side of the cliff, an air-sea rescuer descending a ladder to assess the girls. A precarious and dangerous operation, he reached to Rhiannon, the flesh of her face mutilated and covered in dried blood.

He issued a thumbs up to his colleagues and they swiftly lowered a stretcher to him. Her body was bent backwards, dangling painfully from her shackles, and he secured her to the stretcher around her hips and belly. He ensured she was tied tightly before cutting the ropes that held her in place and the stretcher jerked with her weight, but he held on tight, unwilling to see the poor girl fall, until she was stable enough for him to fit a shoulder harness. He gave another thumbs up and the stretcher was lifted into the helicopter.

French, Spencer and Barker watched the rescue of the five missing girls unfold before them without a clue whether they were alive or dead. They could do nothing to assist, but were patient regardless of their tiredness. The fifth girl lifted into the helicopter, Barker radioed the control room to find out which hospital they were being taken to and beckoned the others, jumping into his car for the short journey to Raymouth General.

"There's no good all three of us going to the hospital." French knew he would never be free of nightmares if he saw the injuries to the girls. "Drop us off at the station, we can arrange for forensics and try and find out where that monster is before he does any more damage."

"I want to see them." Spencer had other ideas.

The whole night and morning of hopelessness that had culminated in the bittersweet rescue of the girls was too much for the usually patient Barker and he snapped. "You have to be the guy who does everything, don't you? You have to be part of every process and you try and outrank me every step of the way. You may be a hotshot in London, Gordon, but here, I'm in charge.

"French is right, that idiot's still out there despite having hurt those girls after everyone told us he wouldn't harm a fly. We have no idea where he's gone or what further havoc he intends to create. For God's sake, stop trying to rule the roost. The only heroes in this game are those poor girls. If they survive."

Taken aback by his childhood friend's outburst, Spencer sulkily disembarked at the police station alongside French and watched Barker speed away to take the glory. "I think he was a bit harsh on me back there, don't you?" Spencer caught up with his colleague, falling into step as he marched up the path to the building. "Well?"

French shook his head, dismayed. "I think he was right, but it's neither here nor there. We need to catch that guy, and sooner rather than later, so come on, stop indulging in your own self-pity because we've got work to do. I'm going to have Lily brought back in, she's the only person who can help us now the trail's gone cold. I interrogated Elliot to death last night, but maybe Roberta Robinson, or Charles' employer, perhaps they have some ideas. The spot he chose must mean something to him."

They reached the incident room and French was straight on the phone, but Spencer remained sullen, brooding on his friend's unwarranted explosion. He had been on Operation Bandicoot before it had even been given a name; if anyone deserved to see the girls alive, it was him. French had no intention of allowing Spencer to wallow in his selfishness and, fed up and tired, he followed Barker's lead, snapping: "Get the fuck on the phone and get everybody and anybody who can help us into the station. I'm sick of playing catch up with Charles Fubarre, of him outsmarting us every step of the way. I want him caught."

Nancy awoke and felt terrible. Her mind was cotton wool, her head dizzy and she was tired and weak. The bed she lay on was harder than her own, but she wasn't sure where she was and when she opened her eyes her vision was blurry. She rubbed them harshly, listening intently to the clattering and voices that ebbed and flowed around her, and soon realised she was in a hospital. Forcing herself wearily up the bed, half-seated, half-lying, she called out, "Nurse, can I borrow you for a minute?"

The young man stepped over, harassed and doing ten things at once. "Ah, you've finally woken. What's up, love?"

"First of all, where am I?

"Raymouth General. You were brought in last night. You took an overdose of sleeping tablets."

He turned to leave and Nancy's strength billowed back. "No, don't walk away, I haven't finished with you."

With an exaggerated roll of his eyes, he crossed his arms and glared at her. "What?"

"I didn't take an overdose. I don't even have any sleeping tablets."

"Look love, I can only go by what I'm told."

Labelled, judged and abandoned, Nancy's hackles rose and she was indignant. "Then you were told wrongly. I want to leave."

"The consultant will be round after breakfast. You can discuss your care plan with him."

"Care plan? What's that all about?"

"For your depression and suicidal thoughts, I think the doctor wants to refer you to the psychiatric team for assessment."

Nancy threw the covers down and moved her legs weakly until they hung from the bed. "I don't have depression and I'm not suicidal. Where are my notes?"

The nurse tagged a colleague as she brightly strutted by and said under his breath, "Got a right one here." And to Nancy, raising his voice as if she were deaf. "At the end of your bed, love, we've been checking your obs throughout the night, but they seem stable, and you haven't had any treatment except IV fluids, which is why you have a cannula in your hand. You're one of the lucky ones."

"Don't you dare patronise me, young man."

He edged closer, lowering his voice in false sympathy. "I know you felt like everything was too much yesterday, but we really can help you."

"Are you hard of hearing? I said I did not take an overdose. If I was admitted due to a drug overdose, then it wasn't me who administered it. Now, how do I discharge myself?"

He sighed. "We really wouldn't advise that, and if you do so and something else happens we may not be able to readmit you."

"Get me the fucking paperwork, will you?"

"That's it. We don't tolerate abuse, verbal or physical, in any form." He glared, shoulders back, head straight - pompous and assertive - before striding to the nurses' station to report her misbehaviour.

Wearing a hospital gown, Nancy manoeuvred off the bed and snatched the notes from the foot of the bed, flicking through the needless paperwork until she found her admission notes. "Diazepam overdose? Where the hell was I? Come on, woman, think."

"That's what I'm in here for, too." The voice was haunting and oddly familiar and Nancy scanned the room to see where it had come from. "It's me, in the bed next to you."

"Roberta Robinson. Oh, now it's all coming back to me. We were at Lily Jenkins' house, she brought that wine through."

"That's right." Roberta shuffled up the bed, woozy. "She must have drugged the wine. Isn't it wonderful that we've got beds next to each other?"

"Why would she drug us? I wouldn't have thought her capable of harming a fly, let alone risk killing two women. And maybe even Elliot, for all we know."

"Well, you were threatening to do a scoop on her brother, that's a good start. As for me, I have no idea. I thought we were friends."

The nurse returned, flanked by two security guards, and brandished a piece of paper. "Self-discharge form. Sign at the bottom and then you can get dressed and these guards will escort you from the hospital grounds."

"For fuck's sake, isn't this a bit overdramatic." Nancy was flabbergasted. The guards moved closer and she held her hands up. "Okay, okay, I'm getting dressed now."

"That's twice you've abused the staff." A guard had hold of her arm. "You're leaving now."

Nancy grabbed the bag with her belongings in, before being whisked away like a naughty child, shouting, "I'm a reporter, you know, and I'll have this in print. You'll be named and shamed for the whole bloody country to see."

The indignity was embarrassing and Nancy fumed as the guards deposited her ungracefully by the main gate of the hospital, the gown unceremoniously displaying her rear to anyone walking behind. She tried to sit on the low wall but a guard pulled her off. "Not on hospital property, there's a seat across the road."

"What are you, the fucking Gestapo? I'd like to retain a modicum of dignity if I can. Can't you see I'm naked apart from this shapeless tent, and this is a main road?" His reply was a finger pointing to the bus stop across the street and she huffed, clutching the flaps of the gown behind her, across the road, regardless of the hooting traffic, and perched on the semi-seat under the bus shelter.

Excruciatingly aware that eyes everywhere were enjoying her vulnerability, she rooted through her belongings for her handbag. She took her mobile and dialled her husband. "Phil, you've got to help me."

"Nancy, where have you been? I've been worried sick."

"It's a long story, but I'm in a bit of a pickle. I've just been thrown out of Raymouth General Hospital and they didn't even let me get dressed."

Phil laughed and she had to admit she probably would too not so far in the future. Vexed, she waited for him to finish ridiculing her, an eyebrow raised. "Sorry, Nancy, but I wish I was a fly on the wall. I'll make a couple of calls and get someone to pick you up."

"Thank you," she said tartly.

"By the way, if you've been out of action overnight, you won't have heard the news. They've found the missing girls, there was a news release on the telly just now. No details yet, but I think you've got your work cut out for the next few days."

"Where were they found?"

"Hanging over a cliff in Raymouth, that's all they've said so far."

"Forget finding me a lift, I'm getting a taxi down to the police station. I'll get dressed in the back."

Chapter 20
Friday Morning

Carl had barely slept after being in charge of the investigation inside the old factory throughout the early hours, but Barker had arranged for every available officer to report to work, regardless of his or her shifts. Although tired, he was excited as he drove to Lily's house. He knocked on the door and waited, then knocked again, harder. Presently, Lily, unkempt and puffy, opened the door. "What now?"

"DCI Barker has asked me to bring you to the station, there have been some developments."

"No, I won't go. I spent the best part of the night sitting on those hard seats and my back's killing me as a result. If Jeremy wants to see me, he'll have to come here."

"Mrs Jenkins…"

"Ms, my title is Ms. I have never been married."

He coughed gently. "Ms Jenkins… Wait a minute, if you've never married, how come your name isn't Fubarre?"

"I changed it when I was eighteen by deed poll." Normally open and kindly, the constant pain and dealing with the police were getting to her and she was abrupt. "I'm not going to the station. If it's that important, then you'll have to arrest me, and you have no grounds to do that."

With a cheeky glint of power, Carl took her arm. "Ms Jenkins, I'm arresting you for obstructing a murder inquiry, if you…"

"Murder? What's Charley done? What's happened?" Carl continued to issue the caution as he followed her into the house and she collected her medications together, dropping numerous boxes of tablets into a carrier bag. "Okay, I get it, you've said your piece and I'm under arrest for the second time in as many days, despite being a law abiding citizen. Can you just shut up now while I get dressed?"

She shuffled awkwardly to her bedroom and left the door open as she changed her clothes, out of sight. "What's Charley done?"

"We've found the missing girls. Three were dead from their injuries when we picked them up and one died in hospital this morning. The last is in a critical condition in Raymouth General."

A sharp intake of breath came from the bedroom and Lily, wearing just a bra and trousers, came out, horrified. She stood, holding her blouse in her hand, trying to understand the dreadful revelation. "Charley killed them? I just can't believe it. Where? Where did you find them?"

"They were tied to a tree on Hawthorn Cliff, do you know the area?"

Lily came closer in a state of shock and sat on her special chair. "Yes, of course I do, wouldn't everyone around here?" She pointed to her back. "It's where I had my accident."

Immediately, Carl withdrew his radio. "I need to speak to Barker, it's urgent."

Barker's day - now twenty-six hours since he had last slept - had started with the bang of finding the girls and showed no signs of slowing down. He had been on the phone to dozens of people, held a tactical meeting with the inquiry team, sent reports to the bigwigs in London who were overseeing Operation Bandicoot, and he hadn't eaten since lunchtime the previous day. He had heard that Nancy Blaine had been drugged and was sorry for her, but she was the last person he needed pestering him. "Nancy, I understand you want a scoop, but I haven't got time. This is a murder enquiry and we've got all hands on deck to find the man responsible."

"You are talking about Charles Fubarre, I take it."

"Who even let you up here, you shouldn't have got past the reception desk?"

"We reporters have ways and means. Look, of course I want an article - what journalist wouldn't - but I've been intensely involved with this case, and surely if it's going to hit the press anyway, it would be more palatable from a local reporter?"

Barker rubbed the cloudy film from his eyes, tiredness grating. "I don't give a jot about who's behind the tabloid stories. What I care about is finding our suspect before someone else gets hurt."

"You think there's a possibility he'll kill again?"

"For heaven's sake, Nancy, French was right: you just don't give up, do you? The press office will be revealing the details at one this afternoon." Barker gestured to the door. "Stop wasting my time and get your information then, like everyone else." Relieved to see Carl and Lily approaching through the glass, he held the door wide, dismissing the reporter. "Please go now, my next appointment has arrived."

Nancy stepped outside and crossed her arms. She had questions to ask Lily herself, and as the woman passed, avoiding eye contact, Nancy whispered, "I'll be seeing you after he's finished with you. What you did last night wasn't very friendly."

Lily kept her head straight and proud as she greeted Barker, shaking his hand, and Carl closed the door behind them. "I had to arrest her again, hope you don't mind."

Sagging, Barker leant against his desk and indicated a spare, cushioned seat for Lily. "Was that really necessary?"

"It's not his fault. I came willingly when I heard you'd found the girls. I'm sorry it's been such bad news, that must be hard for you. Have you found my brother?"

"We don't even know where to look, it's a needle and haystack situation."

"Damn, I need my..." She stopped herself, alarmed.

"You need your what?" Barker stood, awake and eager. "What? Lily, five girls are dead and Charles is still out there. What were you going to say?" He stared at her, waiting. "Forget it. Carl, what did you arrest her for?"

"Obstructing a murder investigation."

"In that case, get the press department to announce immediately that Raymouth Marathon will be cancelled due to the members of the organisation helping the police with their enquiries into a mass murder, committed..."

226

"Stop." Lily held her hand up, beaten. "Enough now, don't involve the marathon in this, please. Charley has my car, and I need my car and my disabled badge."

Barker's jaw fell in disbelief. "He's been in your car the whole time and you never thought it relevant to let us know? Jesus Christ, woman, the charges against you stand firm. What's the registration plate?"

Sighing. "It's a personalised one, L 288 J E N. It's a polar white Mercedes A160 that has been specially adapted for my disability, and the blue card was in the window."

"I'm on it." Carl dashed from the office to circulate the details.

Meanwhile, Barker sank onto his chair, despondent. "Why, Lily?"

"I didn't think it would be important and I don't want to be linked to this case. I have a reputation to keep."

"Not important! Your poncy reputation? Is that all those poor girls were worth. Don't you realise we could have found them alive if we'd known this earlier?" She hung her head, ashamed but not repentant; this was about her brother and she didn't regret giving him a head start to freedom. "What else haven't you told us, and I want to know everything from start to finish, with no grey areas."

Jill had been awake since dawn and copious mugs of tea hadn't hurried the hours until the council opened. She sipped the latest brew and glanced again at her watch, then at the clock on the wall: one minute to go. She picked up the phone and dialled, in case they opened slightly early, and was surprised to hear a human voice instead of a machine. "Oh, I wasn't expecting anyone to answer. Right, well, hello, my name is Mrs Hatch and I'd like to report a certain car - I have the details here, bear with me…"

"Madam, what department would you like?"

"Well, fly-tipping, of course."

The earpiece crackled and clicked, and then ringing on the end of the line. She waited patiently, eager to tell her story, and eventually somebody answered. "Environmental Enforcement, how can I help?"

Jill told the lady of her mishap in her new car the previous day, the inability to find the reverse gear and how she had fallen asleep over a puzzle while waiting for the car in front to move. She explained it had been dark when she had awoken, and she watched what she assumed was a man push a large pile of rubbish over the edge of the cliff. "He had a white car, and the registration, as far as I could make out, was - have you got a pen?"

"Yes, and paper."

"It was L two eight eight J E N. I would have confronted him but I'm elderly and I didn't want him getting angry with me; you never know, nowadays."

"Of course, Mrs Hatch, I completely understand. I shall get onto this right away, and thank you for reporting it, we take fly-tipping very seriously."

Jill smiled as she replaced the receiver, proud of having done her bit, and now... she probably wouldn't speak to another soul all day.

She prepared her nth cup of tea of the morning, unaware that the council, although dealing with the problem, saw no urgency; nobody would have guessed Mrs Hatch had witnessed a multiple murder.

Over the course of the morning the parents of the missing girls were driven to the morgue at Raymouth General to identify their dead children, but the lone survivor had no visitors. Rhiannon Hughes was so lightheaded she struggled to open her eyes, and when she did, realised she was in a hospital. Memories, or dreams, or hallucinations - she wasn't sure - wandered into and out of her mind, and she was aware that she couldn't move, not even to turn her head.

The critical care nurse who had been allotted to Rhiannon for her shift on the Intensive Care ward noticed her patient was awake and tapped the policewoman who waited outside the room on the shoulder as she passed. "She's awake.

Rhiannon," she had reached the bedside, "can you hear me, darling?"

Rhiannon tried to nod but nothing moved and she blinked instead, hoping it would purvey her message. "I hope that was a yes. My name is Karen." Taking her hand carefully to avoid disrupting the wires and tubes that monitored, fed and watered the girl. "You've had an accident and you're in Raymouth General Hospital. You have a tube in your throat to help you breathe so try not to talk, but use one blink for yes and two for no. Can you tell me if you're in any pain?"

What constitutes pain, Rhiannon wondered. Did she know any more? She felt different, but unsure how, and had little concept of what was real and what wasn't. She blinked twice.

"Good girl, we're keeping you on a morphine drip for now as your injuries are severe, but the doctor will reduce it gradually."

"Can I talk to her?" Jo Ellis had followed the nurse after reporting Rhiannon's condition to the station.

"Nothing too stressful. If I hear her heart rate increasing, I'll have to stop you." She lowered her voice. "One blink for yes, two for no, she can't talk until the ventilator's removed."

"Thanks. Rhiannon, do you know where you are?" She wanted to scream 'they've just bloody told me' but couldn't. She blinked once. "Do you remember what happened to you?" Two blinks. "Do you remember being kidnapped?"

The machine to her left beeped quickly and Karen stepped between the two women, soothing her patient as she monitored her speeding heart rate. "I think that's a yes. Please can you leave her now, she's obviously not ready for this yet."

Jo shoved her hands in her pockets, distressed by the condition of the girl they had been seeking, and stepped back to avoid causing her further anxiety. "Of course, but my boss will want to talk to her, and as soon as possible. Her attacker is still at large and we need to get him off the streets."

Karen released a small surge from the morphine drip to pacify the disturbed girl and slowly her heart regulated, eyes closing once more against the world.

Charles sat by the side of the River Stiffkey, having walked for a while through the autumnal scenery to collect his thoughts together. He had perused the newspapers from cover to cover and hadn't found a single report about his display, and the past three months seemed to have been wasted. Of course it hadn't been worth it. Lily would never see the display he had carefully constructed for her, and now he was homeless - town-less, in fact - and being hotly pursued by the police. It was just a matter of time before they caught him, and that was exactly what he deserved.

Thoughts of suicide were never far from his mind, he had nothing left to live for, and coming to terms with breaking his promise to Sammy, not only hurting her, but killing her, was too much. He felt the pain physically.

Charles scanned the natural beauty spot with long reeds and grass, abundant trees overhanging the gently flowing water. Was it deep enough to drown in? Should he try? If he failed it would cause more trouble, alert the police to his whereabouts and lead him directly to jail. What was better, a life sentence, or a life ending? Or were they the same in the long run?

Pitiful defences sang in his mind; he hadn't intended to kill Sammy and was sure the others were alive. Yes, he had slashed Rhiannon's face, but she had brought him to the brink. If she hadn't been so mouthy, been a good girl like the others - like Sammy - he would never have done it.

His psyche tormenting him, the endless questions remaining unanswered, Charles wasn't sure if to live, how to live, whether to die or disappear. He clasped his hands around his head, squeezing tightly against the indecision, and the frustration and bitterness flooded out with his tears.

Nancy had garnered a huge amount of information from the hustling and bustling within the police station and she called her boss with the details, explaining that she couldn't write the article *and* collect more data at the same time. He was terse. "Jonas, I understand what you're saying, but they're doing a press release at one and I wanted you to have the details before, but I'm in the middle of things and I don't want to miss any snippets."

"What I don't understand is why this makes any difference. A press release is a press release, and all the papers will be printing exactly the same dross tomorrow morning, no matter what. There's nothing you can give me that will add to that."

"I'm sure there is, though. Reporters will be coming from London to attend but I'm already here, living and breathing it as it happens. That's got to have an edge."

"Yes, you'll be able to pump out a bigger story but it'll still say the same thing." Jonas eyed the cheese and onion sandwich on his desk, lovingly prepared by Raoul that morning, and wished Nancy would bugger off.

"You don't get it, I don't want my story to be a little bit bigger and a little bit rounder, I want to be top dog in my game, to create a masterpiece that'll make every damned person in England want to buy The Daily Review tomorrow morning."

"We already know you're ambitious, that's one of the reasons we took you on, but you're not going to get anything out of the ordinary for tonight's print run. Just prepare the story and email it to me by ten tonight, as usual. Now, get back to work and let me get back to mine."

Nancy heard the tone and realised he had ended the call, and she cursed under her breath. His lame comments had been a red rag to a bull and she was willing to take the challenge. He may not have realised it yet, but she was the best investigative journalist going and all she needed to prove it were a few awards in her pocket.

Nancy remained seated in the reception area, watching the comings and goings, and presently an older man, maybe mid-fifties, entered, the sickening smell of raw fish wafting with him. She held her hand over her nose as he strode to the counter. "My name's Trev Hollins, I've got an appointment with some French guy."

Stifling a smile, the desk sergeant corrected him. "That'll be Detective Inspector French, sir." Nancy heard and, knowing her old 'friend' was working the case, her interest was roused. While the sergeant called the incident room to inform them of the fisherman's arrival, she sauntered over. "Someone will be down in a minute to talk with you, Mr Hollins. Please take a seat while you wait."

Trev turned, the odour emanating from him, and found Nancy in his personal space. "'Scuse me, miss, sorry."

"Are you here to see DI French?" It was an easy conversation starter.

"Uh-huh."

Nancy thrust her hand forward to shake his. "I've been expecting you, I'm DC Blaine and my Guv asked me to take the preliminaries from you before you go up and see him."

"Oh, right, miss."

"Let's go and sit down, away from all the hubbub. First of all, what connection do you have to the case?"

"You should know, I've already talked to a couple of your lot today."

"No, Mr Hollins, of course *I* know what you're here for, but I just have to confirm you're not a reporter, er, fishing around, excuse the pun."

He tapped his nose - bulbous, red and hairy - and winked. "Gotcha. It was me who spotted the girls this morning. It was awful. I was out on my trawler, bringing home today's catch - all gone to waste, it has, lost a bleedin' day's money through this, I have. Anyway, I saw the colours against the cliff, you know, the girls were in dresses and they sort of looked like the Olympic rings in a mad way. In fact, Will got himself some photos before the old bill was even there."

232

Nancy thought her eyes would pop out as she did a high five in her head, but kept her composure. "And Will is?"

"Your lot spoke to him an' all." He guffawed and Nancy smelt a blast of body odour mingled with the ever-present stench of fish.

"Same story, Mr Hollins, I've got to ensure you are who you say you are. So Will is?"

"I can show you some ID if that helps, then I won't have to go over it all."

"Fake ID is easy to come by, Mr Hollins. This is a national murder enquiry, we have to be sure. Who is Will?" She was sterner and his smile waned.

"Sorry, miss. Will O'Donnell, he's my skipper, he's out in the van trying to knock off what we can of the fish 'cos we was so late docking."

"Do you have his mobile number?"

"Of course."

She waited briefly, but he didn't move. "Well, can I have it then?"

"Oh, right, give us a sec then."

Barker and Spencer pulled the team together to give them the newest details of the case, and Barker had some promising news. "We've had a report from the traffic section. They've studied footage of vehicles on the M25 this morning and have confirmed that the Merc we're looking for first appeared, heading north-east, on the motorway at three a.m. The car stayed on the road, past the Dartford tunnel, and wasn't seen again after the junction with the A12, so we can assume he headed north towards East Anglia. They're now examining the footage available for the A12, and I've informed the guys in London, who are organising extra patrols the full length of the A12.

"However, I must stress that he could have turned off the A12 at any time, or he could be driving a different car, so we could still be on the wrong track. Regardless, it's progress.

"Now, the girls: the post-mortems are currently taking place and early indications show they were alive when they were dropped over the cliff edge." He checked his notes to ensure he gave the correct details and pointed to a rough sketch, drawn with coloured pens, of the Olympic symbol that was pinned to the whiteboard. "This sickens me to the core, but also indicates a powerful message from the suspect. The display is almost certainly a crude attempt to recreate the Olympic rings. Charles has some anger going on, maybe towards the Olympic games itself, but more likely towards the Raymouth Marathon - we all know the link there.

"Okay, so Sying Cheng was in a yellow dress and she was here." He indicated the lower left circle of the diagram. "Rhiannon Hughes, our only survivor, was dressed in green and she was here on the bottom right. For the top row, as you look at it from the sea, Neeraja Sharma, in blue, was to the left. Sammy Cooper, in black, was in the middle, and Keisha, wearing a red dress, was to the right. Their bodies weren't interlinked physically - I think that would have been nigh on impossible to achieve - but the ropes tied them in that order, leading to," he took an A4 image of a photo taken by the coastguard and pinned it next to the diagram, "this nauseating display."

"As you know, I have spent a lot of time, both yesterday and this morning, with Charles's sister, Lily Jenkins. She is currently under arrest for obstructing our enquiries and has agreed to help as and when we need. She's very distressed. However, I'm not convinced of her proclaimed innocence in this case; I wouldn't be surprised if she's not giving us the whole picture as she's insanely protective of her brother. Apart from not informing us that he was driving her car - a fact that could have led to us catching him before he harmed the girls - there's also something not quite right about her changing her name by deed poll when she was eighteen from Fubarre to Jenkins. Carl's been digging on that one, so…"

Carl stepped to the front and flicked a flop of hair back to its spiky home. "It didn't feel right to me, which is why I've brought attention to it. Fubarre and Sons Limited, the disused factory where the girls have been imprisoned, was a large source of employment for the town in the mid to late eighteen hundreds before it's unfortunate decline, which led to bankruptcy in nineteen twenty-four. One would think that the descendants would be proud to bear the name, so why did Lily change hers to something entirely different as soon as she was legally able?

"When I asked her, she told me she'd been fed up of being teased about her ancestors' financial difficulties, but my research has shown that, despite the company going bust, the individual members of the Fubarre family who worked for the business were, in fact, enviably wealthy. Lily leads a very comfortable lifestyle regardless of not having a job. I think there's more to it.

"The choice of Jenkins as a surname is also a quandary. Her daughter's father is named Bishop and the relationship she had with him, as far as we know, is the only sexual one she's ever had. She says her disability impedes on most areas of her life. So why Jenkins? She tells me she picked the name from nowhere, but I don't believe that; your name is your identity, it's important and not something you would choose on a whim."

Barker had a thought. "Maybe it was a favourite pop star, or film star, something like that. An adolescent crush."

"I'll have another word with her, Guv, and any other suggestions will be welcomed. Right, that's me done, back to you."

"Forgive me if I'm missing something here, but why on earth would Lily's name be anything to do with Charles and his actions?" French thought it a ridiculous waste of time.

Barker chuckled. "It's his first gut instinct ever, don't take it away from him."

"With all due respect, Guv, piss off." Carl waited for the tittering to die down. "He's right though, it's playing on my mind, and with Lily being so obstructive when she wants to be, I'm in agreement with him. I don't trust her."

"Fair enough. Barker, you mentioned earlier about the girls being displayed like the Olympic rings; are you getting a psychological profile?"

"There's no need. We know who he is and we can find out his past. He joined the British Army as a Private after an unimpressive education, and in two thousand three was sent to Basra, Iraq. He returned in two thousand four a changed man. How he hasn't been formally diagnosed with PTSD, I don't know"

"PS what what?"

"Post Traumatic Stress Disorder; google it, Carl. I'd have thought you would know about it, considering three of the words describe you to a T."

"I'll let it be known that you are the personal cause of my stress and trauma, and I wouldn't call being gay a disorder." It was banter, but Spencer still screwed his face with distaste.

Barker continued, "It seems he witnessed some atrocities whilst in Camp Dogwood, which sent him over the edge, and he was brought back to the UK in November two thousand four and retired from the army on medical grounds. This could be the trigger that started the slippery slope to where he is now, and the Army are sending his medical records across as we speak.

"After six months on sickness benefits, he secured a job at Arndale Veterinary as a cleaner and has been employed there since. Now, physically he's fit and healthy, and his records show that he hasn't had any illnesses to note, apart from his GP suggesting in two thousand five that he take anti-depressants, an offer he refused. There were no psychological tests, apart from a bog-standard questionnaire, to confirm he had any form of mental health problems, but he did state - hence his doctor's suggestion - that he regularly felt suicidal.

"Finally we come to his social life, or lack of in his case. He's a loner, he's not a member of any organisations that we know of, he doesn't have many - if any - friends, and Lily is the only family member he's in touch with. Basically, he gets up, goes to work, comes home and locks himself away from the world, day in, day out. Weekends: Lily says he's often out, but guarantees he wouldn't go out drinking; our man's not a big drinker.

"He's not got any previous convictions, there have been no complaints made about him. In fact, apart from recently abducting six girls and causing the deaths of five of them, he's quite the good little boy."

Barker ended the brief after a question and answer session and rushed back to his office to check if any relevant emails had come in, eating a family-sized bag of crisps for lunch. He was due to attend the press conference in half an hour and still had to meet and greet Detective Superintendent Brannigan, who had travelled from London that morning to head the panel.

Chapter 21
Friday, 1 p.m.

Jo, who had been assigned to guard Rhiannon Hughes, had contacted French for a second time to let him know that the patient was suitably comfortable and coherent for him to pay a brief visit, and he turned up at one, just as the press release was about to begin at Raymouth Town Hall. "How is she?"

"Bearing up. She's in traction at the moment and will be having spinal surgery tomorrow - don't ask me the details, they all went over my head - and she's already had her dislocated shoulders pinged back into place, but she's had the ventilator taken out and her condition is stable at the moment."

"Can she talk?"

"A little. The nurse told me she's not to become excited; she's got serious injuries that have caused strain on her heart."

French took in the pitiful sight of Rhiannon from the doorway, a young, fit and healthy girl who had virtually been snapped in two, and felt overwhelming sorrow for her. Slowly, he walked closer. "Rhiannon, my name is Detective Inspector French, you can call me Dan. I'm investigating your abduction. Would you mind talking to me for a minute?"

Her attacker had shredded her face and the small amount of skin that wasn't scabbed or reddened from swelling was purple-black. Watching her struggle to talk, in a thin, wispy voice, was heartbreaking. "Yes."

"What can you remember about your time with your abductor?"

In few words, Rhiannon detailed what she could remember leading up to her kidnap, about the cell and the other girls, the drugs he had fed them in tasteless stews. She told a concise story but it wasn't enough to help them in their search for him; it was all past news. "So he drugged you in the room, and the next thing you know?"

"Pain. Excruciating pain. It felt like my body was on fire and every time I moved the agony seared through me. I knew I was hanging from something and I could taste the salt in the

238

air. I honestly wished I could die, there and then. How are the others?"

"I'm sorry, Rhiannon, you were the only survivor."

"That'll piss him off; he hated me."

French was stunned when the girl smiled softly and now understood why she and not the others had been mutilated. "Did he say anything about what he intended to do after he'd dumped you?"

"Sammy was the one he talked to, I think he loved her in some sick way. I tried not to take the drugs, like she did, but it was too hard - too boring - to stay awake twenty-four seven in that shitty, stinking hole. All I know is that his sister was disabled and that he was doing it all for her. He called her Bubby; it made me want to stick my fingers down my throat."

"Did you see him, his face?"

"No, he gassed us every time he came in the room so we wouldn't escape."

"Do you know if he intended to kill you?"

"He said that Sammy and Keisha would live, but because he detested me so much, he said I would definitely die. He was going to slash my throat. What do they call that?"

"Irony? Poetic justice?"

"Yeah, something like that. Is he alive?"

"He's on the run but police forces across the country are searching for him."

"Will he come here and finish me off?" Her heartbeat was increasing, showing she was capable of normal emotion and fear despite her tough exterior, and the nurse edged closer, ready to stop the interview.

"No, we have evidence that he's headed north, but we've got a guard at the door for your reassurance. I know this will be hard to understand but it wasn't personal to any of you girls. What mattered to him wasn't *who* was in the display he made of your bodies, it was about the display itself. From what we can work out, this was about revenge on the woman he believes was responsible for his sister's accident sixteen years ago."

"That'll be Roberta, he swore a lot whenever he mentioned her. He said he was going to make us into 'rings of death'; how did he display us?"

"Like the Olympic rings."

"Oh, inventive then. I can't tell you anything else, I was a zombie most of the time I was there, and I'm really tired." Her eyelids were drooping against her will.

"Okay, sweetheart." French gently laid a hand on hers. "If you think of anything else, my officer is outside and when her shift ends she'll introduce you to her replacement. Talk to them whenever you want."

Spencer had intended to be part of the press conference panel but was overruled by Barker, which hadn't sat well with him, leaving him in a foul mood. When informed that an environmental enforcement officer from the council had also made enquiries that day about the car they were seeking, he had gruffly called them to find out why. As soon as he heard the news that Charles had been seen dumping the girls, he had sent an officer to bring the witness in.

Concerned, Jill Hatch meekly introduced herself and he led her to an interview room. "I thought it was the right thing to do. I thought fly-tipping was illegal so I can't see why I'm in trouble here."

"Mrs Hatch, you're not in trouble, but the suspect you saw last night wasn't tipping rubbish over the edge of the cliff."

"So I'm being prosecuted for making a false report? Typical, I can't do right for doing wrong. Well, I'm sorry, but I stand firm…"

"Mrs Hatch, nobody is prosecuting you, I just need to ask you some questions about what you saw. Exactly what you saw. It wasn't rubbish he was dumping, they were the five abducted girls who have been in the news, four of whom have died from their injuries as a result."

Jill was speechless and, absorbing the shocking statement, her face paled. "They were the missing girls? I was there, I could have stopped him. This is my fault. No... Does that make me an accessory to murder?"

Easily irritated, Spencer kept his voice as friendly as he could muster. "I shall stress again: we will not be making any charges against you. I want to know exactly what happened last night, from what you saw, to what you could smell, to what you could hear. I want you to tell me everything."

Jill reiterated the story she was tired of telling and Spencer encouraged her when she reached the part about the car. "It was a white Mercedes, but obviously looked grey in the moonlight."

"It was white; we're currently searching for both the car and driver. What exactly did you see?"

"If you stopped interrupting me I'd have reached that point by now." She paused, annoying him further. "I opened my eyes and it took me a short while to get my bearings. I felt somewhat embarrassed, but it was a daft situation so I had a chuckle at myself. I was about to start the engine - I'd put the key in the ignition - when I noticed a movement from the corner of my eye. I turned to look and saw the car, and it looked to me like a man was standing over a huge stack of rubbish. Oh, it's awful to think they were the missing girls and I didn't do anything to help."

Abrupt and arrogant, as always. "Keep going."

"You really are a very ignorant man, Mr Spencer. As I was telling you before you rudely interrupted me for the umpteenth time, I thought they were bags of rubbish. Then he stepped forward and kicked one over the edge. I immediately thought he was fly-tipping and searched in my car for a pen and some paper to write the number plate down.

"I didn't see him push any of the other bags - girls, sorry - off, because by the time I'd found a scrap of paper - there was an old envelope in the glove compartment - he was climbing back into his car. My eyes are quite old and my glasses not up to par so I squinted to make out the letters and numbers and noted them as the car drove from the car park onto the road back to Raymouth."

"So he turned right?"

"Yes."

"Could you make out anything of his features while you were looking at him? Think hard now."

"No, he was silhouetted by the moon and was too far away."

"I want you to close your eyes, put yourself back in the moment, think of everything you saw clearly. It doesn't matter how long it takes." It did, he was tired and tetchy.

Jill did as she was told, appearing lost in thought and Spencer wished he could change her batteries to speed her up. "You know, now I think about it, I did see him. I saw him as he drove by, well, his profile anyway."

"Oh? What can you tell me?" Spencer discreetly concealed the photograph of Charles Fubarre that was on the table before him.

"Well, that man you just covered up is Charley, I'm not sure of his surname. He's one of my clients."

"Clients?"

"I'm a masseur, and not in the way your filthy mind is probably thinking, I'm too old for that kind of shenanigan. He served in Iraq and sustained an injury to the top of his back and I give him a full back massage every week, sometimes more often when his pain is bad. He says it helps to keep him off painkillers."

"But we have his discharge notes from the Army and there's nothing at all about any form of injury."

"Mr Spencer, I was in the Women's Air Force in the sixties and I can assure you that what these governmental institutions officially tell you is not necessarily the truth. They cover up more than you could possibly imagine. I could feel with my hands that there was damage to his cervical vertebrae; his spine wasn't in alignment. It was easy to manipulate them back into place by massaging the muscles, but in-between our weekly sessions, he said his shoulder got progressively more painful as the vertebrae slipped back to their damaged positions.

"Anyway, what's Charley got to do with the car; he drives a beaten up Range Rover? You know, now his face is in my mind, and knowing his strong Anglo-Saxon profile - his features are typically Germanic - he has a long nose, see," Jill reached across and uncovered the photo of Charles, pointing out his features as she described them, "and it's quite bulbous at the end."

He couldn't take it any longer. "Please — see, I've taken your guidance about my manners - could you get to the point."

She crossed her arms, indignant. "You've taken no guidance from me, you rude man. The point is, thinking about it, the driver could very well have been Charley, although it never occurred to me at the time." She finished with an impertinent cock of her head.

Supercilious and impatient, Spencer would rather have his teeth pulled than to continue the conversation, but he had a job to do. Why couldn't members of the public just get straight to the point? "Okay, that's confirmed what we already know, so…"

"Well, why didn't you just say 'is that the man who was driving', instead of making me waste my breath going round the houses?"

Now Spencer felt he would rather grate his ears to the scalp than continue and he spoke through gritted teeth. "I didn't want to influence you." He took a deep breath to restrain himself. "Is Charles friendly with you? Does he chat about things when he comes to your house - I assume he visits you?"

"No, I visit him at his place. I've got a portable table. I like that because it means I have reason to get out of the house regularly. Answering your question: yes, he generally chats for ten, maybe twenty minutes when I start massaging him, then he sort of zones out. Lots of people do, they often go into a trance, in fact some even go to sleep."

"What does he talk about?"

"Day to day things, how his sister is - he's very close to her - and how she manages with her disability. I've tried to convince him to let me massage her but I don't think he ever asked."

"Can we be more specific. Has he ever talked about the missing girls to you, or about his plans to display them in the design and colours of the Olympic rings."

"Pardon?" Spencer produced a photo of the macabre display and Jill swallowed hard, shocked. "He did this? Charley did this? I can't believe it, he's such a gentle man."

"So has he ever mentioned any of this in passing?"

"Not that, no, but he does have a huge problem with a woman called... I think her name is Roberta, was a teacher before she retired. I don't know her but Charley paints a sordid picture of her. He says she pushed his sister over a cliff, which led to her injuries. Actually, that would make sense..."

Concerned she was about to launch into another long explanation, Spencer jumped in quickly. "Thank you, Mrs Hatch, you've been very helpful."

"I haven't finished. Now I've seen this picture, I think I know what's going on."

Spencer stood and indicated the door. "Thank you for your time, we're very grateful."

Charles had become hungry for the first time in over twenty-four hours and debated whether to pick up a sandwich from a shop, or visit a remote country pub to have a decent cooked meal. The latter won when he passed a picturesque inn - traditional, welcoming, and typically English - close to the bracing shore of the North Sea.

He had not noticed his appetite until he scanned the tempting menu, and ordered bangers and mash in onion gravy - salivating in anticipation - to have with a pot of tea. The television above the bar flickered lamely with some monotonous afternoon show and he snatched a glance every now and then, uninterested but distracted by it.

The landlady brought the sumptuous, generously sized meal to his table with a beaming smile and he tucked in voraciously to the herbed sausages and creamy, smooth potato, soaking each mouthful with rich gravy. It was delightful and he enjoyed every morsel.

The plate cleared, he approached the bar to pay, but an announcement on the television drew his attention and he stared, horrified. Emblazoned across the screen was a picture of him and the landlady had also noticed, her face now twisted with fear. "Why did you have to see that, you stupid bitch? Now I'm going to have to kill you too."

"Oh no you don't." The gruff voice from behind startled Charles and, terrified of being captured, he grasped his knife from its holster underneath his jumper and spun around, whipping the knife back and forth furiously. He caught the man in the stomach and he doubled up, but instead of stopping, Charles was frenzied. With the landlady's screams in the background, he plunged again and again, the pub's best regular falling lower with every strike.

The man, now an empty body, his life over, slumped onto the wooden floor, crimson blood seeping onto the beer-sticky carpet, and Charles had a choice: fight or flight. Without a moment to think, he raised the knife high and ran towards the landlady, who scarpered, trying to impede her attacker with everything and anything she could throw in his way.

Her weekly zumba sessions and knowledge of the pub layout served her well and she was out in the open, sprinting for her life, not looking backwards, her terror so great. Beaten, Charles thrust the bloodied knife back in its holder and dashed to the car, trembling as he fumbled with the key and ignition. Now the police would be hot on his trail and he was more confused than ever.

Unfamiliar with the area, he relied on the sun to guide him west, away from East Anglia and away from the dreadful crime he shouldn't have committed, and all the while he berated himself for having lost control. Why had the damned news programme broadcast his face? Now everyone would be looking for him, eager to take him out. Why hadn't he left without the bloodshed? He wasn't a killer, simply a nobody with a creative mind who had made something pretty and profound for his sister. Why was the whole world against him?

Jill Hatch and Nancy Blaine sat near one another in the reception area, Nancy tapping on her laptop, writing the article to include the extra information she had garnered from the press conference, complete with copies of Will O'Donnell's photos after finally getting hold of him. He had been glad to supply them on the promise his name would accompany them if they made it into the newspapers, which, of course, they would; the images were priceless.

Jill leant across apologetically. "How long have you been here?"

Without looking up, Nancy replied, "All day, so far."

"Are you a witness?"

Annoyed by the disturbance, Nancy shook her head. "Sort of." She stopped typing, wondering who was speaking to her. "What are you here for?"

She expected a tale about a cat up a tree, but was soon enwrapped with Jill's story. "So that's why they asked me to come in today. The thing is, I've worked out what was going on in Charley's mind. I know him, you see."

"What do you mean?" Jill had Nancy's full attention now.

"Well, I tried to tell Mr Spencer but he was so boorishly dismissive - such a pompous and arrogant man - that I gave up. I decided just to wait here in case I saw somebody who was a little more open to hearing things from a psychological viewpoint."

"You're a psychologist?"

"No, but I read a lot. I read all the time, and I absorb, not skim. And with the benefit of knowing Charley personally, I know exactly what he's done and why, and I have a good idea of what he's going to do next. I just hope nobody else dies before I find someone who can spare five minutes to listen to me."

"Tell me, Miss - I'm sorry, I don't know your name, but mine is Nancy Blaine, I'm working on the case."

"Jill Hatch, and hello Nancy, it's lovely to meet you, and I'm grateful you're not as dismissive as everyone else always is." She spent a couple of minutes explaining how she knew Charles and about his back problems, and how she had listened to everything he had told her about his sister, not realising the woman had once been a local celebrity of a kind. "Looking back now - retrospect is a wonderful thing - I can see that this has been building up for a long time within him. He used to tell me he was going to create a masterpiece to make his sister proud, and he would always chuckle to himself, adding coyly that it would stun the world.

"If I'd known Roberta was something to do with the marathon committee, I would have suspected something exactly like what he's done, but to me she was just a name, somebody he detested for what sounded like good reason."

"I don't understand how crudely displaying five girls, an act which killed four of them, could possibly count as revenge to Roberta. Why would that hurt her, apart from the obvious confusion and revulsion that pretty much everyone in the country feels right now?"

"He was going to do this on the sixth of October, and Hawthorn Cliff is part of the route the Raymouth Marathon takes. Plus, his sister's accident happened there. That place has him trapped in a scared child's mind. He's adamant Roberta pushed his sister over the edge, which he claims to have seen in person, and he can't erase the memory.

"Think of it like this: you know if you're in a car accident, or some other horrific personal disaster, you tend to recall the events in slow motion, and other senses - smells, sounds, textures - also bring you back to the moment at the drop of a hat. That's what Hawthorne Cliff does for him and the smell of the sea, of the fauna, the sound of the waves lapping - we experience those every day in Raymouth - keep his anger at boiling point.

247

"Well, Charley, for whatever reason, had to display his long-planned arrangement early, but it's set him off balance and he's now bouncing off the walls with no former plans to help him know what to do next. Quite simply, he's a loose cannon and he's capable of anything. Mark my words, Charley will either kill at random over the next twenty-four hours or he'll kill himself."

Astounded, Nancy was silent for once, and found herself developing a conscience. "How sure of this are you?"

"One hundred percent. But they won't listen to an old woman so I don't know why I'm bothering to try telling them. People assume that once you pass the age of fifty you no longer have a brain."

Nancy wanted desperately to type it all down, to finish the article and have the newspaper she was so proud to work for stun the nation with the concise and terrifying premonition. But even her notorious selfishness couldn't force away the feeling that Jill needed to be heard. "You said you know him; do you think that if you confronted him he'd listen."

"Charley and I have a wonderful friendship. I don't know if I could stop him, but I'd certainly be willing to try."

The timing was perfect: French burst through the main doors and raced through the room, and Nancy was on her feet immediately, following him. "Not now, Nancy. Here, have this one for free, Charles has been seen in Norfolk and he's killed someone else."

"He's on a spree. He's lost it." Jill was saddened by the news.

"French, stop and listen, will you." Nancy grabbed his arm before he could key the security code into the internal door's locking system. "Jill here," she pointed to the solemn woman, "she needs to be heard. Where are you going?"

"It's going crazy in the incident room. I've just been to the hospital to visit Rhiannon, but then this happened and they needed me back."

"I think that if you find out where he is, Jill could help him see reason. Jill, tell him what you told me."

French was staggered by her persistence. "Nancy, for fuck's sake, I haven't got time." Before she could stop him, he punched the code in, jerked the door open and slammed it behind him.

It took a split second for Nancy to realise she and Jill were on their own, and a rush of adrenaline flooded her. "Come on, Jill, if they won't listen, we'll just have to do it ourselves."

"Lily, he's killed again, this time a man in Norfolk." Barker rushed into the interview room that Lily hadn't left; the cells would be far too uncomfortable in her condition.

She hung her head, full of guilt but unsure why. "Why's he doing this?"

"There's no time for regrets or recriminations, I need you to tell me where he's heading. Think back to things he's said, places he's mentioned. The site of the murder - and it was most definitely murder - was on the outskirts of a small town in North Norfolk called Hunstanton. He could have gone in any direction, so I need you to tell me where you think he'll be heading."

"How would I possibly know?" Abrupt and unhelpful.

"Just think. We believe he's on a spree and anybody who gets in his way is in danger. He won't stop until either we get him or he kills himself, he's completely out of control."

Lily wanted to help now, despite still somehow hoping he would escape to a life of painless freedom, but this was so sudden. Just this week he had been at her house, sharing a pot of tea as she told him all about her committee meetings. Did she know Charley? Had she ever known him or was everything he had told her a lie. How could he be doing this, just like Charles Fubarre - the first Charles Fubarre - had allegedly done over eighty years before? She was quiet, unable to find anything to give Barker.

"Lily, please help us. Help his next victim. He's dangerous and you know him well enough to guess what he's doing."

"That's the thing, though, I don't. I never listened to him and that's the truth. To me he was a pain that I couldn't get rid of, with his ridiculous insistence that Roberta was responsible for my accident. I stopped listening to him years ago, blanked him out, ignored what he had to tell me. And now he says he's doing this for me. Did he tell me and I didn't hear? I was always too busy with some committee or other. Maybe he told me, I just don't know."

Barker gave up; she was as good as worthless. "Fucking self-piteous crap. Perhaps you are the reason - the cause - of all this, and perhaps you deserve his punishment." He stormed from the room, abandoning her to the torture of her own regrets.

Chapter 22
Friday, 2 p.m.

Nancy plugged her phone into the car and put her headset on, and as soon as Jill was settled, she headed north without knowing her destination. She pressed redial and her husband picked up after two rings. "Phil, I've got no time to explain, I need your help. Charles Fubarre has just murdered again, this time in Norfolk. He's on a spree and I'm on my way north to find him."

"No you're not, it's too dangerous."

"I need you to hack into the police radio, I need to know of any sightings to help me work out where he's going."

"Nancy, that'll take ages, do you realise…"

"I don't care, just do it. I'm on the A21 at the moment and I'm not alone, so don't be worrying, she's the safest person in the country to be with right now."

Jill smiled as she watched the scenery hurtling by, travelling faster than she had done since she stopped riding her Triumph Bonneville T120 - rebellious days against her overbearing mother - in the early sixties before starting her family. She hadn't had so much excitement in years.

Phil finally spoke. "I'll do what I can but please be careful, I couldn't bear to lose you."

He cut the call and Nancy floored the accelerator; speeding tickets could go hang. "If he's in Norfolk, where would he go?"

"He'll be heading west and I'll bet it's to Manchester, Fubarre and Sons had a second factory there. It wasn't as productive as the one here and closed years earlier, during the first World War. Henry Fubarre wasn't a nice person."

"Henry Fubarre?" Nancy was navigating her way onto the M25, unsure whether to go west or east.

"West, Nancy, you can exit at the M40, then before Birmingham get onto the M42, then it's plain sailing on the M6. That'll take you close to the Manchester ring road and we can ask from there how to get to the industrial estate the factory is on."

Nancy, intrigued yet impressed, tried not to take her eyes off the road, but it was hard. "You know where the factory is?"

"I told you, I listen where everybody else is already thinking of what they'll say next. More people should try it, it's amazing what you can learn. He brought the area up on my computer once - I only have one for when my kids visit, they'd be gibbering wrecks without the internet - and did that google thing where you can see the streets as if you're there."

"Street view, but that's only available with the net and we haven't got WiFi. Press redial on my mobile and speak to my husband, he's called Phil. Get him to have a map of Manchester ready for us. And see if he can find out exactly where the factory is."

Jill smiled and picked up the phone; she had never used a mobile. "Why not, there's a first time for everything, even at my age."

"Anyway, what's this about Henry Fubarre? I'm guessing he's a relative, but how does he fit in?"

"John and Henry Fubarre, two brothers, had the Raymouth factory built in eighteen eighty and it seemed to be an overnight success. They quickly became one of the most prominent employers in the area and business was booming."

"He told you all of this?"

"Just the names, then I visited the library - another thing that's threatened by society's desire to have everything available at an instant. Anyway, in nineteen and two they'd become successful enough to consider opening another factory, and at the time Manchester and Liverpool were booming in the textile industry. Lancashire was even dubbed 'Cottonopolis' due to the trade.

"They bought some land near what was then Duke's Canal - nowadays it's called the Bridgewater Canal - and they built a factory to match the one in Raymouth, the same plans and builders were used, and the subsidiary held its grand opening in nineteen o-three. Henry Fubarre was at the helm due to the fact he didn't have a family to uproot like John did. John is Charley's great-great-grandfather, by the way.

"The new business was instantly a competitor to be watched and the Fubarre brothers became rich men, and when Henry finally took a wife at the grand old age of fifty-two, his wife - the daughter of a fellow prominent businessman and in her early twenties - was able to live in the lap of luxury. She bore him a child in nineteen o-four, a boy named - aptly - Charles, and by all accounts he was a spoiled brat, not wanting for anything. After all, Henry was grateful to have finally had a family and his wife was too young to know any better in her silly, privileged world. By all accounts, they spoiled Charles senseless."

"It's like hearing an encyclopaedia talk, listening to you." Nancy was gobsmacked, she had never known anyone to retain such detail. Was it true that nobody listened nowadays? Well, she was heeding Jill's every word, digesting and absorbing. "So what happened then?"

"World War One. Henry Fubarre was a selfish man and didn't want to share his wealth and facilities, so when the government began forcing companies to make supplies for the war, he sold the factory to an eager competitor. That was in nineteen sixteen, and he invested his money in alternative ways that would be more beneficial to himself and his family. He took his wife and son to live in Raymouth and John, annoyed at his brother's unpatriotic ways, employed him on a lower level and wage than he'd been previously which, unsurprisingly, caused bitterness. However, his son - school age now - seemed to thrive with the sea nearby, and as they did anything he wanted, the narcissistic family remained there.

"Charles grew up to be a hapless youth, in and out of trouble all the time and never punished due to his wealthy relatives opening their purse strings to buy him out of trouble. Aged fifteen he discovered sex, which was ultimately his downfall. He was accused of murdering a prostitute a year later, having raped her repeatedly before stabbing her and dumping her body outside the factory; a clear message to his father."

"Message of what?"

"He wanted attention. Dear old daddy gave him no time and, by that time, his mother was what they then called insane, but would now be diagnosed as depressed. He sent the message 'look at me, I'm here' and it gave him the reward he'd wanted after his father used his most prestigious contacts, along with a bit of bribery, to get Charles off the hook. Once his name was cleared, John and Henry found him a role in the business to keep him out of trouble.

"Of course, Charles never understood what a gifted life he led, he took all the financial benefits and hanger-on friends for granted, and a year later another prostitute's body was found, mutilated this time, quite horrifically. They all knew it was down to Charles and he barely bothered to deny it, but rather than have shame brought on the family name, they agreed with the police to send Charles to a mental institution for the rest of his life."

"Goodness, I've heard about that kind of thing, but that's terrible. So Charles was locked away." They passed a sign for the M23 and Nancy wished it was for the M40 in her eagerness for the drama that hopefully awaited them. "Does this fit in with Charles now, though, or was it just a history lesson?"

"It very much fits with him now. He told me that he felt madness ran in the family and frequently asked me if I thought he was. I always said no, but sometimes his anger towards Roberta seemed like overkill, and those times I did wonder if he was a candidate to go over the edge.

"Now, however, knowing his heritage, feeling trapped by the police, and having killed girls that I honestly don't think he intended to hurt, he's firing on all cylinders and he'll feel lost without an organised, detailed plan to adhere to; as an ex-Army man he needs order to survive. Right now, in what is probably a delusional state of mind, he will believe that this madness that runs in his blood is his destiny, that he has no choice anymore but to destroy anybody who gets in his way."

"And those pompous bastards back at the station wouldn't listen to you. All I can say is that it's their loss and our gain."

As much as possible, Charles kept to the back roads, aware the police would be teeming on the main routes now they knew his rough whereabouts. He had travelled west across the country and was now passing through Saddleworth Moor. It wouldn't be long until he arrived in Manchester.

Ahead, a Mini Cooper was parked in a lay-by and Charles pulled off the road and stopped behind. The passenger door was wide open and nobody nearby, so guessing the owners had either parked to take photos or have a toilet break in the shelter of the scattered bushes, he opened the driver's door to see if the keys were in the ignition.

They weren't, but he noticed them in the door pocket and seconds later had started the engine, slammed the door, and was hurtling along the narrow lane under the disguise of the new car. The owners would no doubt report the theft to the police, but by the time they took action, he would be nearing his destination, lost amongst the many thousands of vehicles and people of the heavily populated city. He followed the signs for the M67, which would take him into the heart of Manchester.

He was approaching the motorway when a feeble wailing came from the back of the car, and he was horrified to notice a newborn baby in a car-seat, dressed in pink frills. His heart sank and, without other options, he drove on the verge and leant into the back, unharnessing the child. He brought the little girl to his lap and stared at her, cute and cuddly, without fear or hatred: an innocent baby. Could he kill her? Should he?

Lily, Spencer and French were in Barker's office, each man helpless in their distance from the search for the suspect. They had heard that Charles had stolen a Mini Cooper and kidnapped a baby, while the parents were doing their business under cover of the bleak wilderness of the haunting moors, and was possibly heading to Manchester.

Despite a young child's life being at risk, Lily insisted her brother would have no interest in the city. She saw no point mentioning that her forefathers had once owned another factory there a hundred years before, a bad historic wound that she had no intention of reopening. Dismissive, she said, "The best thing you can do is wait for the next sighting to see which way he's heading."

"He must have said something before now. Surely there's some reasoning behind his escape? Lily, if you're hiding something you have got to tell us now, if we don't get him quickly that poor child may be added to the list of casualties."

"Stop making out like I'm responsible for all of this, will you? Charley's a grown man and he thinks for himself. We've never been close. To tell the truth, he's nothing but a thorn in my side. I sub him financially and I have to make his decisions. Without me he'd have been lost years ago and I resent having to cope constantly with a grown-up child. I don't know what he's doing and even when you've asked me another fifty or a hundred times, I still won't know."

Barker's phone trilled, breaking the frustrated silence, and he snatched the receiver, announcing his name before listening. He slammed it down with a gruff 'okay' and began to pace, unable to sit wasting time they didn't have. "She's gone. A baby girl was found fatally stabbed on the A635, near to Saddleworth Moor. It looks as if she was thrown from a car window. The local police believe the child is the one Charles kidnapped."

The highly charged atmosphere was replaced by sorrow. Charles Fubarre had already won the sick game they were playing. "Those poor parents." Barker could remember his own sons as babies, needy yet compelling, vulnerable in their innocence. "They'll wish they'd held on a little while longer for the rest of their lives."

Using his radio scanner, Phil had managed to pick up the police band and had been carefully listening for any updates. He had relayed to Nancy that a Mini had been stolen and given her the registration number, and half an hour later, as she careered along the M6, he sadly told her about the baby. With the handset on loudspeaker, Jill heard every word and silent tears fell with sympathy for both the newborn who had merely begun her life before having it cruelly taken away, and for the parents, who would never forgive themselves for what had happened to her.

"Jill, pull yourself together. You're the key to getting him to give himself up, you can't flake on me now."

"I'm not flaking, as you so eloquently put it, I just find it very sad that it's come to this." Jill had realised in her latter years that she should never apologise for her emotions. At least she still cared.

Nancy uncharacteristically took the old woman's hand and clutched tightly with reassurance. "I know, it's all so pointless."

"I could blame myself, you know. I know what he's doing now, why couldn't I see it before?"

"You're the kind of person who tries to see the good in everything, you have a sunny soul. Charley was your friend as well as your client and you loved and trusted him for that. Nobody could have predicted this."

"Maybe so, but I dearly hope he doesn't kill again before we find him. If he can kill a poor child so brutally, he's gone beyond any reason. For all we know, he might want to kill me, and to be honest with you, living in a world where things like this happen on an unfortunately regular basis, I'm not sure I'd mind if he tried. Gone are the days when you could leave your doors unlocked, when your children could play on the street without threat. You can't ask people directions without seeing fear in their eyes. It's a very sad world we live in."

"I know, you're right there and I'm a waste of space for hankering after any story I can get, regardless of how much pain people are in."

"What do you mean?"

"I lied to you, or misinformed you, whatever you want to call it. I said I was working the case, which I knew you would misinterpret to mean I was a policewoman. Well, I'm not. I'm a journalist, I work for The Daily Review."

Nancy expected admonishment and shame but instead Jill chuckled. "Being a journalist isn't a problem, but working for that dreadful rag is. Okay, we're nearing Manchester, shall I call Phil to see if he's located the factory?" Nancy nodded, and Jill - now amazingly competent with the top-of-the-range phone, having soaked in Nancy's concise instructions - dialled, posing the question when he answered. Still on loudspeaker, Phil said, "At Junction nineteen head north on the A556 and carry on to the A56, through Altrincham, and once you're nearing Sale, call me back and I'll direct you from there."

"Got that, thanks Phil." Jill ended the call and beamed at the reporter, proud of her new technical skills.

Giving compliments usually embarrassed Nancy, but she was amazed by her companion's fearless zest for life. "Jill, has anyone ever told you that you're a remarkable woman?"

"I'm not remarkable, I just care. And so do you, you just haven't realised it yet. When you can stop long enough to see the grass on the ground and the leaves on the trees, see the budding flowers and watch them unfold to show their beautiful glory - once you can see what's always been there in front of you - none of this will matter any more because you'll have found peace."

Nancy would normally laugh at silly sentiment, but something about Jill's calm statement made profound sense. She indicated left and steered.

Carl ran into Barker's office without knocking - something only he was allowed to do - and breathlessly related the latest information to his three superiors. "I've been looking at the history of the Fubarre family and they had a factory in Manchester. I reckon that's where he's heading. Here's the address." He dropped a post-it note in front of Barker. "They closed down ninety-seven years ago, but the company that took over, Reece's Cotton, is still thriving."

"Gordon, alert the guys in London and get every sodding police car in the country hot on his tail. Lily, you knew this, didn't you?"

"The factory was sold nearly a century ago, why on earth would I consider it to be relevant?"

"I've had it with you, you're nothing but a pathetic waste of space. French, get her out of my sight." As an afterthought he added, "And increase her charge to aiding and abetting murder."

Once Lily had been removed, Carl added that he had read about a man named Charles Fubarre, their suspect's namesake and distant relative. "Rumour has it that although he was never charged, he murdered a prostitute in nineteen-nineteen and a second a year later. Wealthy daddy put his hands in his pocket and paid Charles's way out of jail, but he spent the rest of his life in a mental institution in Eastbourne. Apparently he was a talented artist and the few pieces of his work that are still in circulation are worth a fair amount of money."

"I might read about it when it comes out in book form." Sarcastic, Barker wasn't interested in the creative side of a murderer. Painting, drawing, writing; anyone would be good if they had the time and resources lucky Charles Fubarre the First had been fortunate enough to have at his murderous hands.

Charles reached the premises of Reece's Cotton, tired, relieved and home at last. The building was an exact replica of the one in Raymouth except, in contrast, it was alive and buzzing. To avoid courting attention, he drove close the back door, the equivalent to the one he had used when holding the girls hostage, and abandoned the stolen car haphazardly at the edge of the car park. He darted towards the building, dodging in-between the variety of vehicles, and clambered over a fence to reach the empty courtyard behind.

Checking around to ensure nobody was watching, he tried the door and was relieved to find it unlocked. He let himself in and made his way through the familiar, albeit brighter and cleaner, corridors until he found 'his' room. At last he could relax. Moments later two suited men entered and Charles panicked. "What are you doing in my room?"

Equally surprised, Ranjeet stopped, an unsure smile on his face. "I could ask you the same thing." Charles removed the knife, caked with drying blood, from its holster and waved it, threatening and dangerous, and the two men stepped back. "Hey, it's okay, mate, we'll go. No harm done, eh?"

They retreated, grasping behind them for the door handle, and Charles stepped forward menacingly. "I don't want anyone in this room again. This was Henry's room before and now it's mine. If you tell anyone I'm here I'll kill you, I swear."

Chapter 23
Friday, the Beginning of the End

Nancy noticed the discarded Mini as soon as they rounded into the premises. "My god, Jill, you were spot on. What do we do now?"

"We find his room. I think I know where to look."

"How, goddamn it?" Nancy struggled to keep up with the sprightly pensioner who was trotting breathlessly towards the back of the building.

"He was always going on about his room, detailed it to me several times, and like I've told you so many times before, I listen. He said he used a small back door and with this being a replica of the Raymouth factory, it's bound to be where he told me it was. Blast, there's a six-foot fence. I can't climb that."

"Yes you can, I'll help you. There's no point me going in without you, he'll have hacked me to pieces in seconds." Hearing herself speak, it suddenly hit Nancy how much danger she was in and she briefly thought of Phil, how he would cope if she wasn't there. He had tried telling her and she had labelled him needy. The truth was that he cared, just like Jill did. Dismissing her thoughts, she cupped her hands together and bent down. "There, I'll give you a push up, and then stay at the top until I'm on the other side and I'll help you down."

Jill had barely been active in years, a short stroll here and there, an effortless wiggle to music in the kitchen as she cooked her lonesome meals, but today had been incredible and if Nancy said she could do it, then she could do it. She stepped on the younger woman's hands and heaved herself to the top of the fence, shaking a little as she straddled it, and watched her lithe partner-in-adventure effortlessly clamber first up, and then down on the other side.

"Miss, get back over the fence, there's a madman in there." Ranjeet and his colleague were desperate to escape the sweaty, unkempt intruder who clearly had a screw loose, with crazed eyes and a bloodstained grey jumper.

Ignoring his warning, Nancy helped Jill down into the yard. "That's who we're here for."

"Are you the pigs - sorry, police - then?"

Nancy and Jill shared a mischievous glance and Jill nodded. "Yes."

They trotted on, Jill the leader, and she located the door so easily that Nancy would have sworn on her life that the woman had been there before. Her heart raced, too high on adrenaline to feel fear, and she followed the grandmother through a maze of corridors, eventually stopping by a closed door. "If I've got my bearings right, this is where he is. Stay outside, he's less likely to panic if he sees me alone."

"Jill, this is a big risk, I'm not sure I want you going in on your own." A thunderbolt of affection hit Nancy and she realised Jill was the mature influence she had needed for so many years, for her gentle guidance and endless patience. For her love. "The truth is, now I've found you, I couldn't bear it if something happened to you."

Jill smiled in her humble, unselfish way, reassuring and in control. "Charley won't hurt me." She opened the door quietly and stepped inside, and Nancy crossed her fingers, praying to whomever that nothing would happen to the old woman.

"Charley, it's Jill."

The knife was in his clenched hand, rage pulsing at his temples. "What are you doing here? Why are you here? Have they sent you? Are you going to hurt me?"

"Shush." She confidently, yet slowly, stepped towards him. "Shush, now. I'm here to sit with you, nothing else. You can tell me your stories if you want, all about the things you get up to and your past, your history, but it's fine if you just want to sit in the quiet. I just want to be with you because I know you're very scared at the moment."

Jill eased herself onto a chair, tired after the uncommon exertion, and Charles followed her lead, perching on the edge of a table. "How did you know I was scared?"

262

"You know me, Charley, I always feel it when you're hurt."

A minute of peacefulness passed. "I've done some bad things, Jill, but I didn't mean to be bad, I just wanted Bubby to be proud of me. Then I got scared because everything went wrong. Those girls weren't meant to die, especially Sammy. I think I loved her."

"You probably did, there's a condition called Stockholm Syndrome, where a prisoner relies on and maybe falls for his or her captor, and I guess this is the same kind of situation in reverse."

"Oh." He was quiet for a while. "If you know what I've done, why aren't you scared of me?"

"Because I know you're terrified and I want to hold your hand, to be with you and love you like a mother would. I promise I'll let no one hurt you, Charley, and I know in return you'll look after me too."

Steadily, unsure, Charles edged closer to her, wanting to be held, to be loved, but scared she would reject him like people always did. But when he felt her loving arms draw him into a hug, he melted into her shoulder, a vulnerable child, scared of what had gone and what would happen. She clutched him tight, a rock for him to lean on.

Without warning the door burst open and an armed policeman stormed into the room, rifle poised and ready to shoot. "No, get out," Jill screamed, but it was futile. In the background Nancy was yelling desperately that she had tried to stop them from coming in.

"Charles Fubarre, get your hands off that woman immediately."

Jill stood and shielded the little boy locked in a man's body. "Put your weapons down. He'll come quietly, but only if you stop behaving in an intimidating way."

"Get out of the way, lady, he's a dangerous killer and you'll be his eighth victim if you're not careful. I repeat, step out of the way."

"If I move, you'll shoot him and I'm not prepared to have that. Lay your weapons down and I promise he'll come without a struggle. Won't you, Charley?"

It happened too quickly for Jill to realise what was going on: the sniper knocked her out of the way, falling to the floor, and without a word of warning his colleague pumped three bullets into Charles. She spun round, gasping 'no', trying to catch him as he fell, but her strength was diminished and in slow motion his broken body fell to the ground, blood from his wounds seeping into a pool around his abdomen and head. "Charley." She bent down, cradling his head in her lap as the last scrap of life left his body. "Why? He would have come with you. You didn't have to kill him."

"He murdered a fucking baby girl in cold blood, ma'am, what would you do?"

There was no point answering the man who had hung, drawn and quartered her friend - her child - and judged him without knowledge or understanding. Again, for the zillionth time, she accepted the world - what it had become - wasn't for her. Gently she laid his head on the ground and kissed her fingertips, transferring the sentiment to his cheek. She scrabbled to her feet and solemnly, slowly, walked away.

Chapter 24
Sunday 6th October

Raymouth was deathly quiet, the opposite of how it should have been, and Lily uncomfortably made her way from her hire car - arranged by the police while her Mercedes was impounded - to the promenade, where she knew from gossip that her fellow marathon committee members were meeting before heading to a café nearby for a light lunch. The weather would have been perfect - not too hot, not too cold, with a gentle breeze - for the marathon, but public and police pressure had been too great and they had cancelled after Raymouth's latest celebrity, the notorious Charles Fubarre, had been caught and killed.

She wanted to feel sad that he had come to such a destructive end but couldn't; it was actually a relief. Years of wondering about his mental stability had culminated in the revolting acts he'd had the nerve to justify using her name, and not having to hear, incorrectly, that Roberta was the cause of her unfortunate accident again was a reprieve.

Charles's soulless body lay in the morgue awaiting the cheap cremation, without a funeral or service, that was planned for the next Wednesday, his ashes to be binned afterwards, not collected to be scattered in a beautiful and meaningful spot. She hadn't been to see him; she didn't want to.

None of the Raymouth Marathon board members, nor any from the other numerous committees she was part of, had been in touch, her name tainted by her brother's actions, but if she didn't face them now she would end up a hermit in her home, seeing and hearing from nobody. They would scorn her presence but she had done nothing wrong.

She hobbled towards the group, assisted by the walking stick that she tried not to use, and Elliot noticed her. "Oh. Lily." The others stared, but she held her head high.

"I think you forgot to tell me about the meeting." She appeared so much braver than she felt.

"It was no oversight, Lily, we just didn't want you here." Roberta was disgusted she had dared to show her face. "You're off the committee, it's been to the vote. You are the single-most reason that almost six thousand people aren't pounding these streets for charity today."

Lily scanned the familiar faces, people she had thought were friends, and wished she could hide from their scorn. "Do you all feel that way?" Not brave enough to sit on either side of the fence, she was answered with mumbling murmurs and she looked hopefully to her oldest ally for reassurance. "Elliot?"

"Not here, Lily." Underneath his glasses, his cheeks reddened.

"So I'll be the friend you don't admit to from now on, will I? And why? Because my brother - my thirty-six-year-old, responsible for himself, brother - went crazy. How is that my fault? I've helped with the marathon for the past ten years, both with time and money, doesn't that count for anything?"

The group avoided eye contact with her, muttering under their breath, but Lily didn't intend to be defeated and sat on the wall between the town and the beach, her spine jarring from the cold stone.

Jill finished giving Jeremy Barker a full back massage at his home and his back was free of knots and tenderness. He had met her, having heard of her incredible bravery, the day after the horrifying chase and she had not wasted time in telling him of her working hobby. His wife, as a reward for having had such an incredibly stressful time at work, had secretly arranged for the treat as a surprise and, when given the news, he had been delighted.

He felt wonderfully relaxed, relieved life had settled back to normal, and he led Jill to the kitchen to meet his family; two sons bounding about in their crazy way, alongside their over-excitable dog and his long-suffering wife, Trudy.

"I'll definitely hire you again, Jill, what you've done to my back must be some kind of black magic."

Jill tapped her nose. "White magic, Jeremy, we don't want any nasty rumours starting about the silly old recluse who sits at home all day, casting meddlesome spells and wishing hatred."

Trudy was collecting sandwiches, fruit and prepared salads into a cool-bag and she paused, a six-pack of fizzy drinks in her hand. "We're off to the beach for the afternoon, why don't you come with us?"

"That's a lovely offer but I've got a friend coming over."

Jeremy liked Jill, she reminded him of his recently bereaved mother; perhaps the two women should have coffee together one day. "Bring him or her along."

"More's the merrier!" His seven-year-old rocketed by and they laughed.

Jill looked at the sweet family, happy and carefree, and at the placid weather through the window. "Why not? Nancy won't mind, I'm sure. I'll go home and put my equipment away. Shall I meet you there?"

Lily had been completely shunned from the group, who had gone for their meal after making it blatantly clear her company wasn't desired, but she remained seated by the wall, now on a bench, overlooking the sea. If she lost her committees, there would be nothing of any worth left to her disabled and pain-filled life. She knew they could see her lonesome form from the café, that they would think her pathetic. Maybe she was, but her need for their company was worth the embarrassment. She was sure they would relent in the end.

Ignorant to everything except the gentle white-tipped waves lapping at the stones of the shore, she hadn't noticed Nancy approaching behind her. "Lily Jenkins, or should I say Fubarre, what are you doing here alone? Have you drugged your companions?"

Lily had many apologies to make and this was a good place to start. "Nancy Blaine, I didn't expect to see you again. Look, about the sleeping tablets…"

"Yes? My fearsomely sore head the next day after a wasted night in hospital. What about it?"

"I'm sorry. I'm deeply sorry. I know why you wanted the story and maybe exposing my brother and his evil wrongdoings would have been the right thing to do after all. I was confused and it was wrong."

"Heartfelt. I doubt you do that very often." Nancy noticed that Jill, puffing a little from the walk, had caught up. "Do you have any interest in meeting the woman who - heroically, I might add - tried to save your brother's life?"

Lily looked at the older woman, her cheery smile and humble manner. "Jill Hatch, I've heard all about you, it seems you were terribly brave last week. Thank you for doing what you did. Charley was always bugging me to go and see you, and told me how highly he thought of you, so I'm glad you were with him in the end."

"Charley was a good man. He was troubled and I wish I'd seen the signals before it went this far, but please don't hate him. His mind needed some help." Nancy sat on the wall, the compounded stone sparkling under the sun, and Jill sank onto the bench beside Lily, taking her hand. "You loved Charley in your own way, and I know how much he loved and relied on you. He's at peace now and so should you be."

It was as if Jill had opened a dam and tears coursed down Lily's cheeks. "You were just his masseur, but not only did you know him on a far deeper level than I ever did, but you cared for him where I just saw him as an irritation. How do I ever forgive myself for that?"

"By understanding him now and trying to see the good that you missed. It's never too late to say sorry."

As the two women consoled each other, Nancy watched Barker and his family park in the lay-by, and they climbed out, the two youngsters zooming over the grassed verge and darting down the steps to the beach. Barker reached the huddle of women and greeted them, introducing Trudy. "Lily's sad because everybody has shunned her because of what Charley did."

Barker, who had reluctantly decided not to continue with the charges against her, could understand. If she had been honest earlier, eight people, including her brother, would probably still be alive. "She had it coming."

Timidly, Lily glanced up at him, her sad eyes watery. "I guess I owe you an apology too. I didn't know that Charles had seen the register, that's the truth, but considering I never took the precaution when he was around because I trusted him… I know I must bear some of the responsibility. I'm sorry I withheld so many things from you, Inspector Barker."

"Detective Chief Inspector." It was a childish slap but, regardless, he was pleased of the apology.

"So why *are* you sitting here on your own, Lily?"

She pointed to the café, explaining she had been ousted from the committee. "To be honest, even though I know I deserve their treatment, my life will be nothing without the charitable work. It's always kept my mind from my disability in the past."

The café doors opened and the party, fed and watered, spilled onto the pavement. Only Elliot looked at Lily and they stared at each other for a while, intense. She willed him to forgive her for what she couldn't control and when he tentatively approached, she smiled softly.

Awkward. "We've got too many years behind us to let this come between us. Lily, they're all ignorant, you know that, and it will take a while, maybe years, for them to see you in a good light again. But I promise I'll work on them and do what I can. We're all to blame in our own way, but everybody likes to have a scapegoat, unfortunately." He reached out and they held hands, calm in the understanding their friendship could bridge anything.

Jill beamed for her new friend, with every intention of making her a client, pleased that forgiveness was winning. Leaving them with a modicum of privacy, she addressed Barker. "The girl, Rhiannon, have you heard how she is?"

"She's been left paraplegic and her anger is raw, but she's a survivor. She'll get through this."

With a cheeky wink, Jill chuckled. "Perhaps, now you've experienced my services, you could recommend me to her. A good massage does everyone the power of good."

No longer a reporter, now registered to be a full time student on a massage course at the local adult education centre, much to her husband's relief, Nancy had been right: Jill's good heart and gentle, understanding and forgiving ways would conquer all.

Nancy leant back, absorbing the warm sun on her neck, and smiled.

The End

Biography

Ricki's lifelong interest has been the psychology of a killer, specifically in the past few years of serial killers, and this is strongly reflected in her writing. Her stand-alone novels include bestselling Unlikely Killer, Black Park, Bonfire Night, Deadly Angels, Hope's Vengeance and Bloody Mary. She also writes short stories and articles, with many in print or on the internet, and scripts for film, television, radio and stage. She lives in South Yorkshire with her younger sons.

www.rickithomas.com